Fire and Ice

'You're dying for it, aren't you, Nina?' said Andrew, as he handed the young waiter a condom. 'Are you ready, lad? She will be.'

As Nina stared at the hotel carpet she felt the waiter's hands fumbling about and then a big rubber-clad penis push against her until it found what it was looking for.

'Not too quickly, please,' said Costas to the waiter. 'I want to get my money's worth from this. Nina, get down on your elbows with your head on the floor.'

She felt like an actress in a porno film, being told which way to move to give the three men the best view. Despite her humiliation, thrills were rippling through her. She knew she was giving a good performance.

Fire and Ice
Laura Hamilton

BLACK LACE

Black Lace books contain sexual fantasies.
In real life, always practise safe sex.

This edition published in 2005 by
Black Lace
Thames Wharf Studios
Rainville Road
London W6 9HA

Originally published 2000

Typeset by SetSystems Ltd, Saffron Walden, Essex
Printed and bound by Mackays of Chatham PLC

ISBN 0 352 33486 X

Chapter One

'*B*e lucky, darling,' said the cab driver as Nina paid him off outside the hotel.

'Thanks, mate.'

I'm going to need it, she added inwardly.

Belgravia was off her usual patch and the old red-brick hotel with its discreet sign a world away from the bigger, brasher hotels she knew from clients' cocktail parties and the annual company dinner. Nicer than those, she thought, but not as hip as, say, the Portobello in Notting Hill, or as chic as somewhere like Blake's.

Not that she knew what sort of place would choose to take a hooker for the afternoon.

From auditor to hooker over the space of a weekend was a pretty radical change – except this was a one-off.

Unless I really like it, she teased herself.

The doorman saluted her with a deferential 'good afternoon' and held the door for her. She took a deep breath and walked confidently into the lobby and asked for Andrew.

The receptionist didn't bat an eyelid as she directed her to Room 404. Why should she? Nina was smartly dressed in a pinstripe suit that she often wore to

1

work. Sure, the skirt was short, some cleavage peeked out of the jacket and her shoes were uncomfortably high stilettos. But there was no clue that she was anything but a businesswoman going to a legitimate meeting.

Of course, the receptionist didn't know that under the anonymous suit was a black lace basque, strapless to emphasise her creamy shoulders, with the bra cups reaching just a tiny fraction above her nipples. Nor that her legs were encased in lace-topped stockings held up by suspenders, and the scrap of lace which served as knickers was little more than a G-string.

Nina felt good. The contrast between her outer and underwear turned her on. The mere fact of wearing stockings and suspenders was exciting.

Not to mention getting paid a hundred pounds an hour for the next four hours. That was a turn-on in itself.

Money is power, she reminded herself.

The mirrored lift gave her a chance to check her face. She'd put on a little more make-up than usual, but nothing too vulgar. After all, she was going to play the part of a high-class hooker, not a common tart.

Her blue-grey eyes stared back at her, rimmed with kohl and fringed with black mascara'd lashes. She never used foundation and had just applied her usual tinted moisturiser to her creamy, pale skin. A slick of russet blusher along the cheekbones and a terracotta lipstick completed the look.

She had contemplated putting her glossy chestnut hair up into a French pleat but, as someone who had never bothered much with styling her hair, she decided it was best to leave it alone. In any case, she always felt the blunt-cut chin-length bob with its heavy fringe was pretty classy.

As the lift arrived on the fourth floor she settled her jacket around her shoulders and pulled it down firmly to show as much as possible of her cleavage, then without a backward glance walked as briskly as the shoes allowed along the corridor to Room 404.

Andrew counted out the money: 'Three sixty, three eighty, four hundred.' He handed the roll of notes over to her. 'I brought twenties – I thought you'd like a big wad.'

'Yes, I certainly do,' said Nina, deadpan, lowering her eyes to his crotch and back up to meet his.

He smiled, bringing into play the delicious lines that started from the corners of his eyes and ran right down his face. Just looking at him was enough to up her pulse.

Not that he could be called handsome. For one thing his nose sported a bump in the middle, obviously having been broken at some stage. That, combined with his thick, dark brown hair and unusual almond-shaped light brown eyes, made him look more distinctive than conventionally attractive.

His best feature, though, was a mouth that belonged on a statue of a Greek god, with full lips that looked as though they had been sculpted from marble rather than formed from mere flesh.

'I don't think I can manage to get all this down my cleavage, though,' she said, picking up the money.

'That's not where I want it – I want your clothes off,' he told her. 'Put that money away.'

She stuffed it into her handbag. 'You want me to take them all off? Or just the top layer?'

He raised his thick eyebrows. 'Don't worry, I'll tell you when to stop. And take your time. Tease me.'

Taking off his jacket, he moved over to the bed and lay down, his hands clasped behind his head. She suddenly felt self-conscious as she started to undress while he stared at her appraisingly. Her fingers faltered as she started to undo her buttons.

3

'Will this help?' He switched on the radio. 'Dance for me, Nina. Strip for me.'

To her intense annoyance, Nina blushed and fumbled even more. She started to sway her hips but felt ridiculous. 'I don't think I'm going to be very good at stripping,' she apologised.

'For Christ's sake. For four hundred pounds you'd better be,' he said harshly. 'This isn't just a game, Nina. Make me want you more than I've ever wanted a woman before. Dance for me, and make it good.'

This isn't just a game. His voice had gone cold as he spoke to her. God knows what I'm doing, she thought, panicking slightly.

In the lift she'd congratulated herself on her confidence and power. Now, only minutes later, she'd turned back into a wimp.

Do the job properly, she told herself sternly. After all, she had moved her hips seductively for herself in the mirror enough times to turn herself on. Surely she could do it for Andrew.

The music was some old sixties song – Carole King, she thought. It was fairly slow but rhythmic, and Nina concentrated on it and started to move with the beat, moving her hips from side to side and running her hands down her body. Gathering her hair up behind her head, she turned her back to the bed, letting her hair cascade slowly as she showed Andrew her swaying backside. There was a mirror in front of her and she saw she was looking good. Her fear of making a fool of herself melted away and she started to dance properly, as though she was in a class at the Dance Studio.

She thrust her hips in a circle as she lifted her hair once more. He was watching her in the mirror. Slowly undoing the buttons of her jacket, she turned to face him again and pulled the jacket apart, giving him the first sight of the black lace of her basque and her

4

swelling creamy cleavage. Already her nipples had hardened. She wondered if he could see that. She danced a few steps closer to the bed. He was gazing at her, nodding, and she could see he was getting excited. His nostrils were slightly flared and he was breathing more shallowly.

He wasn't the only one. She was turning herself on as well. Pulling off the jacket, she twirled round so he could get a glimpse of the white flesh of her back. Facing him once more, she ran her hands lingeringly over her breasts, appreciating the cleavage the wiring gave her. Then she moved her hands down and lifted the skirt high enough to show off the lace-topped stockings and suspenders.

'Come here,' he commanded quietly. She danced over to him provocatively, hands on hips, now feeling confident. He was excited; he was within her power. She could make him come at any time if she wanted to. Or she could make him wait.

He was on the edge of the bed now, and as she reached him she lifted her skirt so he could see, above the stocking tops and suspenders, the tiny lace knickers framed by the bright brown curls of her pubic hair. She stood just inches away and gyrated her hips.

Andrew said nothing. His hazel eyes were fixed intently on her crotch. As Nina looked down she could see the bulge in his trousers. Yes, she was doing a good job. Not such a bad job on herself, either. She wondered if he could see the juices she felt slowly creaming her knickers.

Backing away from him slightly, she turned and unzipped her skirt, then wriggled until the tight material slowly dropped to the floor. Stepping out of it, her excitement went up a few more degrees. She didn't feel like a common stripper – or a common prosititute, come to that. As she stood naked except for the lacy

5

suspendered basque and stockings, she felt like the sexiest woman in the world.

Her inhibitions had completely fallen away with the pinstripe suit. The music changed to a more up-tempo number and she lost herself in the gyrations of her dance, moving and shaking her body in a way she'd never been able to do on a dance floor.

Not just moving it but stroking it, pushing up her breasts, licking her shoulders, caressing her nipples, making love to herself. Turning her back to him again, she bent over and wriggled her arse, which was bare apart from the lacy string joining the crotch of her knickers with the waistband. As she did that, Andrew stood up and grabbed her.

'I want to fuck you now,' he muttered, undoing his zip and dropping his trousers. 'You should be on the stage, Nina. How about it? Haven't you ever fantasised about stripping in a club, being watched and lusted after by complete strangers?'

As he talked he thrust his hand inside the tiny lace crotch of the knickers and felt her viscous wetness.

'I guessed it. You've excited yourself as much as me,' he whispered. 'Bend over. I want you from behind.'

As she heard him tear the foil of a condom packet, she hooked her thumbs in the lacy strings to take off her knickers, but he stopped her.

'Leave them on,' he said, holding the string to one side and pulling her arse back against him, the head of his penis nudging against her. She widened her legs and leaned further forward, holding on to the bedside table for support as the full length of his cock slid with ease inside her.

He started to shaft her slowly, his hands on her hips. Looking down, she could see her breasts almost spilling out of the cups of the basque and her stockinged legs tensed from the height of the stilettos. It made her imagine what she looked like from behind, what he

6

was seeing as he thrust in and out of her. Her calf muscles, shapely enough but emphasised even more by the high-heeled shoes; her round, firm buttocks bisected by the lacy string he'd pushed aside.

She felt curiously detached from him, only able to feel his cock and his hands. When they had fucked before he had talked to her, but now he was silent apart from his steady, rhythmic breathing.

Into her mind came a fantasy of being fucked by a complete stranger, or maybe more than one. She was ordered to bend forward, her eyes facing the floor, while they thrust inside her and fucked her selfishly, impersonally. She was just an instrument of their pleasure whose feelings were unimportant.

The fantasy heightened her excitement as Andrew drove deep into her. She wriggled her arse and moved in little circles for him.

'You're thinking about something other than me,' he said. 'What is it?'

'I was thinking, you could be anybody,' Nina murmured. 'You could be a complete stranger just using me, my body just a vehicle for your enjoyment, and waiting after you could be another stranger. Maybe not even strangers, men I know, but I couldn't tell which one was fucking me at any time.'

Andrew breathed more heavily and she felt his warm chest with its curly hairs bear down on to her back, as he leaned on her and pushed in even further, his hands coming round and cupping her breasts.

'Would you like that to happen to you? It can do, if you want. I can get men to do that to you. Yes, one of them would be me, but you wouldn't know which one. Shall we do that? It could be even more exciting. You could be tied up so you couldn't get away. Or you could be blindfolded and taken from the front as well.

'None of those men would care if you came or not. They'd just push inside you whether you were ready

7

or not, and fuck you as quickly or as slowly as they wanted, for as long as they wanted.

'They wouldn't care about you, whether you were enjoying it or not. But you would, wouldn't you? You'd love it. Even if you weren't ready for it, you'd soon get wet. It wouldn't take long for you to come. God knows you're not far off now, are you?'

He was right. The combination of his words and his thrusting cock had brought her to the brink of orgasm. He moved his hand down to her clitoris and rubbed her, swiftly and surely. Within seconds she felt that sudden twitching in her vagina, that intense build-up, and knew that she was coming, and nothing could stop it, nothing.

'Now, Nina?' She was vaguely aware that Andrew too was breathless, tensed up to come himself. But like the men she had fantasised about, all she wanted was her own pleasure.

'Now, Nina!' he repeated from somewhere far off, as she felt her whole body engorged and swollen, as her lips opened and pouted and her eyes half closed, and the giant breaker wave of pleasure took her. Helplessly, her cunt contracted rhythmically and she felt as though her very centre had taken up residence there for the time being.

Andrew withdrew from her and she staggered and almost fell on to the bed. She looked up at him with a small smile and he lay down beside her.

'Was everything all right for you, sir?' she asked, remembering her role.

'Oh yes,' he said softly. His hands came up and stroked her face. 'And for you?'

'Fantastic. You're a great fuck.'

'I bet you say that to all your clients.'

They laughed and he turned on his back with a contented sigh. Nina snuggled up against him, realising he was still almost fully dressed.

'I think you might take some of these clothes off, as you've booked me for another – what – three and a quarter hours,' she teased.

'Perhaps I was a bit optimistic saying four hours,' he hazarded. 'There's no way I can keep that pace up for the rest of the afternoon. I think we'd better take a break for a bit. How about a drink?'

'Please. I'm dying of thirst. What do I drink in my new job?'

Andrew laughed. 'High-class tarts only drink champagne. How about I drink it out of you?'

'No way! It'd be too cold.'

'You weren't supposed to realise that,' he said in mock disappointment. 'I liked the thought of giving you a shock by pouring a slug of icy champagne inside you.'

'Sadist.'

'Not really – just a few tendencies in that direction,' he said with a sly smile. 'None you'll ever complain about, I bet.'

As he phoned room service, Nina surveyed the room. It was decorated in muted blues, with subdued floral wallpaper, the heavy-slubbed linen of the curtains and bedspread adding a more contemporary look. A leather-topped desk with a captain's chair stood at one end of the room, faced by a dusty-blue velvet settee and armchair. The carpet was thick and deep blue, and the pictures on the walls were good-quality prints. Altogether it spelled unostentatious luxury, and she guessed that hiring the room had cost as much as hiring her.

'So, how was it for you?' asked Andrew. 'What did you think of your first chance to act out a fantasy?'

'Brilliant. Just getting into the taxi and giving the address of a hotel I was going to have paid sex in made me horny,' she admitted. 'And coming into reception and asking the receptionist for your room was great. It made me feel like I really was a prostitute.'

He smiled. 'And what luck getting a stud like me for a client.'

'Yeah, yeah. I don't think I could do it for a living, though.'

'Just as well. If you were really a whore, I'd like to have you once in a while, but I don't think I'd be going in for a real relationship with you.'

Nina laughed. 'I liked stripping as well, once I'd got going.'

He nodded appreciatively. 'Yeah, you were pretty hot. Mind you, you were pathetic at first.'

'Don't remind me! But once I started looking in the mirror it was just like a jazz dance class, then after that, I sort of got carried away.'

'Yes. You're a good dancer.'

He reached out and stroked Nina's chest, above the swell of her breasts in the basque.

'How many fantasies have you got in that head of yours, Nina? I mean, even in the middle of acting out a whore fantasy you have another one of being fucked and degraded by faceless men. How many of them do you want to act out?'

She shrugged. 'God, I can't answer that. I told you, till I met you I had nothing but fantasies. The most non-existent sex life anyone ever had.

'Do you know what they call me at work? The Ice Queen. Can't blame them, I suppose. After all, I've been there for a year and a half without having a relationship, even a one-night stand.'

It had actually been almost two years since she'd had sex. Working as an auditor in a big City firm, she'd had plenty of offers from both colleagues and clients, but she had always refused. Nicely and politely, of course, but that hadn't stopped her getting a reputation. Not the one most girls dread, of being too easy, but the opposite.

Once, she was at the photocopier outside the tea room and heard two men talking about her.

'She's a fucking ice queen, that one,' sneered John Daly. 'Never known her go out with anyone. Not only from here, but at all.'

'Down at Personnel they say she's a dyke,' sniggered Mike Thatcher.

'No, she's bloody frigid. Ice queen, that's her. What she needs is a good shag.'

Nina walked away, pissed off that they were talking about her like that, but half amused. She felt like going back and saying, 'Yes, I do need a good shag, but I've never met a man who could deliver one, and I'd give a hundred to one that you two wouldn't be any different.' John Daly, who'd lost his libido along with his hair, used to walk round the office singing, 'Sit upon my face and tell me that you love me,' until he was told to shut up or get out. And everyone knew that Mike Thatcher's wife had been having an affair for years.

OK, if that's what they thought about her, that was fine by her. She didn't want sex getting in the way of work, anyway. If ever she was going to get a good shag she wasn't going to get it from anyone from the office.

Andrew interrupted her reverie. 'How do they know you haven't got a secret life?'

She laughed. 'Well, I have now. That was a bit of a thrill on its own, telling them I had to have today off and knowing that they'd all be mega shocked if they ever found out what I was going to do.'

He shook his head and ran a finger down her face. 'You know, it's still hard to believe this sort of thing is so new to you. You're a really sexy lady, but you might as well be a virgin for the little experience you've had.'

11

He looked at her intently. 'If you'll let me, I want to help you act out all your fantasies. As long as you really want me to.'

'Are you kidding? I feel as though I've just woken up, like Sleeping Beauty. I've been missing out all these years and I've got a lot of lost time to make up for. There's no way I'm going to turn you down.'

She laughed. 'God, I sound like a little girl lost in a fairytale world. Ice Queen, Sleeping Beauty . . .

Andrew smiled. 'I remember telling you the first time we had sex I thought you were a real firebrand. It's hard to believe anyone could think you're made of ice.

'I want to initiate you into all sorts of experiences, to do all the things you've ever dreamed of. What about having sex with a woman, for instance?'

He leaned up on one elbow, looking at her. 'You might even prefer it to sex with a man.'

She shook her head. 'No way. I like the fantasy of making love to a woman, but I think I'd know by now if I was a lesbian. I might even hate it.'

He laughed. 'Only one way to find out. There's no point having dreams you don't try to make come true. You know what they say – life's not a rehearsal.

'It's up to you. I can help you move into your fantasy world – if you're sure it's what you want. I can take you through the maze of sexuality and lead you out the other end.'

Nina's brain whirred, wondering exactly how literally she should take what Andrew was saying. How far did he want to go into her fantasies? She felt a bit scared – but only a tiny bit. She was sure he wouldn't make her do anything against her will. But what exactly was he going to do to her, or ask her to do for him?

For a split second she was tempted to say no, let's end this now, better to forget about it. Safer, anyway.

Safe, like the celibate path she'd been following. If she hadn't met Andrew and carried on like that, she'd

12

never even have known what proper sex was. And now she'd had a taste of that, she wanted more.

Just the thought of this fantasy life was filling her with a sexual energy she'd never known before.

So she smiled and kissed his face.

'Of course I want to do it. I want you to take me to all the places in my dreams.' Her smile broadened. 'You're doing quite well so far.'

'Right.' His fingers ran down her basque to the juice-stained crotch of her knickers.

'I think you might as well take these off now – they're like a wet rag.'

Nina laughed. 'What about the rest? Do you want me naked?'

'You're kidding. That's beautiful. Does dressing up turn you on?'

She remembered how excited she'd been when she got back from the shops after her sexy underwear buying spree and tried on all her purchases. So excited that by the end of her dressing-up game she had had to lie on the bed and rub herself off through the blue silk . . . but she didn't have to tell Andrew about that.

'Yes, it does. You didn't have to ask that, did you?'

She got up and wriggled out of her knickers, throwing them at Andrew. He sniffed at them.

'Mmm, musky. God, they're wet.'

'That's your fault,' protested Nina.

'Bullshit. You excited yourself with your striptease, didn't you?'

'Yes, but whose idea was it! Anyway, I think I'll just freshen up ready for the next round.'

She blew him a kiss as she went into the bathroom. The champagne would be arriving soon, so she was pleased to have the excuse to leave the room.

After using the toilet she ran hot water to rinse off the sweat from her armpits and to rid her pussy of the rubber smell.

While she soaped herself, she smiled at the excitement of playing her role. She still couldn't believe the way her life had changed thanks to Andrew. How she'd exchanged a sex life limited to masturbating to her many fantasies for real, man to woman, orgasmic bliss – with the added promise of being able to act out those fantasies that had turned her on so much.

Having sex had always been a non-event for Nina. She'd always thought, this time it'll be fine, but the silent snogging and groping had always led to a brief and, for her, unsatisfying penetration.

It wasn't till she met Andrew that she realised it was probably partly her own fault. She'd always treated having sex as a sacred rite where talking wasn't allowed; she'd never progressed from the silence of adolescent fumblings. Never thought to tell a man that what he was doing was right, or wrong, to stop or not to stop, for Christ's sake. Never thought to say be more gentle, or harder, faster!

Angry and frustrated, she'd wait impatiently for the man to leave so that she could make herself come imagining one of the fantasies that came unbidden into her mind. As she touched herself, sometimes watching in the mirror, seeing her deep-pink nipples harden, feeling her clitoris swell and respond so easily to her stroking finger, she dreamed of a man who could make her feel the way her fantasies did.

Andrew had asked her out after she and her colleague Max had finished looking through the books of his shipping firm as part of the audit. She was surprised. They'd had little contact with each other, as most of her dealings had been with the accountant.

He was a bit old for her, probably about 38. A public schoolboy, Nina guessed, with a rather odd way of speaking, almost like a foreigner who had learned perfect English, but with a slight transatlantic accent.

Sure, he was a bit smooth – but compared to most of the men she knew who could do with the rough edges knocked off them, he was a treat.

More significantly, he was always good humoured, even when he seemed to be under pressure. He had an ironic turn of phrase which amused her and he didn't make her feel a nuisance, as so many clients did, when she'd had to query things with him directly. Nina had been sorry when her investigations on site had drawn to an end, but it was then, on her last day there, that he had asked her out.

Their first date had all the potential to be disastrous. Nina chose a film which she had to admit afterwards was a complete dud. He confessed that he'd guessed all along it would be bad, but had gone along with her choice. It was raining when they came out of the cinema and they got soaked running to the nearby tapas bar. That turned out to be noisy and smoky and they had to shout at each other as they discussed work and auditing and shipping while washing their tapas down with two bottles of Rioja, but as the wine went down so did their awareness of their surroundings.

He phoned the next day and they laughed about the bad film, bad weather and bad choice of restaurant – and the fact that they still managed to have a great time despite it all.

The next time Andrew chose a play at the National Theatre, which they both liked, followed by an American Hot each at Pizza Express. They explored each other's cultural likes, which in Nina's case were mainly music that Andrew dismissed as 'mainstream Britcrap', novels; especially modern and romantic, *EastEnders* and *Friends*. Andrew was more into theatre and blues and contemporary classical music, which was a closed book to her. He liked French films and modern art, while Nina only went to the cinema for the latest blockbuster, and her idea of art was Monet rather than Jackson Pollock.

Really, they had nothing in common. But they got on even better than the last time.

The night they met at the Italian just down the road from her flat in Clapham it was obvious that she had to ask him in for a drink, and Nina braced herself for the usual disappointment.

But it wasn't. He had undressed her slowly while stroking every part of her body. Instead of the solemn mime she was used to, he whispered to her continuously. As he touched the inside of her thigh, he exclaimed over the satiny softness of her skin. He marvelled at the cleft of her buttocks as he stroked all around them, and the hardness of her nipples. Then his fingers moved to that pink bud of flesh that had swollen in response to his caresses.

'I bet this is what you want, Nina. Do you want me to stroke you here?' he murmured. 'Perhaps just a bit of lubrication . . .'

His fingers stroked down, down and up into her vagina.

'You're nice and wet, Nina. I knew you would be. I could tell you were excited. I guessed you'd be a firebrand.'

Now he was stroking her clitoris with his wet fingers. Nina had never felt as excited when she had touched herself before. The centre of her being had moved to that small point of flesh, which had become so unbearably hot it felt almost numbly cold. Cold as ice but, paradoxically, hot as fire.

His words were pushing her to the brink. She knew she was on the point of coming – for the first time ever with a man.

'You love sex, don't you, Nina? How many men have you had? Have a lot of them talked to you like this? You like being talked to, don't you? What's your favourite position, Nina? How can I make you come quickly?'

'I'm coming – any minute now –' gasped Nina.

'Already! You're like a bitch on heat, Nina. All your nice clothes, education, career – just a front for a woman who lives to fuck. That's right, isn't it, Nina?'

'Yes. Oh yes, tell me that. Just don't stop talking, Andrew.'

'You want me to keep talking? That's exciting you so much? You're desperate to come, aren't you? What if I moved my finger now?'

Abruptly, he stopped and looked down at her. Nina could have burst into tears.

'Oh, for God's sake! Please, Andrew, don't stop.'

He frowned. 'I think you should be able to do better than that. "Please, Andrew"' he mimicked, his voice falsetto.

Nina looked at him; his mouth smiled but his hazel eyes looked mockingly at her as he waited for her answer.

'Please! What do you want me to say?'

He put his head on one side. 'Guess!'

Nina sighed. 'I beg you, Andrew! Is that what you want?'

He nodded. 'Yes – again!'

'I beg you, please touch me again,' said Nina in a small voice.

'Will you promise me to do anything I want after I've made you come?'

'Yes, anything!'

'OK, one more time. And sound like you mean it.'

'Please, I beg you, I beg of you to touch me.'

'OK.' He had resumed stroking her, as she sighed and lay back, quickly burning once more. 'I think that all the things I want to do, you probably want to do too. I think you need more than just a good fuck. I think you want to do things that are a bit different. I

17

think there are things you've dreamed about that you should make come true.'

'Yes, that's right.'

'You fantasise a lot?'

'Yes, all the time . . .'

'Like what? Would you like to be fucked by two people at once? Do you want to know the taste of another woman? Do you want to try a little pain?'

She didn't hear any more as his words and his fingers together took her over the edge of her climax and she came like a rocket, her body shuddering again and again, till she could stand it no more and had to stop his moving hand with hers.

Then his cock had entered her with ease, the first time she'd not had to suppress a wince because she wasn't wet enough. He'd moved quickly, excited himself by his words.

Her cunt had moved instinctively against him, almost as if grateful to feel a man inside giving pleasure rather than discomfort or pain. As he thrust into her urgently, it was her turn to whisper to him, to tell him that he had given her the best climax she had ever had, and that it was just the first, and she couldn't wait for the others to follow, the others he could give her not just with his fingers, but with the long cock that was driving into her liquid slit now, and with his beautiful mouth; and that she wanted this climax to be perfect for him, and that too would be the first of many.

After he came they held each other and talked, and she confessed to him that it was the first time she had come with a man. He laughed disbelievingly at first. It was hardly surprising that it was hard to accept that anyone could have reached 28 without having had an orgasm except through masturbation. Reluctantly she told him about her own secret life, her fantasies that made touching herself so quick, so easy, and the best pleasure she'd had from sex – until now.

For hours they had sat and talked and she let him drag out of her many of her fantasies. His astonishment at her unusual sex life had given way to tenderness. He told her he would never have guessed how vulnerable and inexperienced she was. Nina had felt almost ashamed as she told him, but also excited as she quickly sketched out the thoughts she had when she wanked. He felt her excitement and started touching her again and then they made love again after that, slowly and tenderly, and he brought her to orgasm again, this time through sweet, patient and gentle penetration, touching her and talking to her all the time.

They'd had sex a few more times since then, each time as good as the first. Then he had suggested they should act out one of her fantasies. She had told him she'd fantasised about being a prostitute and Andrew had whispered to her a story about her being paid for sex while he stroked her to climax.

'Let's make an appointment now,' he'd said as he left her in the morning. 'Come to a hotel room with me. How much do you want?'

Nina had laughed. 'I don't know! What's the going rate? How long do you want me for?'

He stroked her cheek. 'We might as well make an afternoon of it. Let's say four hours, a hundred pounds an hour. How's that?'

'Very generous! But, really, there's no way I could take that sort of money from you –'

'That's the whole point, Nina,' Andrew said impatiently, his eyes darkening. 'This is business. I'm a businessman. I want you at one o'clock next Monday at the Belvedere Chase Hotel in Belgravia – do you know it?'

'I'll find it,' said Nina in a small voice. 'Shit, I'm not playing this game very well. It's not like you're doing this for your own benefit.'

The cloud left Andrew's eyes and he laughed. 'Well,

I hope I am going to get some benefit out of this. Especially at that price.'

He put both hands on her shoulders. 'If you want to be a whore, you want to get paid for it. OK?'

'Yeah, sure, whatever you say.' She kissed his cheek, then his lips.

'Good.' He brought some money out of his pocket.

'Don't pay me now!' she said, dismayed. 'It's part of the fantasy, checking the money first, before I let you –'

'Just shut up for two seconds!' he interrupted. 'This isn't for your services. It's for you to buy some sexy underwear with. I hope you don't mind my saying so, but you desperately need a fantasy wardrobe if you're going in for a fantasy lifestyle.'

Nina had been crushed momentarily, but she knew of course that her usual white bra and high-leg briefs set wouldn't really do for a prostitute – even one just for an afternoon.

After Andrew had left she looked at the roll of notes he had given her. It obviously wasn't just one outfit for Monday he'd meant her to buy, but more outfits for this 'fantasy lifestyle'. So she'd gone on a spending spree, going from department stores to a specialist boutique in Chelsea, a sex shop and even the chain stores, until she was happy with four outfits that she reckoned would see anyone through a few fantasies.

The door closing brought her back to the present as she finished drying herself. It must be the champagne. She smoothed her hair, rubbed in the complimentary hand cream, and left the bathroom with one last backward look in the mirror. But when she turned round, Andrew wasn't alone.

'Nina! You've taken your time. Come and meet Costas, my oldest friend – in both senses of the word.'

Andrew strode the few paces towards her and encircled her wrist tightly with his hand, preventing her from making the swift return to the bathroom she was going for. He drew her over to a small, wrinkled, incredibly old man, sitting on the settee and smoking a cigar.

He rose as she approached and bowed his head at her. He was short, probably no more than five-foot-two, dressed in an expensively tailored suit. But the best tailoring in Savile Row couldn't have concealed the fact that he was astonishingly old – the oldest man Nina had met in her life.

Brown splodges covered his bald head. His large nose was hooked and his lips fleshy. Thick glasses magnified his eyes, whose brown edges had faded into grey. They were fixed on her, and she could see that despite his age there was intelligence in those eyes, a shrewd appraising intelligence – and maybe a glint of malevolence as well.

'Charming! Very charming! Sit beside me, my dear,' said the old man in a thick foreign accent.

'Costas is from Greece, Nina. He's the oldest man alive still running a shipping fleet. He taught me everything I know about the business.'

Andrew beamed at Nina. 'I always call him my godfather. Costas has been more than a father to me.'

Costas said something to Andrew that Nina didn't catch, and she realised he had spoken in Greek. The younger man laughed and answered in the same language. The Greek smiled, his thick lips widening but not opening, and his eyes screwing up behind his glasses.

Nina smiled at him. 'It's nice to meet you,' she said, feeling awkward at exchanging polite conversation with a stranger while wearing a basque and suspenders. 'I heard the door go but thought it was room service. I'll just get dressed.'

Andrew struck his head with his hand. 'God, what am I thinking of? I forgot we'd ordered room service, and I didn't even ask if you wanted anything, Costas! We're having champagne. How about you? And Nina, stay as you are. I'm sure Costas will get as much pleasure from looking at you as I do.'

She perched uncomfortably on the edge of the settee next to the old man, aware of the velvet upholstery on her bare arse.

'Brandy, please, Andrew,' the old man answered. 'I don't touch anything else these days. It's bad enough to smoke these,' he waved his cigar, 'without poisoning myself with alcohol as well. When I was younger, I denied myself nothing,' he went on, turning to Nina while Andrew moved to the phone. 'Wine, brandy, cigarettes, women – but at my age I have to be careful. I won't tell you how old I am, because you will probably have noticed that as people get old they always want to boast about their age, as though it were an achievement.' He chuckled derisively. 'Age just happens to you. I have been more interested in the things I have made happen for myself. I have made fortunes and lost them, but fate has been kind enough to leave me plenty for my old age.'

His wrinkled hand reached out and traced a wavering line down Nina's cleavage. She tensed her muscles. Only a great act of will stopped her from shuddering and backing away. However much money he might have, it was impossible to feel anything but disgust at his touch. But she felt Andrew's eyes on her and she steeled herself to show nothing.

'I have enough to pay for pretty women like you, anyway,' he said. 'Not that I am much good at sex now, you know. But with a bit of help, I can sometimes manage.'

Nina felt physically sick. OK, she'd wanted to play a prostitute, but for Andrew. She couldn't believe he'd taken her at her word and arranged for her to whore for this old man as well.

She tried to signal outrage to him with her eyes, but he was just looking indulgently at the old man.

As though he felt her eyes on him, he turned to her, but if he knew what she was trying to express he ignored it.

'She is pretty, Costas? You approve of her?'

'Andrew, she's lovely. Your skin is so soft, my dear.'

His hands moved over the swell of her breasts pushed up by the basque. His dry, papery fingers felt like sandpaper rubbing over her smooth skin. She could almost hear the rasping noise she was sure it was making. His gnarled hands pulled down the cup of the basque to expose her nipple, and he pulled it roughly.

'Yes, beautiful.'

There was a knock at the door and Nina made to get up and run to hide in the bathroom but Costas was still squeezing her nipple.

'Stay!' commanded Andrew, as though she were a dog, and with a louder voice shouted, 'Come in!'

Nina froze.

The door opened and a young waiter came in, pushing a trolley carrying a tray holding an ice bucket with the champagne, two glasses and a large balloon glass of brandy. He stopped abruptly at the sight of Nina and Costas on the settee.

'Over here,' said Andrew brusquely, indicating the coffee table right in front of where Nina was sitting. The waiter was blushing. He was young, still with adolescent spots, and had obviously never before seen anything like the weird scene he was witnessing. Nina could tell he was embarrassed as he hurriedly took the tray from the trolley and put it down right in front of her, but she saw he risked a sly glance, his eyes moving quickly from the black stockings to her curly chestnut fleece and up to the cups of her boned basque where Costas was still fingering her nipple. She saw admiration and desire in his eyes, mingled with his embarrassment.

'She's pretty, eh, young man?' cackled Costas.

'Y-yes, sir,' stammered the waiter, studiously wiping the glasses with a white cloth.

Costas laughed. 'How old are you, boy?'

'Eighteen, sir.'

'And is this your first job?'

'Yes, sir. I've only been here a couple of weeks.'

'Well, you'll get used to seeing lots of pretty girls in this job. But maybe not like her.'

'No, sir.' The waiter opened the cage of the champagne cork and worked it loose, but his nervous hands let the cork shoot out too quickly. He hurriedly tried to pour the drink into one of the glasses as foam tumbled from the bottle.

'OK, thanks, I'll pour,' said Andrew, putting a note into the waiter's hand. 'You can go.'

'Thank you, sir,' mumbled the mortified young man, wheeling his trolley quickly out the door.

'Well, Costas, you embarrassed him,' laughed Andrew. 'Or was it you, Nina?'

She was blushing as furiously as the waiter, her mind a seething mass of emotions.

First she felt humiliation at being pawed by this ugly old man; humiliation at being exhibited to a spotty waiter like a prize cow.

Also she felt fear. What was Costas going to do with her? Surely he wasn't going to fuck her. She couldn't believe he was up for it at his age.

And if he did, what sort of old, flaccid little cock did he have? God knows what tricks she'd have to get up to in order to excite him – and what if she didn't succeed?

But apart from humiliation and fear, she was ashamed to realise that what was more important was the excitement coursing through her body. Those two

24

emotions had aroused her powerfully. She closed her eyes and felt her cunt tingle with desire. Not desire for Costas, that would be impossible. But the desire that sprang from her degradation, that of being fondled by such a disgusting-looking person, and that of being flaunted like a whore in an Amsterdam window in front of the waiter.

There was no way he would have thought she was anything but a whore. No woman would let herself be touched up by such an old man without being paid for it.

Costas lowered the bra cup on her other breast so both nipples were projecting proudly over the top of the basque.

'Ah, that's better, my dear. Your nipples are hard now. I'm glad I can still excite a beautiful girl. And make her blush!'

Andrew had finished pouring the champagne and handed a glass to Nina, and passed the brandy to Costas.

'To all of us!' he toasted, raising his glass. 'To a pleasant afternoon. And of course to continuing success in our business, Costas!'

They raised their glasses and drank. There was a brief silence. Then Costas turned to Nina.

'Come and sit on my lap. I want to touch you.'

He motioned for her to sit sideways across him, with her head resting on the end of the settee. Andrew had already pulled up an armchair and was sitting opposite them. Nina could not imagine what was going to happen. Suddenly the old man's hand thrust swiftly but not roughly inside her pussy, and pulled out again almost as quickly, making her gasp.

'Well! Should I feel complimented, my dear?' Costas showed her his hand glistening with her wetness, soaked by the juices of her humiliation and excitement.

The old man raised his hand to his mouth and licked at it.

'Ha! Nearly as good as Greek honey! Have you had Greek honey, Nina?'

'No, I haven't,' she said in a small voice. Costas put his hand to her own mouth.

'Go on, taste it!' he commanded. She put out the tip of her tongue and licked his fingers, tasting nothing but cigars and expensive aftershave through the slick wetness, but she smiled and nodded politely.

'All of it,' he said, a subtle smile playing round his lips.

Another thrill of degradation made her sex muscles spasm and she put her tongue out and licked the rest of her own sap from his trembling fingers.

He picked up his brandy.

'This tastes better, though.' He took a puff of his cigar. 'And this – not better, but different.'

His wrinkled face cracked even more as he smiled at Nina. 'Do you like cigars, my dear?'

She shook her head. 'No, I don't smoke at all any more.'

He smiled again. 'You might like one this way.' As he spoke he moved his cigar down and Nina moaned as he roughly fretted her clitoris with it and then rubbed it along the length of her sex to her wet opening.

'Christ, Costas, I always thought you had presidential ambitions,' joked Andrew. He moved his chair as though to get a better view as the old man laughed.

Nina lay completely still as he pushed the cigar inside her and started to move it in small, lazy circles. She sucked in her breath sharply as he thrust it further up into her, down slowly, then up again with a deliberate and firm stroke. A shudder of fear ran through her at the thought that he might push the whole thing inside her, lit end as well.

26

Again he pushed it into her like a small penis and her vagina contracted with excitement. As though he had felt her spasm, he looked at her with amusement as he thrust again, and then she was suddenly empty as he took the cigar out abruptly and moved it to his lips.

'Now this, the taste of your honey on a cigar – this is best of all,' he pronounced. 'I think you do like cigars after all, Nina!'

Nina smiled, her body willing the cigar to go back to fill the opening that now felt so empty. Unconsciously she thrust herself forwards for attention, embarrassed as she saw him smile at her movement.

She realised that the wrinkled old man who had so disgusted her now had the upper hand. Instinctively she'd shown him she wanted his caress, so turning the power over to him.

Taking a deep pull on his cigar, he puffed the smoke right in her face.

Nina was stung as much with humiliation as her eyes were by the smoke. She drew her head back and coughed.

'You want it now, Nina,' he said calmly. 'And just a minute ago you thought I was a repulsive old man. Didn't you?'

She felt her face redden with shame and embarrassment, and didn't dare to answer.

'Didn't you?' he repeated, his voice less friendly than it had been. Nina was suddenly afraid.

'Yes. I'm sorry,' she whispered.

Costas laughed and patted her thigh. 'Don't be frightened, my dear. I'm used to it. Women who know me pretend they like me, but what they really like is my money. Women who don't know me shudder when an old man touches them. But you know we Greeks are fond of sex, Nina, and we know how to make a woman forget everything but what is happening to her body, regardless of who is doing it.'

He paused and took a large swallow of brandy. Nina, still rosy with embarrassment and desire, watched through half-closed lids as he dipped the end of his cigar in the brandy and took another drag. Then he dipped it in again and moved the cigar down and once more toyed with the bud of flesh that had grown hard and smooth, as hard as the cigar that was nudging it. She felt that he was being too rough with her but he soon moved away, tantalising the flesh between her clitoris and her wet slit for a while before sliding it with ease inside her. But almost before she could get used to it, he withdrew it and moved it slowly back the other way.

When he reached her erect clitoris this time, the cigar felt more gentle, wet now not with the brandy but with the creamy viscous liquid of her sex. He stroked slowly and then more quickly.

Nina felt the tension mounting inside her. Again he moved, this time backwards and forwards several times, and then once more thrust the cigar into her waiting opening. Backwards and forwards the cigar went as Nina abandoned herself completely to sensation, no longer caring how old Costas was or how ugly, or the fact that Andrew was watching. All she cared about was the pleasure in her clit and her pussy, both waiting for the next caress.

The men had resumed their conversation, which excited her even more. It was as though Costas were playing with her almost as a chore while he continued with what he really wanted to do, which was talk to Andrew. She couldn't concentrate on their conversation but as Costas moved to concentrate on her clitoris, she heard Andrew say the name 'Bill Clinton' and Costas laughed, but she didn't know if he was referring to Costas's prowess with the cigar or whether they were having a conversation about politics. They could have been talking in Greek or in English, she couldn't have said which, and she didn't care.

Abruptly the cigar stopped moving. Nina's eyes opened in dismay and she turned towards the old man's face.

'You know what to say.' It was Andrew who spoke, his voice bland. She looked at him, but his eyes were unreadable, his face on her.

'Please,' she whispered, still watching.

He sat waiting, impassive, apart from the muscles of his face, which tightened as though in irritation.

'I beg you, Costas, please go on.'

Andrew's face relaxed, but his eyes were still cold.

Then the cigar was moving more quickly inside her and the Greek's other hand was rubbing her clitoris and she felt the pressure mounting unbearably until she thought her insides would burst open and then there she was, on the brink of the abyss, looking down for that wonderful moment before it swallowed her up, as her body reached a fantastic, all-encompassing climax. She didn't even know that she was making little sounds in her throat until it began to subside, and she heard soft groans coming from her lips in time with her panting breath and pulsating vagina. But it was too late to care about appearances and she just took the last drop of pleasure from Costas as he moved the cigar now so gently, and his fingers moved from the white-hot tip of her clitoris and instead pressed gently down on the mound above it, stroking down softly but firmly so that she could extract every last sensation from her climax. Slowly, he eased off the pressure and stopped gradually, seeming to know when she had wrung the last drop of pleasure from his hands.

As her eyes came back into focus, she saw him look down at her breasts, their shallow rise and fall now slowing also as she started to calm down. Then she felt him remove the cigar and saw him survey it as he raised it to her mouth.

'You've made a mess of this, Nina! But you've had a good time, yes?'

She nodded. 'That was fantastic.'

She guessed what they were both waiting for. 'Thank you.'

Both men laughed.

'That's what I like, Andrew. To be thanked by a lady. But don't worry, Nina, you can thank me properly in a minute.

'At least,' he added, 'you can try. As you get older, my dear, the body doesn't respond as well as it used to. But you are so beautiful, and I was so pleased to see your enjoyment just now. Watching is unfortunately the most exciting thing when you get to my age. But it's better than nothing.

'Andrew likes to watch, as you have obviously noticed. You know, Andrew, if you would like to make love to Nina first, I may find things easier.'

Andrew frowned.

'Jesus Christ, that would be like making love in front of my father. I can't believe you mean that. Anyway, as you just said, I like to watch too.'

Costas shrugged. 'Well, one other thing can excite me – let's talk business first! I think we need to make a few changes to protect our joint venture – let's go over them.'

With an effort, he extricated himself from Nina, and with an old-fashioned solicitousness patted her legs down on to the settee as he rose slowly.

'Don't go away, Nina. Let's sit at the desk, Andrew, so we can look at these papers properly. I'll sit on this side, so I can see Nina when I look up.'

Nina watched lazily as Costas got his briefcase and pulled out a pile of papers. She wasn't listening to the discussions the two men were having. In fact, she felt so sated that she couldn't really raise any interest in

30

anything. Her only focus was her body and the pleasure she had just experienced from such a strange source.

Reaching over to the coffee table, she picked up her barely touched glass of champagne. She sipped it greedily, her mouth and throat feeling suddenly bone dry. She got up to pour herself another glass, marvelling at the change in her since she arrived at the hotel just – she looked at her watch – two hours earlier.

Then she had been excited at the prospect of acting out the role of a prostitute with her boyfriend. Despite the sleazy connotations, it was just an innocent adventure.

When Costas walked in the room, innocence had walked right out.

You should be ashamed of yourself, a little voice in her mind whispered. You're disgusting.

But she didn't feel shame. She felt sexy, bold and uninhibited. Although she had had no control over what had happened, she felt something had been liberated inside her.

Despite being a pawn in the old man's power game, she felt oddly stronger. With contentment, she looked down at her body and traced the cleavage of her breasts with her finger.

Looking up, she saw Costas's eye on her, a small smile on his wrinkled face. For the first time she smiled at him spontaneously, but it wasn't just a friendly grin. It was a lazy, sensuous, knowing smile, one that promised that she would try to give him the same satisfaction he'd given her.

He had already turned back to the documents and was arguing with Andrew. That was fine. She had earned a rest. Picking up the champagne, she nestled back on the settee, and then, remembering that Costas wanted to look at her, propped her head up on one arm and bent one leg so that when he looked up, he would be able to see how wet she was, thanks to him.

31

Chapter Two

*S*ipping her champagne, Nina looked back on her previous sexual encounters. She now felt she could think of them with indulgent amusement, rather than with the distaste and embarrassment they had elicited from her before.

In just a few short weeks she had metamorphosed from a woman whose sex life consisted solely of masturbatory fantasies into a real sex object.

Sex object. The words brought her up short. Wasn't that what she was becoming – and wasn't she better than that?

Sure, it had long been one of her fantasies, to be a wanton vessel for others' pleasure, to be used as an anonymous tool for men's gratification. But the words themselves made her wonder if that was what she really wanted from her relationship with Andrew – or any other relationship.

Hell, what Costas had just done for her hadn't solely been for his pleasure. As he had said, the main source of excitement for him at his age was playing the voyeur. However, he had given her the most explosive orgasm she had yet had without Andrew, and had celebrated her enjoyment with her. She felt that her excitement had been important to him as well.

But then again, what he had been celebrating was also his power over her; his ability to manipulate her body until her mind had gone completely; to force her body into helpless rapture. That was power. She remembered Andrew making her beg him to bring her to orgasm the first time they had made love. Both men were used to wielding power in business, and perhaps that pervaded their whole lives, even their sex lives. Yes, maybe she was just a helpless sex object compared to them.

So what? said her new, sexual self. What could be better than this wanton enjoyment; this feeling of complete abandonment to sensation?

Nina remembered her old self having sex. The first time, as a student, was with her boyfriend Peter, who she had known throughout her school years. They had been girlfriend and boyfriend in the sense that they went around in a crowd who had all paired up, mostly casually, for disco nights and hanging around the park in the school holidays. They lived in a world of in-jokes and sayings, laughter and teasing, and knew each other too well. That was probably why sex was a disaster between her and Peter.

All the gang had gone away to college, mostly in different parts of England. Nina had gone to take a course in accountancy in London and Peter had gone to St Andrews in Scotland – so far away! But she felt she missed her girlfriends more, although she spent hours writing gossipy letters to all of them, and reading their news back. At first she was lonely at college, which was why she was so pleased to see Peter in the first Christmas holidays.

She was finding London a hard place to live in. The college was near the centre of town, but all the students lodged some miles away, and she didn't know anybody near her.

In class she found it difficult to make friends. She had a veneer of easy friendliness which hid the fact that she lacked the confidence to be herself in this new environment.

Many students were shy and hung back from joining in with the crowd, but there were always kind people who made an effort to make them part of the group. But because she seemed so confident, others assumed that she just didn't particularly want to be friends; that she was as self-contained as she looked.

Not all the gang had gone home for Christmas, and she found herself seeing more of Peter alone than she had ever done. They slipped back easily into the old joshing routine, and she began to feel happier than she had done since the start of the autumn term.

Maybe that was why, on that Christmas Day, she was so relieved by the comfort and familiarity that being with Peter again had given her, that she didn't resist his hands as she'd done in the past. They had petted before, but she had only allowed him to go so far.

As usual they sat in the dim light of the bedside lamp, while the music played not too loudly so as not to disturb Peter's mother. They talked about their Christmas and wondered what their other friends were up to, and looked forward to New Year's Eve when they would meet up with more of the gang at a party.

They played out the usual routine as they kissed and his hands moved to her breasts, his hands pulling her sweater up and her bra cups down. He fingered her nipples, rather roughly, because she had never told him that he was hurting her, and that he should touch her more gently.

He continued as usual by stroking up her thighs till he reached the forbidden zone at the top of her legs.

For the first time she didn't slap his hand away. Although she could hardly feel his caress through the thick seaming of her jeans, it excited her, more than she had expected. Breathlessly she wondered if he would try to go any further with her, not knowing if she wanted him to or not.

Peter seemed to hesitate as she offered no resistance to his hands. He unzipped her jeans and stroked her belly. He tried to pull her knickers down, still seeming to wait for her resistance, but she waited as well to see what he would do next.

He pulled at her jeans and she helped him, lifting her bottom so he could pull them clear of her hips. Peter was getting excited, she could tell, as he snatched roughly at the thick denim to pull them down to her ankles. He didn't bother pulling them off completely, leaving her to kick inelegantly at each ankle to get the trousers off, while Peter, now breathing heavily, pulled her knickers down to her thighs. Then his hand dived between her legs, feeling inexpertly for her opening, and she heard a noise almost like a growl as he found it, because she was wet. He rubbed roughly at her vulva and then hesitantly inserted a finger into the wet opening. It felt big and rough to Nina, only used to feeling her own hands or a tampon pushing into her sex. He grunted again and put another finger in, sawing backwards and forwards vigorously.

It wasn't what Nina had imagined when she had dreamed of the first time a man would enter her, but she was excited nonetheless. She knew now that it was going to happen, and when Peter moved his fingers out of her roughly and dragged his own jeans and pants off, she pulled her knickers down over her knees. But before she got them past her feet, Peter flopped heavily on top of her and she felt his cock hard against her. It was harder and bigger than she had imagined. He still

35

had his thick plaid winter shirt on, which felt rough against her exposed midriff and belly.

'You're ready for me, Nina,' were Peter's only words before she felt his hand fumble again against her wetness as he pushed his cock inside her.

For a split second before the pain started she felt indignation. This was supposed to be a seduction, and here she was with her sweater pushed up around her neck, her breasts hanging out of her bra cups, and her knickers around her ankles. Then, as Peter pushed against her, the pain engulfed her and she forgot about anything else.

For ever, it seemed, he pushed into her like a battering ram but failed to break the hymen which was stopping him from getting inside her. Apart from that pain, Peter was a lead weight on top of her, squashing her on to the bed with his face buried in her shoulder, hurting her. Suddenly the pain eased a tiny bit and at almost the same time Peter gave a muffled shout and reared up and pulled out of her, flopping back down as his come flooded her belly.

For a few minutes they lay there, Peter breathing heavily and saying 'Oh Christ' at intervals, and Nina wishing she had stayed at home. She didn't know what was expected of her next, but she wanted to get this horrible mess off her body.

Finally he raised his head and smiled at her. It was a horrible smile; a bit sheepish, a bit defiant, but mainly triumphant. 'That was pretty good, wasn't it?' he enquired. Nina was lost for words. Pulling up her knickers, she dashed to the bathroom.

Once the door was locked she tore her panties off and ran hot water into the sink. She wiped her belly frantically to remove the slimy, creamy mess that was everywhere. It smelt disgusting to her; an astringent smell like bathroom bleach. It was clinging stubbornly to her best sweater and running slowly down her body like the trail of a gigantic slug. Then she saw the blood.

Of course, she had known what would happen when she lost her virginity; it would hurt, and she would probably bleed. But the sight of the vivid red in her knickers, like her period come too soon, brought home to her what she had done.

She wasn't bothered about the loss of her virginity, but had always assumed it would be a romantic event. Instead it had been a confused, painful fumble, where instead of feeling like the most desired woman in the world she had felt like a rag doll, clothes moved out of the way to reach the necessary parts, as though nothing above or below her breasts and sex was important.

As she soaped herself thoroughly, the tears welled in her eyes. But Nina knew she had to be sensible about this. It hadn't been romantic, it hadn't been enjoyable, but it was bound to get better. Wiping her eyes and blowing her nose, she dried off, dressed and went back to the bedroom.

Peter had dressed again, inasmuch as he'd put his trousers and pants back on. Prepared to overlook his poor performance, Nina was astounded with his greeting.

'Christ, Nina, look what you've done!'

Amazed, she looked at him. He was pointing to the duvet cover, where a big red stain had spread like a rose on the plain green cotton. She giggled, and looked back at him, expecting him to be joking. But he wasn't.

'How the hell am I supposed to explain that? Mum'll guess what's happened!'

Nina realised that he was really annoyed. *He* was annoyed with *her*! He had pushed against her, hurt her, for five minutes of his own pleasure, and now this was all her fault!

'Well, it's probably time you started doing your own washing, you big wimp. Run it under the cold tap, that's the way to get blood out. Then put it in the washing machine.'

'You go and run it under the tap,' he said sulkily.

Nina gave him a withering look, though she felt sick.

'You go fuck yourself,' she said to him. 'You might manage that all right. You certainly weren't any good for me.'

And she left.

Of course, they had to see each other again when the rest of the gang came home. At the New Year's Eve party Peter tried to make amends. As everyone kissed at midnight, he whispered, 'I don't know what went wrong, Nina. Come round tomorrow. It'll be better.'

But she didn't go round, either the next day or any day after. They met up in the group but that was it. Her girlfriends asked her what had gone wrong, but she just shrugged and intimated that she'd met someone in London. They weren't too curious; all they wanted to talk about was their own new friends, the different boys on their courses, who they fancied, who they thought fancied them.

And that was that. In time there were others who took Peter's place, but it was a while before she let one into her bed. That time wasn't as bad as her first experience, as John was more mature – he was a research student and five years older, and had obviously done it before – but he wasn't particularly considerate. She tried a few times and then stopped seeing him. She became close to a couple of girls on her course, and didn't bother about the lack of sex life. Every so often she would go out with someone else and as far as she knew her friends assumed she was having as much sex as they were.

It had gone on that way for the next few years. In every other respect she had a fulfilled life. Her career had gone well. During her student years she had grown to appreciate London and the cultural life the big city offered, so she accepted a job there. She had always known she wasn't a genius, but she was a methodical and careful worker, and her rise through the ranks had been modest rather than meteoric.

Now she had a job she really enjoyed, working as an auditor for different firms, which involved going into their offices and checking their accounting systems, so she met new people all the time. She'd managed to scrape up a deposit and, closing her eyes, signed over her soul for a mortgage on her own flat in Clapham, which she loved.

She'd kept in touch with Angie from college and a couple of friends from her last job and had a modest but big enough circle that she moved in. But that circle hadn't provided any boyfriends who had lasted more than a few dates, or at least more than one sexual encounter.

Sometimes Nina wondered if she had spoiled herself with her own fantasy life, where the tableaux that played themselves out in her head were so much more exciting than the sight of a man undressing himself. Neither had there ever been a man who could touch her as well as she could herself, who was as gentle as she was to start with, who knew how to build her up to a climax as she could herself. As she watched herself in the mirror running her hands over her body, imagining that she was doing it because she had been ordered to by some captor, she excited herself so much more easily than the men she had tried to make love to.

But Andrew had entered into her fantasy life. He had given her orders, as had the anonymous hero of her dreams. He had excited her verbally as well as physically. And he had touched her as well as she could touch herself.

Starting from her reflection, she realised that the old man was looking at her. He and Andrew had obviously finished their work, as he was packing away the papers in the capacious briefcase. He smiled at her and sighed.

'That was exhausting, Nina! But I think maybe I have a little energy left, and I think it's my turn for some pleasure. Does that seem fair to you?'

'Of course,' she admitted, still doubting that he could actually manage the sex act. She looked steadily at him, wondering if his whole body was covered in the almost reptilian wrinkled skin of his face and hands, if he would undress and lie down on top of her, what his chest would feel like against her breasts, what his penis would be like.

But Costas just sat down heavily on the settee next to her.

'Don't take it personally, my dear, but I'm too old to fuck you,' he explained, as he undid his belt. 'But maybe you can make me come with your mouth.'

As he undid his fly and pulled out his cock, Nina felt dismayed. It was barely hard, small and wrinkled. Despite having felt a perverse excitement at the thought of him fucking her, now she was filled with distaste again. She had always been fastidious about what she would put into her mouth, somehow never really believing men's cocks were as clean as they ought to be. Of course, Costas was a rich man, he was dressed in expensive clothes and smelt of designer cologne, and she couldn't doubt that he'd showered that morning. But still, the thought of tasting him there, and having to suck at him until he came, was disgusting.

Once again she felt Andrew's eyes on her, willing her to do her job.

Perhaps it would excite him, seeing her pleasure his old mentor. The thought that he might get turned on by her performance stimulated her. She would do the best she could to bring Costas to his climax if it would excite Andrew. She would act the part of the slave girl carrying out her master's wishes.

40

She kneeled as though in supplication in front of the old man who looked steadily at her with his hooded eyes, her bra cups lowered to expose the whole of her milk-white breasts with their erect nipples. She reached out, as though humbly, and stroked his small and flaccid member.

'It would be better, Costas, if you could lower your trousers,' she said softly. He smiled and stood, nodding, and his trousers dropped around his old legs to his ankles. The slack flesh hung loosely from his thighs but Nina noticed that only in her peripheral vision. Her mind was concentrating on the performance to come, one she hoped would not be disappointing either to Costas or to Andrew, who was watching intently.

The revulsion she had felt at the thought of taking this old, old cock in her mouth had not left her, but she didn't allow herself the slightest tremor of distaste as she once again touched the soft flesh. There was the merest quiver of a response as she stroked down and gently passed her hands over the sac of his balls, a loose baggy monster of flesh encasing his two shrunken testicles.

Slowly she lowered her head and very gently and delicately licked the head of his penis. She heard a noise coming from his throat and, encouraged, licked all around it. The skin was dry and she worked her throat to make enough saliva to moisten it properly, as she of all people knew the importance of lubrication. She distributed her spit all around his cock, paying special attention to the little vein at the top leading to the eye, which made it jerk every time she ran her tongue up it.

Then she cupped his balls with one hand and lightly ran her mouth over them as though kissing them. Her tongue then began the journey up the slowly hardening shaft, with tiny, lapping little licks that took for ever to reach the top, little cat-like licks with her soft tongue, increasing the pressure just a little as she reached the little vein and the head of his penis. Then she moved down and once again started the slow upward process, moving at such a slow pace that she hoped Costas would imagine that his cock was huge, and so turn him on. Indeed, it was certainly bigger than when she'd started, and hard enough to put in her mouth.

Her tongue finished the last little lick at the eye of his cock, this time wiping up some salty juice, and she looked up at Costas, her tongue still out, and licked her lips. She made her eyes speak desire to him, and he was smiling and breathing more heavily now. Yes, she was doing a good job.

She ran her tongue right around her lips to moisten them and carried on looking at him for as long as she could as her mouth closed gently over him, until she had to lower her eyes and move her head down to enclose him completely in her mouth. Then instead of just moving her mouth up again, she resumed her tiny licking movements, but at the same time her lips exerted enough pressure on him as she moved up the shaft again. She heard him sigh and knew she was doing it right. This time when she reached the top and sucked more firmly on him as she went down again, she realised that his cock had swelled to its full size.

With one hand she held the root of his cock firmly as once more she licked upwards, and this time when she reached the top she licked again around the head of the shaft.

She could still sense Andrew watching, and before her mouth closed again over the old man's cock, she licked her lips lasciviously and pouted, wanting him to wish she was doing the same to him. She started to imagine him pushing Costas out of the way and falling on her himself. Excited by the thought, she stroked Costas's thigh with her free hand in time with her sucks and licks.

'Ah, there you are! I need some help, young man,' Costas was saying. Startled, Nina looked up to see that the young waiter had re-entered the room with his trolley. She hastily lifted her head away from the old man's lap, only to have Costas's papery hand push her down roughly.

Not before she had noticed that the youth was blushing furiously, his skin matching the glowing red of his pimples.

'Yes, sir?' he enquired in a low voice.

'I'm not as young as I used to be, and I need a bit of help to satisfy myself. Have you ever had a woman before?'

'Well, yes, sir.'

'Then would you be so kind as to fuck this young woman for me? From behind, on all fours – doggy fashion, I think you call it in England. Is that acceptable to you?'

The waiter said nothing. Nina looked up. His prominent Adam's apple was moving up and down as he swallowed vigorously, obviously not knowing what he should do.

'Come on,' said Costas impatiently. 'Look, will this cover it?' He pulled some notes out of his pocket and waved them at the waiter. 'I would have thought that fucking a beautiful young woman would be enough payment, but if this is what you want –'

'That's not it, sir, exactly,' gasped the young man. 'But – of course I'll do it, and I could do with the money – but isn't she a tart, sir?'

'Yes, what of it?'

'Well, I don't want to catch anything. That's not worth any money, sir.' He stood as though afraid of what Costas would say.

Nina was frozen. The spotty, ugly young waiter was talking of her as though she were a woman of the streets, a cheap tart who'd fuck anyone in the back of a car for ten pounds, who could be carrying all sort of diseases. He was frightened of catching a disease from her. And was even expecting to be paid to fuck her.

Once again, pain and humiliation coursed through her body and mind. She closed her eyes and had to squeeze back tears.

She realised that Andrew had handed the young man a condom and he was taking off his trousers. Then she heard what Andrew was saying.

'Are you ready, lad? She will be. You're dying for it, aren't you, Nina?'

I could just get up, get dressed and walk out, she said to herself. He could have his bloody money back. How much degradation does he think I can take?

Yes, and if you do, it'll be over, said another part of her mind.

Costas raised her head and smiled at her, and she shrank from the mocking triumph in his eyes.

She thought he had already got his own back when he puffed the smoke into her face, but he was exacting every drop of revenge he could.

'Now, my dear, just use that wonderful mouth of yours to lubricate me, please,' he said. Nina, cowed, once again spat as much saliva as she could on to his now fully erect cock.

'Thank you. Now if you would just turn round here –' He moved her shoulders so that she kneeled sideways in front of him '– and just put your hands on the floor. That's it, on all fours, that's perfect.'

As she stared at the hotel carpet she felt clammy hands fumble against her sex, and suddenly a big rubber-clad penis pushed against her as he found what he was looking for. Rudely he thrust inside her and she almost cried out. He was big, not particularly long but thick, and she felt her body expand around him.

'Not too quickly, please,' said Costas. 'I don't want

this over in two minutes. Try not to pop your cork as quickly as the one in the champagne bottle.'

'No, sir.'

Andrew laughed at Costas's remark.

The waiter's oversized polyester shirt billowed over her back as he started to move more slowly backwards and forwards.

She heard Costas groan. 'Take that shirt off, for God's sake. I can't see anything.'

Andrew laughed again and said something to the old man in Greek. The waiter had stopped abruptly, still inside her, and the shirt flapped around her back as he shrugged it off and then began moving inside her again.

'Hold her hips,' ordered Costas. Nina couldn't see him but presumed his scaly hands were touching himself, touching his cock, wet with her saliva. His voice had hoarsened and she imagined she could hear his hand rasping up and down. 'Pull it out further, not altogether, but as far as you can without slipping out. Nina, get down on your elbows and put your head on the floor.'

She felt like an actress in a porno film being told which way to move to give the best view. As she lowered her head she imagined the sight she presented to Costas, her arse up in the air, still framed by the black suspenders, the waiter's thin white hands on the side of her hips, and the rubber-clad cock going backwards and forwards. She moved her head to one side to try to watch Costas but he was sitting further along the settee so he could get the best view of the fuck he'd paid for.

But despite herself, thrills were rippling through her, knowing they were both playing their parts so the old man would get his money's worth. As the waiter pushed her forwards, she knew it was so Costas could see the length of thick cock that almost, but not quite, left her wet sex. Then as he pulled her back on to him and slammed into her, she knew it was so Costas could feel the power he had over her.

And it wasn't just the performance that was making her body respond. The rhythmic hammering of his cock in and out of her and the pressure on her G-spot was sending waves of pleasure through her.

She could hear Costas breathing harder and guessed he would come soon. As the waiter pulled back, almost out of her, she rotated her hips as she'd done earlier for Andrew so that he would feel her sex moving just slightly around his cock, and so that the globes of her arse were quivering in a delicate circle. She wondered if Andrew would notice, and whether he would mind that she was using the same trick as she did for him. Just like a prostitute, she thought, going through the same motions for every client.

The waiter also breathed more heavily, and as he pulled her back she rammed herself backwards hard, so that his cock slammed further into her than ever. She was enjoying feeling so full, almost distended with the thickness of his cock. Although Costas thought she was within his power, she could demonstrate hers too. Still wriggling her body, she moved her head from side to side, letting her hair swing over her shoulders as she thrust back and forth in unison with the waiter.

She sensed a change in him too – that, like her, he was now only doing what came naturally, with no thought to who was paying or giving the orders.

'Look at me!' Costas gasped. As Nina turned her face towards the settee, she realised he had moved up to sit just above her head. His clawlike hands were moving desperately and then suddenly her face was hit by his stream of come, more than she would have thought any man would have a right to produce at his age. The familiar acrid smell assailed her nostrils and the viscous mess dribbled down her cheek but she didn't care any more, because she was coming herself. Her eyes closed and she gave a low moan as her muscles started to spasm, and she felt the waiter move up a gear and finish with her.

He collapsed on top of her, prostrating her.

'Get up, that's enough,' ordered Costas. 'You're hurting her. Well done, my boy. You can clear up and go now.'

The waiter scrambled to his feet, still panting. Now the moment of climax had passed, he was again the embarrassed youth who had first entered the room. He dressed hastily, and Nina was amused to see that he hesitated as to whether to remove the condom, and where to put it, and decided it was easier to leave it on his slowly subsiding cock. Clearing the bottle and glasses, he made to move his trolley out of the room.

'Hey, you forgot your tip!'

Costas picked up the wad of notes he'd pulled out of his pocket to tempt the waiter with in the first place. Looking strangely at Nina, the waiter leaned over and took the money.

'Thank you, sir.'

'OK, good job. Don't tell the boss what you've been up to.'

The youth was out of the door before Nina had even finished wiping the sticky mess from her face. Costas turned to her with an ironic smile.

'Well, that was fine for me, Nina. What was it like for you?'

'It was fine for me too,' she replied, slowly returning his smile, still lying on the floor.

'Good! How about you, Andrew?' He turned to the younger man. 'Did you enjoy the little scene?'

'Of course,' said Andrew. 'I could watch Nina any time. But especially when she reaches her climax.'

He stood over her, looking down. She couldn't read the expression in his eyes.

'You see, Costas, she flushes here –' His black leather-clad foot moved against her chest, just where the swell of her breasts ended '– and here.' This time his shoe was high on her cheekbone. Nina kept very still and very quiet, suddenly tasting fear.

'And the other thing is, she gets extremely red down here.' And now Andrew's foot was pushing her thighs apart and the toe of his shoe grazed over her swollen clitoris. 'And of course extremely wet here.' For a breathless second the thought flashed across Nina's mind that he was going to ram his shoe right into her, but he just nudged her swollen lips. She closed her eyes and then he was crouching down by her shoulders and stroking her hair.

'The other things is, Costas, Nina has a very vivid imagination.'

Nina looked up into his eyes. Now they were transparently affectionate. She breathed out with a little girlish laugh. Andrew laughed too, and kissed her.

'God, you taste of come,' he said in mock disgust. 'Go and get washed or I won't kiss you again. I might as well have sucked you off myself, Costas.'

'No, that would be going too far,' chuckled the old man. 'Nina, congratulations. I want to give you a little present.' His hand went into his pocket, and just as for the waiter, he brought out a wad of notes. 'I'm sure Andrew has paid you well, but let me give you this. You did well.' He reached forward and pushed the notes down the front of her basque. Then as she rose he patted her behind affectionately but a little absent-mindedly.

'I must go, Andrew. See you at the office tomorrow. Nina, goodbye and thank you.'

He took her hand and kissed it, then went towards the door with his briefcase. Andrew followed, arranging a time for their meeting, and Nina went to wash again.

48

As she scrubbed the come from her face and the rubbery smell from between her legs, her mind felt curiously blank. What have I done? she tried to ask herself. No response. I shouldn't have done it! she reproved herself. Still her mind was disinterested.

I don't know what to think, she admitted to herself as she dried off. One thing she did know was that she had had three orgasms in the last few hours. Anything else was irrelevant.

Andrew came in and slipped his arms around her waist.

'How many years have we made up for today?' he murmured. 'Not many. Perhaps one week of your wasted youth. But never mind, Nina, we'll get there. Tell me, have you enjoyed yourself?'

She looked at him in the mirror and laughed. 'Come on, you just told Costas you know only too well when I enjoy myself.'

'Oh yes, but climaxing doesn't always mean enjoyment. Don't tell me you didn't hate Costas touching you at first!'

'Of course! Why, did you know I would?'

'I guessed. And I bet you hated even more the thought of sucking him.'

'Yes! And I didn't want that spotty youth inside me, either! And when you told him I was dying for it, I nearly walked out.'

'What stopped you?'

She shrugged. 'The thought that all of this might have ended.'

He looked at her consideringly.

'It wouldn't have done. Look, if you weren't happy with it I'd rather you had walked out. Don't think you have to do anything you don't want to do.'

'Shit, Andrew, part of me wants to do things I don't want to do. If you see what I mean.'

He nodded, smiling. 'Of course I do. But really, the

49

last thing I want is for you to hate it. The idea is that you enjoy it.'

'Which, as you know, I did. Anyway, I liked you watching.'

'That was part of it, I expect. But haven't you always known in your fantasies that sex can be good with an old man, or an ugly young man, as well as Mr Right?'

'Sure, in my mind.'

'But once you're caught up in it, it doesn't matter, does it? Whether you're being fucked by a spotty boy who thinks you're a disease-ridden tart, or by a cigar, or –'

Nina turned to face Andrew. 'What does that make me? When we first made love you said I was like a bitch on heat. Is that what I am? Is that why it doesn't matter who or what is inside me?'

He laughed. 'You know why I said that. It was because it excited you. And no, you're not. You're normal, Nina. It's abnormal *not* to like sex. When you're coming to the brink of orgasm, what difference does it make to you if it's a cock or a cigar, a young man or an old man, a handsome man or an ugly man? It would be abnormal to insist on only making love with a handsome hero – like me.'

'Yeah, I suppose,' she said hesitantly.

He kissed her freshly scrubbed face and then moved his mouth on to hers and kissed her tenderly.

They made their way back into the main room.

Andrew looked at his watch as Nina got dressed.

'Well, time's up! You should have been the one to say that.'

'I almost forgot how we started out here,' she admitted. 'Well, thanks for the money, anyway! I almost forgot, there's a stack of notes in the bathroom that Costas gave me!'

Andrew got the money out of the bathroom and handed it to her.

'Count it,' he suggested.

She flushed. 'I don't think I can do that twice in one day.'

'Go on!'

'Oh, for God's sake – there's almost two hundred pounds!' She looked at him suspiciously. 'Does Costas know I'm your girlfriend, or does he think I really am a call girl?'

Andrew looked slightly abashed. 'Well, I told him there'd be some entertainment laid on, but I didn't tell him my girlfriend was going to be the entertainer. So, yeah, he thinks you're a prostitute.'

'Oh, please.' Nina stared at him, open mouthed. Then she couldn't help it – she laughed.

'Well, I wanted to play the whore, so I can't really complain because I was taken for one. I must have been convincing enough, anyway.'

'Not bad,' he admitted. 'Don't worry, he'll find out that you're not really on the game. You'll meet him again on Friday, if you're up for it.'

She looked at him dubiously. 'Up for what? Not an action replay of this afternoon?'

He laughed. 'No, I promise it won't be. I'm meeting him and some friends at a club – there's plenty of entertainment laid on there.'

'What sort of club?' she asked apprehensively. 'What sort of entertainment?'

Andrew touched her cheek. 'Just a Soho strip joint.'

'Oh really? Is that all?' she said drily. 'Just your everyday sort of Soho strip joint? Is that all?'

'Actually, no, it's not your everyday sort of strip joint,' he said, amused. 'It's quite different from most. I think you'll find it interesting.'

'Yeah? And what about these other friends? They wouldn't all be men, by any chance, would they?'

He shook his head. 'No. Don't worry, I haven't

51

forgotten the fantasy about men lining up to fuck you, but give me a bit of time to arrange things.'

She poked her tongue out at him. 'Don't think you have to make all my fantasies come true. Some are probably best kept in the imagination.'

'That's right. Anyway, what do you think? Do you fancy a strip club?'

She shrugged. 'As long as it's better than the hen night I went on once, which was totally gross.'

'This will not be at all like that, I promise.'

'OK. And it won't be an orgy, either?'

He looked at her quizzically. 'What about all your orgy fantasies?'

Nina suddenly felt a bit lost and confused. 'Oh God, I don't know. Oh, for God's sake, I'll come. Of course I'll come.'

He laughed and gave her a hug. 'Don't worry. I won't let you get into anything you don't want to. I'll pick you up about eight on Friday. And I promise, there'll be nothing to worry about.'

No, she wouldn't worry, Nina told herself, as they kissed goodbye and she left the room. She wouldn't worry all the way home, at least! Maybe she wouldn't even worry tomorrow.

As Friday drew nearer, though, she knew she wouldn't be able to help being apprehensive. Deep down she knew Andrew wouldn't let her get into anything she didn't want to, but she couldn't help feeling a shudder of fear go through her.

She shook herself. You're being irrational, she told herself. You're just imagining it for an added thrill.

Then she remembered Andrew's shoe in her face, and the way the light would go out of his eyes as he gave her an abrupt command, and shivered.

She shook herself mentally. For God's sake, she told herself, he's great fun, he's amusing and urbane, intelligent and cultured. And rich. And the best fuck ever.

The doorman ushered her out of the hotel politely and she rounded the corner only to bump into the waiter. 'Sorry,' they said simultaneously, before even realising who they'd each collided with. She gave him a small smile, and he detained her with his hand.

'I want you to take the cash he gave me,' he said boldly. 'I didn't need paying for what I did. It was brilliant.'

He pulled the money out of his trouser pocket. Nina waved it away.

'Look, he paid me too. And so did An– the other man. You keep it.'

'It doesn't seem right. It's one thing paying a woman for it, but I don't see why I should get paid. I should have paid you.'

Nina laughed. 'Look, if it makes you feel any better, I'm not on the game. It was just a one-off. So there's no reason why I should have got anything either.'

The young man looked at her, puzzled. 'If you're not on the game, what the bloody hell were you doing in there?'

She smiled indulgently, feeling worldly and sophisticated. 'The younger man's my boyfriend,' she explained gently.

The waiter moved away from her as if stung. 'Boyfriend! How on earth can anyone make his girlfriend do what you just did!'

He was watching her with horror. 'What sort of hold has he got over you? Making you do it with a stranger, and that horrible old bloke?'

'It's not like that.' She knew she could never explain. 'It's just sex, you know.'

His eyes were looking at her with pity. 'I'd ditch him if I were you,' he declared. 'You're worth more than that.'

Nina was touched. She smiled at him gently again. 'Let's just leave it, OK?' she suggested, then walked away swiftly, but not before she heard him say, 'Bloody weirdos!' Laughing to herself, she stopped a taxi, and couldn't help smiling as she gave the driver her address.

Maybe she was weird, but she wasn't thinking about that now. She was looking forward to a quiet evening in with a good video and a takeaway pizza. Tonight she wouldn't be touching herself in front of the mirror. She wouldn't be thinking about anything tonight – especially not the forthcoming orgy, she told herself blackly.

She knew though that every day until Friday she would be wondering about it, looking forward to it, fearing it, getting excited about it. But not tonight, she told herself again, with a mental slap on the wrist. Tonight she'd earned a rest.

Chapter Three

*T*uesday was a busy day at work. It was always the same, Nina reflected bitterly – if you took one day off you had to work more than twice as hard the next to catch up. It was worse than taking a proper holiday, when tasks were rearranged in advance so that someone else did the work.

There was no denying, though, that she was almost grateful that she had no time to think about the previous day.

She'd felt good when she woke up that morning, stretching in bed like a cat, her sex contracting pleasurably when she remembered the events of the day before. The face in the bathroom mirror seemed to have acquired a new, knowing look. Walking to the tube station she felt she was moving almost arrogantly to an inner rhythm, like John Travolta at the start of *Saturday Night Fever*. As she held on to the rail above her head in the crowded train, she felt again the power that had surged through her in the hotel room.

But her confidence ebbed when she caught the appraising eyes of a fellow commuter on her as she happened to glance down. He didn't even look away when her eyes caught his. She felt herself blush and turned her head, pretending to read the ads. Maybe she was giving too much away by her body language.

Jesus, I'm only standing on a train, she thought furiously.

And then as she walked on to the escalator, one of the two young buskers singing Beatles songs turned and followed her with his eyes, without missing a beat on his guitar.

So she was glad to have to concentrate on work. She couldn't spare a minute to think about whether she should feel pleased or ashamed with herself. Not even at lunchtime, when her plans to meet her friend Angie had to be shelved. Nina called to apologise.

'No problem,' Angie reassured her. 'I know what it's like when you've had a day off. What were you doing, anyway? Anything exciting?'

'Oh yes, but I can't explain now,' hedged Nina. 'Look, I don't suppose you'd fancy coming over tonight for something to eat? I need a proper girlie chat.'

'Tell you what, how about tomorrow night? I've got step tonight and we usually go for a drink after. Is that OK?'

'Fine. I'll get some food in.'

'And I'll bring the wine. About seven?'

'Brilliant.'

Without a date that evening, Nina worked till half-past seven, finally feeling as though she had caught up with her analysis of the accounts of Clyde, Surrey and Co., the firm she was working on. Just as she was about to call it a day, Max whistled his way into the office and flopped down at his desk.

'God, the whole day at Mr Sleaze's office is just too much!'

Nina prickled. 'Who are you talking about?'

'Andrew Marnington, who else?'

'Actually, I happen to think he's very nice.'

56

'You're kidding! He's a real smoothie. I think there's something not quite right going on over there.'

Nina hoped he hadn't noticed she was blushing.

'What do you mean, not quite right?'

'I don't know yet. There are a few invoices that don't seem to add up.' He pulled a thick file from his brief-case. 'I must be missing something. Or perhaps I'm just seeing things that aren't there because I don't like him.' He yawned. 'Anyway, I've had enough. Come and have a drink, Nina. They didn't even give me a cup of tea this afternoon.'

'I'm beat, Max.'

'Oh come on. You'll have to give in one day. Just a drink, that's all! I won't try anything on. I really just want to sit and have a beer with someone.'

His big, innocent-looking grey eyes looked plead-ingly at her. Max had asked Nina out so many times it was almost a standing joke. She liked him, but only as a colleague. They worked too closely together and besides, although he was attractive, with his thick, cropped dark blond hair, she preferred men with a more Mediterranean look – like Andrew.

'Go on, then. One drink.'

'Unless you fancy another one afterwards . . .'

'Don't start, Max, or I'm going home.'

'I'm not! Come on! Let's go.'

It felt odd to be sitting in The Bush alone with Max. She'd been there enough times with a crowd to cele-brate someone's birthday, or the Christmas bonus, but she'd always turned down Max's invitations. She didn't want him to get the idea that there could be anything between them.

What the hell, she thought, loads of people go for a drink after work and there's nothing in it.

'So what was it yesterday – interview?'

Nina chuckled. Odd days off always led to the same comment.

'No chance. Just a bit of shopping, relaxing, you know?'

Max took a swig of his beer then sat back, both arms stretched across the top of the seat. 'No, I don't know. What do you do when you're not at work?'

Nina started to get the uneasy feeling she'd had on the tube. She and Max had got on well since they'd been working together over the last year, but he'd never shown any interest in her private life before.

'The usual things, believe it or not,' she said tartly. 'You know, reading the papers, books, going to the gym, swimming, going out with my mates. What did you expect?'

He wrinkled his nose. 'Sorry! It's just that you never talk much about what you do at weekends and so on. Look, I really would like to have more than a drink with you.'

'Max. No. How many times? Anyway, I'm going out with someone at the moment.'

He pouted. 'Guessed it. You look different. Sod it.'

Nina laughed. 'You haven't got anyone at the moment, I presume? I suppose I can't blame you for trying it on with the nearest person.'

'That's not why I asked. I really like you.' He leaned forwards. 'You seem more relaxed lately. I guessed you were probably going out with someone, but thought maybe you were just feeling a bit more sort of mellow, so it was worth asking. Don't be mad.'

'I'm not. Thanks for asking. But please, leave it out in future.'

He held his hands up in surrender. 'OK! As long as you tell me when you've broken up with this guy. I'll be your shoulder to cry on. Then we can take it from there.'

'Max!'

They both laughed, and Nina felt the pressure lifting. But she wasn't happy about looking different, or more relaxed. She didn't want the whole firm talking about her love life. She could just imagine it: 'The old Ice Queen's getting it regular now – no wonder she's a bit more cheerful,' and so on.

'This is between you and me. Don't tell the world I've got a new bloke. You know what they're like at work.'

'Don't worry about me. But I bet people will notice. Quite honestly, Nina, you look like you're being shagged senseless at the moment.' He smiled. 'It really suits you.'

'Piss off, Max. If you're not going to shut up, I'm going.'

'OK. Let's change the subject. Hey, I don't really want to talk about work, but – you didn't notice any odd invoices between Anmar Shipping and Limanos Hellas, did you?'

Andrew's company – and Costas's.

'No, none. I was checking the cargo documents, remember.'

'Yes, that's what's so strange. I found a couple of invoices that seem to refer to cargoes, which means they should have been in your files. I don't understand why two shipping companies are invoicing each other for cargoes – presumably they carry their own. That's why I went back today to check through a few more documents.'

'Well, I suppose it's to do with their joint venture.'

He stared at her. 'What joint venture?'

Flustered, Nina picked up her drink. 'I don't know anything about it. I just heard him mention it.'

'Who, Mr Sleaze?'

'Max!'

'Very interesting.' He knocked back his beer. 'I wonder what that's about.'

She shrugged. 'Don't ask me. Anyway, I'm sure there's nothing shady about it.'

'Yeah, there's probably a simple explanation. I think I'm just working too hard. I need another drink. How about you?'

'I seem to remember we were only having one,' said Nina sharply. 'I've not finished this yet – go get yourself another one if you like. But I'm leaving in ten minutes, whether you're ready or not.'

'Can I drink a beer in ten minutes? Is the Pope Catholic?'

She did like him, she thought, but as a pal. That was all. Anyway, she was busy with Andrew.

At least the tube was fairly empty by the time she left Max so she didn't have to put up with straphanging in a crush of bodies. Thankfully, she slumped into a seat, buried her head in the evening paper and managed to think about nothing but the news until she was home. A quick shower, beans on toast, and she settled down with a glass of white wine in front of *NYPD Blue*.

What the hell have I done? she asked herself.

Alone for the first time all day, a wave of shame swept through her as she reflected on the events of the previous afternoon. Like the morning after a heavy drinking session, when the euphoria of the booze-fuelled evening has gone, self-loathing kicked in. Alcoholic remorse, they called it.

She was experiencing something like depravity remorse.

'Shit, I'm even *blushing*!' she muttered. 'For God's sake, sort yourself out. You either want to do this or you don't. And if you don't, just get on the phone to Andrew now and tell him it's over.'

But perhaps I don't have to do that, she continued musing. Maybe I could just tell him that although yesterday was fantastic, I don't want to live out any more fantasies. Just to go out with him normally; just have ordinary sex with him.

Would he accept that? No way. He was pleased with

himself for taking her over the edge of normal sexual experience into a darker, more decadent world. He had obviously loved watching her come with Costas and the waiter. Not only was he a voyeur, he also admitted himself that he had slight sadistic tendencies. He wanted to be in control. There was no way he'd just put up with an ordinary man-woman relationship.

So what were the real options? First, to finish with Andrew, and to hope that now she'd discovered her sexual power the next man she met would not disappoint her as all the others had done. After all, she told herself, it was probably partly your fault that you never had a proper screw. You never took any initiative. You thought of sex as being something that was done to you, in a dark and silent room.

Now she knew she could turn a man on by stripping for him and touching herself, and she wouldn't be afraid to tell him to talk to her to turn her on. She even had a fantastic wardrobe for sex.

Yes. But there were other new experiences in store with Andrew. He'd talked about pain. What did that mean? Would he tie her up and whip her? Or put her over his knee and spank her? And he'd talked about sex with a woman. Could he arrange that for her? The thought was starting to turn her on.

She thought about one of her favourite fantasies, a party where she was the centre of attention of a group of men and women. They tied her to a table and covered her with the remnants of a feast, smearing jelly over her breasts, strawberries on her nipples, cream on the soft inside of her thighs and around her pussy. First they'd lick off the food, tantalising her with tongues on her nipples and clitoris, lapping all the cream from her cunt. Then someone would pick up a cucumber and push it a little way inside her, untying her legs so she was better able to receive it, with a man holding each of her legs and a third fucking her with the cucumber while the rest watched and made comments. There were still women licking over the rest of her body and sucking on her nipples, and then there was a big cock dangling in front of her face and she opened her mouth and began to suck, and then felt a woman's long hair brush over her opened thighs and her tongue and teeth working gently on her clit and then she came, helpless to cry out with her mouth full of the strange big cock, helpless to stop the sensation and having to carry on coming until the cock suddenly spurted inside her mouth and she had to swallow and only then beg for a let-up.

'Jesus, I don't really have to think of all that any more,' she muttered to herself, realising that despite all the satisfaction she'd had yesterday she could still turn herself on with her fantasies. Aware of the wetness between her legs, she rubbed herself through her thin cotton trousers, arousing herself even more.

She called up Andrew's face, running her mind over his long, sexy eyes, broken nose and the wide-lipped smile. She saw him watching her as Costas thrust his cigar into her, as she spread her thighs for the waiter to enter her, and as she danced over to him in her striptease, and realised she wanted more of that face looking at her. No way was she going to finish with him.

Nina imagined watching his face as he concentrated on tying her to hooks hanging from a wall so she was standing spreadeagled before him, naked. He was looking meditatively at a riding crop he was holding, and then he lifted the crop and brought it down on her thighs and belly, the look in his face a mixture of cruelty and compassion. Afterwards he kissed away her tears and told her he loved her.

And all the while her hand was rubbing frantically through her knickers and trousers. Even though she'd had sex with three men and a cigar the day before, she'd turned herself on enough to need to come now, just thinking of that face.

Just a functional wank, no finesse necessary, she thought, feeling the dampness at her crotch and her clitoris hard and plump. She tensed her legs and came with a sigh, wryly noting that despite the events of the previous day her muscles contracted just as powerfully as ever.

'It's so hot all of a sudden!' exclaimed Angie, flopping down on Nina's settee, holding aloft a carrier bag clinking with bottles. 'I can't believe how the weather changed today. It was chilly this morning but by the time I got back from lunch, I could have done with a cold shower.'

She shook her long black hair behind her head and picked damp strands from around her face with a look of distaste.

'I know, it's amazing,' agreed Nina, relieving Angie of the bag. 'God, what's all this? Two bottles of wine and two beers? On a week night?'

'Yes, well, we don't have to drink it all. But I am desperate for one of those ice-cold beers.'

'Me too,' said Nina, getting the bottle opener. She pushed a dish of tortilla chips and guacamole towards Angie. 'It'll go better with this than the white wine I had ready.'

'Yum, Mexican. I should've brought two Sols and a couple of slices of lime.'

'This is great. Cheers. Here's to a cosy evening without men.'

'Cheers,' responded Angie. They drank in silence. 'Mmm, that's better. Drinking to an evening without men's a bit of a joke, though. I haven't had anyone for ages and you definitely spend more evenings without men than with.'

Nina flushed. 'That's a bit below the belt,' she

objected. 'I never found anyone I wanted to spend many evenings with – until now, anyway.'

Angie looked at her appraisingly. 'The mysterious Andrew.'

'He's not mysterious. Well, not exactly. He's just very nice. He's got this really interesting face. Gorgeously interesting.'

'Wow. So apart from his face, what's special about him – his money?'

'No!' said Nina indignantly. 'Cheek. No, it's just, it's hard to explain, it's – well, sex. It's terrific.'

Angie raised her eyebrows. 'It must be. You look different somehow.'

'Don't tell me – I look like I'm being shagged senseless.'

'Well, I wasn't going to say it, but since you mention it . . .'

'You might not have been going to say it, but Max did.'

'Well. at least he doesn't beat around the bush,' laughed Angie.

Nina looked at her watch.

'Time to get the gourmet cuisine underway – I'm starving. Come and talk to me while I open the packets.'

'Surely you've slaved over a hot stove ever since you got in from work!'

'Of course! In your dreams.'

Nina got Angie opening a bottle of the red wine to let it breathe while she boiled water for pasta and emptied the ready-made mushroom, chilli and tomato sauce into a pan. They had been friends since college days and so always had plenty to talk about – news of old friends and gossip about their jobs. Nina chopped avocado, tomato, red onion and artichoke hearts to go on a bed of mixed salad leaves, tossing it at the last minute with garlicky dressing. In minutes the meal was on the table, the wine was in the glasses and the two friends clinked them together.

The main course was cleared from the table, the second bottle of wine was called into service and Nina was cutting into a ripe piece of Brie before Angie asked, 'So what did you do on your day off on Monday?'

Nina paused with the cheese knife still plunged into the cheese before she said carefully, 'I went to a hotel as a tart. I wore a black basque and stockings. I did a strip for one man, who fucked me, then gave a blow job to the oldest man I've ever seen in my life, and then got fucked by a spotty waiter while the old man wanked all over my face. I got paid six hundred quid.'

Angie's mouth was open in shock. 'Is this a joke?'

'No. Pretty good money, eh? Oh, and the old man made me come with a cigar and his hands.'

Angie's face was still a picture. 'Nina, have you got a secret life I don't know about?'

'Yes. I'm not a closet prostitute, if that's what you're thinking. I've got to talk to you about this, Angie. I just need someone to tell me I'm not being a complete idiot.'

'Talk about *what*? What's going on?'

Nina poured another glass of wine, drank deeply to give her courage, took a deep breath and told Angie everything. Not just what had happened two days before, but for the first time she told someone apart from Andrew what a disappointment sex had always been for her, how she had got used to satisfying herself. She began nervously, not knowing if Angie would be disgusted, but feeling a need to confide in another woman, and a need for reassurance.

Angie wasn't disgusted, but fascinated. She listened to Nina's story with barely an interruption, apart from the odd question or prompt. Her eyes never left her friend's face while she told her strange story, especially when she told her in detail what had happened just two days ago.

'And on Friday he's taking me to a strip joint with some friends of his. I don't know what's going to happen afterwards. I'm scared it's going to be an orgy, and though I've always fantasised about being in one, I'm still afraid.'

'God, so have I!' breathed Angie. 'I'm so sorry for you, Nina – sorry about your sex life before, I mean! I wouldn't have imagined it – you always seem so confident. Who would have thought you'd never even come with a man!'

'I know,' said Nina wryly. 'It must seem really bizarre to you. After all, your sex life has hardly been unadventurous.'

'I don't think you can really throw that at me after what you've just told me,' laughed Angie. 'You've had more experiences in one afternoon that I've had in the last couple of years. I have never been fucked by a cigar or a waiter. Except on holiday, of course.'

'I presume you're referring to a waiter, not a cigar.'

'Of course. Nor an old man. Well, the oldest was about fifty.'

'That's old enough, Ange. After all, mine wasn't exactly voluntary. How did you get to fuck someone that old?'

Angie looked slightly embarrassed. 'Well, since we're swapping secrets, it was Mr Pearson at college.'

'You're joking! Why?'

Mr Pearson had been the statistics lecturer, not a particularly attractive man, small and bald with wire-framed glasses, who certainly had not appeared to Nina as a sexual predator.

'John Merton bet me I couldn't get him into bed when we were pissed one night. But it was easy as anything, and he was bloody good too. He kept calling me Miss Jones, which really turned me on, saying things like, "Would you mind raising your hips just a little, Miss Jones?" and "Am I right in thinking you're going to climax now, Miss Jones?" '

'No! Why didn't you tell me?'

'I felt a bit mean afterwards. He was so nice, and it was really exciting, much better than with most of the guys. Especially than with John Merton.'

'Oh God, don't remind me. I remember him at the last Christmas dance.'

They both laughed.

'So what's he got lined up next?'

'He's just mentioned the strip show and meeting his friends, but there was all that stuff about women and pain and so on.'

'Oh, wow. I wish I'd met him first. Can I have him after you?'

'Yes, if I get fed up with him. But you don't think I'm getting myself into something stupid?'

Angie considered. 'If you'd just met him, I'd say yes, it sounds dangerous. But you've met him at his office through work. It's not like he's someone you just met in a pub. He can't do you any harm.'

'Exactly. I'm relieved you agree, though. But the real pain in the bum is I seem to be attracting other men at the moment. I've never noticed men looking me up and down before, but suddenly I seem to be sending out unconscious messages that say "Fuck me"!'

'Pheromones! Sex signals! You can't help it. You're a walking sex bomb. Don't worry about it. I'd like to be sending a few out myself.'

'I would have thought you did, all the time.'

'No, it really only happens when you're having a lot of sex – or thinking about it a lot. I'm going through a fallow period at the moment.'

They both drank contemplatively, then Angie said, 'Well, come on, let's have a look at this sexy underwear!'

Nina blushed. 'Oh, really? Come on, then.'

As they left the table to go to the bedroom, Angie caught her foot round the table leg and almost fell. 'That wine's gone to my head!' she exclaimed. 'It must be the heat.'

'It's more likely because we've drunk a bottle and a half already. And that's on top of the beer,' said Nina drily.

Angie grinned. 'Well, a good story always needs plenty of lubrication to swallow! Come on, let's have a fashion parade.'

'I'm not putting it on for you,' laughed Nina as she opened her bottom drawer where she'd stored the new clothes. 'This is what I wore on Monday.'

She laid the black basque, lacy pants and stockings on the white duvet.

'Wow! That must be the sort of thing real prostitutes wear,' said Angie, picking up the stockings. 'I like these lacy tops, though stockings are bloody uncomfortable.'

'Well, I wouldn't wear them for work, but I loved wearing them for sex. I was turned on just putting them on,' confessed Nina. 'It was definitely worth it. Anyway, this is my favourite.'

She brought a blue silk set out of the drawer, a plain camisole with shoestring straps and tiny boxer shorts which fastened at each side with silk-covered buttons. Angie breathed in sharply.

'I bet that looks fantastic on!' she said. 'And imagine someone undoing those buttons.'

'That's what I thought,' said Nina simply. 'And here's the pure outfit.'

It was white, of course, a satin half-cup bra and briefs set, with a matching suspender belt and white stockings.

'That's a bit boring,' said Angie.

'Yes – but –' Nina picked up the briefs and showed

68

Angie that the crotch was cut away. 'I thought it might be a good idea.'

Angie laughed. 'Oh, yummy. Someone can just lift your skirt and fuck you anywhere, as though you weren't wearing any knickers. Oh God, imagine somewhere public, you know, like on a train. You could do it between stations. It'll be great for the orgy.'

'That's not all,' said Nina. 'I wasn't sure about this one.'

'Wow!' Angie stared in silence. The last outfit was of soft black leather. The top was halter necked, with wired bra cups, cropped off just under the bust. There was a silver zip going all the way down from the top of the neck with a little silver chain to pull on. The pants were matching leather hipster shorts, also with a zip from top to bottom.

'That's fantastic,' breathed Angie. 'That's my fantasy gear. I've always imagined being dressed in black leather and holding a whip. Not that I think I could really hurt anybody, but I wouldn't mind pretending.'

She picked up the bra top and held it to herself, looking in the mirror.

'I'd probably hate it,' she went on. 'But you know it's nice to imagine.'

'Don't I just know! You're talking to an expert here,' laughed Nina. 'Why don't you try it on?'

'I couldn't,' protested her friend, putting the top down. 'Trying on other people's underwear is – well, it doesn't seem right.'

'Hello! This is me you're talking to! It's not like it came from Oxfam! Go on, put it on,' urged Nina. 'I'll put the blue on and we really will have a fashion parade.'

'I must be drunk,' muttered Angie, as she undid her button-through dress and let it drop to the floor. Nina noticed that like herself she was wearing serviceable but boring white undies, but they looked good against the tanned skin. She slipped off her bra and picked up the leather halter neck and unzipped it.

'My hair's in the way,' she protested as she pulled the leather over her shoulders. Nina helped by holding Angie's long black hair up while the snug leather top went on. Angie managed to engage the zip at the bottom and pulled it up by the chain.

'Of course, your bust is bigger than mine,' she said wistfully.

'True, there's a bit of slack there,' admitted Nina. 'But it still looks great. Put the bottom on.'

'You too!' said Angie indignantly. 'I thought we were doing this together.'

It took Nina no time to pull off her wraparound skirt and T-shirt. She wasn't wearing a bra and pulled the blue camisole on. They both hung back, a bit embarrassed about taking their knickers off in front of each other.

'This is ridiculous,' Nina observed. 'Come on, knickers down.'

Angie giggled and swifly pulled her white knickers to the floor and grabbed the leather ones, unzipping them. Nina also started laughing as she dropped her own cotton briefs and unbuttoned the blue silk. The silk was much easier to handle than the leather, so Nina was ready while Angie was still working the leather shorts up over her hips.

'Unfair!' pronounced the dark girl, as she finally settled the shorts in place and started to zip them up. 'Ouch! I've caught my pubes!'

Nina couldn't stop laughing. 'I guessed there'd be a catch in those things. Oh, a catch, do you get it?'

Angie giggled again. 'It's all right for you. It's really hard to do these up. I must have bigger hips that you.'

'A bigger bum, I think,' chuckled Nina. 'Look, you hold the top together and tuck your pubes in, and I'll do the zip.'

She closed the shorts easily and raised her eyes to her friend's. Face to face, just inches apart, Nina suddenly stopped laughing and felt a shudder of desire go through her. Stop it, she told herself. She's your friend. Andrew has promised me a woman. This is different.

They both turned to face the mirror.

'So what do we look like?'

Her eyes told her. They both looked fantastic. Angie's tanned body in the zipped-up leather outfit was stunning.

'Turn round,' Nina insisted, pirouetting her friend. 'Your bum is beautiful in that. It is bigger than mine, by the way,' she teased. Angie put her head over her shoulder, straining to see.

'It doesn't look huge, does it?' she asked anxiously.

'Of course not! With your hair coming down past the top, all you can see is hair, leather bum and suntan. You'd turn anyone on.'

Angie smiled brilliantly. 'Yes, and just look at you!'

Again they surveyed the mirror. Nina knew only too well what she looked like in the blue silk; the last time she tried it she was so turned on she had to bring herself off right there in front of that mirror.

The camisole was a perfect fit, loose enough not to flatten her breasts but tight enough that her nipples showed through. It was short, ending just at the waist, and the panties were low cut, so the swell of her hips was pronounced. Her creamy flesh was flattered by the colour. Nina turned back and forth.

'Yes,' she said simply. 'Pretty good, eh? What a pair we are.'

The contrast of the two in the mirror was exciting her. It's time to stop this, she told herself.

'Well, shall we get the playthings off and get back to the wine?' she asked. Angie nodded ruefully, pulling at the zip at the top of the halter.

'Yes, fun's over. I love dressing up, though . . .'

71

She trailed off, zip still only half undone.

'Actually, I don't want to take them off. If it's all right with you.'

Nina raised her eyebrows. 'You want to borrow them?'

Angie shook her head and laughed. 'No. But it's nice just hanging out in clothes like these. I love the feel of this, and I love how I feel in it. And I love seeing you in that.'

She left the room. Nina suddenly felt breathless. What was going on?

Angie returned straight away with their wine glasses, topped up.

'Anyway, it's so hot, the less we've got on the better. To hot days and steamy nights!'

'Yes, I'll go for that,' said Nina as they clinked glasses. She sat cross-legged on the bed. 'Well, if you want to look at yourself, this is the most comfortable place!'

Angie drank deeply. She set her glass down on the bedside table and got on to the bed on all fours, looking at herself in the mirror.

'My imagination's running riot looking at us dressed like this,' she breathed. 'Aren't you imagining things, Nina?'

'Well, I've told you that I spend a lot of time imagining,' she stalled. 'So what's on your mind, Angie?'

Angie crawled closer to Nina, still on all fours, and spoke in her ear.

'Kissing you. And undoing those buttons of yours. Stop me if you want.'

Nina's heart leaped. 'Angie, you're my best friend. Is this a good idea?'

'Probably not. But you've really turned me on, talking about what you've been doing, and now seeing us both like this has really got me hot.'

'You've done this before, haven't you? With a woman, I mean?'

Angie nodded. 'It's not something you tell your friends. You think they're going to be waiting for you to jump on them every time you go to the loo when you're out. Anyway, you always seemed a bit too tight-arsed.'

'Oh, cheers. So what's it like?'

Nina was feeling decidedly turned on.

'Depends. It's been brilliant and totally disappointing. I've only done it three times, and once was with a man as well – I was just the entertainment for the night. They were married. That was pretty good, though, and then I got fucked by him as well, which was a bonus. The first time was a real letdown – I'd just hit on this temp at work because she was a lesbian and I really fancied trying it with a woman, but she was too uptight.'

Angie's voice softened dreamily. 'The last time was amazing, though. I got chatting to a woman in a feminist bookshop near Charing Cross. I told myself I'd gone there to find some new women's fiction, but really I was just out to pull. She was bi as well, and great looking, short red hair and a lot of attitude. I saw her a few times, and the sex was terrific. But she was from the States, and went home. I wish she was still around.'

Nina felt as aroused by Angie's stories as she was when Andrew murmured fantasies to her while they had sex.

'God, Ange, just the thought of it makes me feel really horny. But it doesn't seem right to fuck your best friend. I mean, if you were a man, I'd feel the same – that it'd come between us somehow.'

Angie sighed. 'I suppose so. Shit, I'm not begging you for it, Neen. You just got me turned on with your stories, and then trying this on got me even hotter, and

73

the heat makes me feel really sexy. Just let's have a little kiss.'

'Sure.'

Still cross-legged, Nina turned towards Angie. Their faces were only inches apart and their lips met in seconds. Nina closed her eyes. Just the thought of kissing another woman was enough to make her cunt tingle even more than it already had been. Angie's lips were soft and her breath sweet and winey. She hesitated before going further. Then Angie's tongue snaked into her mouth and her own came out to meet it. Then they were tonguing each other hard, and somehow Nina lost her balance – whether Angie pushed her down she didn't know or care – and she was lying underneath her best friend and they were rubbing against each other. Angie's bone was grinding into her and she arched upwards to push her sex against it. The smell of the leather mingled with the scent of Angie's shampoo and the faint tang of fresh sweat sent Nina's senses into overdrive. The heat wasn't the only reason she was sweating.

'That's enough, Ange.'

Her arms lifted Angie up and out of range of her mouth. Her friend laughed. 'I thought I might come for a minute – how about you?'

'Yeah, for a minute. But it's still not a good idea.'

'You're in charge,' said Angie, shrugging.

Nina laughed. 'Makes a change from when I'm with Andrew.'

'Or with any other man, from what you said.'

Nina frowned. 'That's right. I'm sort of liberated now – except I'm always being told what to do.'

'Sounds good to me,' said Angie. 'But you ought to have a turn at being in charge. You've got to take control of your own sexuality, not just let Andrew look after it for you. That'll make you feel more confident with other men too.'

'Mmm. I'll bear it in mind,' said Nina absently. 'Coffee?'

'I'd rather have a vibrator, if you've got one handy,' Angie suggested.

Nina shook her head. 'Sorry, I've always made do with my hands.'

Angie sighed. 'OK, I'll wait till I get home.' She unzipped the leather top, exposing her brown breasts, and shrugged it off her shoulders, then wriggled out of the shorts. 'If you ever get tired of these, don't give them to a charity shop.'

Nina wrapped herself in her towelling robe and went into the kitchen to put the kettle on. My God, she thought, as she put the decaffeinated coffee beans through the grinder, this is bizarre. I've known Angie for years, but if it hadn't been for my experience with Andrew none of this would have happened. It's like he's waved a magic wand over me. Things don't just happen to me because he makes them, they happen anyway!

Will tomorrow bring another sex hangover, she wondered? Would Angie suffer from it too? Anyway, after all the booze a real hangover would probably drive other thoughts out of her mind. Sod it, she decided, as she poured water on to the coffee, she wasn't going to punish herself with remorse again.

Chapter Four

*T*he sultry weather broke with a thunderstorm on Friday afternoon, but instead of clearing the air the heat returned, leaving the streets of London steaming. Andrew had offered to pick Nina up to take her to the club, but it seemed pointless for him to go from his flat in Regents Park down to Clapham just to get back to Soho, so they'd arranged to meet at Leicester Square tube station.

Nina regretted her independence when she dressed. She'd planned to wear the blue outfit under a short lilac slip dress with a flippy skirt, but while two sets of shoestring straps would look suitably sleazy – she hoped – in the strip club, she realised that newly liberated or not, she didn't have the confidence to wear it on the tube.

Instead, she put on a white button-through gypsy top with cap sleeves and a drawstring neckline, which she could loosen when she got to the club to show off the blue straps and maybe a bit of shoulder, with a little print skirt in blue and white which went with both top and undies. She moussed her hair and scrunched it with her fingers while she dried it to give a slightly mussed and tangled look instead of her usual sleek bob. A dab of tinted moisturiser, mascara and a pinky-brown lipstick completed the look. She felt good.

The rain might as well not have fallen. It had completely evaporated and the air was heavy once more as Nina set off on her second trip to the tube station that day. As usual there was a little group of winos on the benches on the edge of the common, mumbling incoherently or arguing among themselves. As she walked past one old boy intoned his usual 'Be happy!' She smiled at him but then his companion lifted his bottle from his lips and shouted at her, 'Hey, darling, I bet you've got a nice hairy mary!'

Nina wished the ground would open and swallow her up.

'Fuck off,' she hissed, glancing round nervously. Thank God there was no one around. The tramps guffawed drunkenly. She scuttled down the steps to the station, mortified. Apparently it wasn't only nice men who picked up on the pheromones.

Jittery, she waited for the train, trying to calm herself down with some deep breathing. It was a coincidence, she knew. Tramps just say that sort of thing. As the train approached, the wind blowing through the tunnel cooled her blushing cheeks. Relax, she told herself.

The carriage retained the smell of the thousands of sweaty commuters who'd piled into it during the day, but the night-time crowd was good humoured, groups of boys and girls determined to go for it on Friday night, the girls dressed up and made up and the boys dressed down. A few couples turned in their seats towards each other and spoke with their eyes rather than words. There were men in overalls going on to the late shift, and of course a silent child begging.

Where did they come from? she wondered. Maybe Bosnia or Kosovo. They looked like Muslims, with their headscarves and dark complexions. London absorbed so many displaced people, refugees, asylum seekers. The break-up of the Communist bloc had changed the whole of Europe, not just the east. She gave the girl a few coins.

Half the Friday night revellers left the carriage with her at Leicester Square and Nina felt carried away in the anticipation of having a good time that fizzed through the crowd riding the escalator.

She saw Andrew as she pulled her Travelcard from the machine, leaning against the subway wall and staring into space. He was wearing a black T-shirt and khaki jeans, his muscular arms looking tanned against the black of his short sleeves. His hands were in his pockets and he bent one leg at the knee so that his loafer-clad foot rested on the tiled wall behind. In profile his broken nose and craggy brows gave him a slightly menacing appearance. Nina felt the heat of the night concentrate itself in her.

Loosening the drawstring around her neck she pulled the gypsy blouse down just past her shoulders, exposing the two thin straps of her silk vest, just as Andrew turned. He smiled and raised his eyebrows as he walked towards her, pulling her close to him and kissing her forehead.

'Pretty gypsy,' he said appreciatively. 'You should just be a bit darker – but you look good. Your hair's nice, sort of wild. Hope you're managing to keep cool.'

'It's not easy,' said Nina opaquely, looking at the crinkles around his eyes and feeling completely the opposite. 'I could do with a drink.'

'Yeah, let's have one before we go to the club. It's a bit limited there.'

Nina felt as though they had to physically push their way through the heat as they left the station. It was so oppressive it was like walking through water rather than air. The traffic was locked outside and horns were blaring, drivers losing patience as they sweated in the queues.

They turned down Old Compton Street and walked along with the crowds through the scents of garlic and coffee and beer erupting from the bars and restaurants and shops.

'London changes so much in summer. It gets noisier and more upfront, like New York, or Buenos Aires,' said Andrew. 'The heat just transforms it. I love it like this.'

He squeezed Nina's waist. 'It's so sexy. Everyone wearing less clothes, out looking for a good time – don't you think so?'

She wondered for a second whether to tell him what had happened with Angie, thanks to the heat and wearing less clothes, but decided they'd both savour it better when they were turned on later after they got home.

Or at the orgy, her inner voice muttered.

'It's brilliant,' she agreed. 'You're right, wearing summer clothes makes you feel looser, more aware of your body.'

'And other people's,' he added, looking pointedly at her breasts.

Andrew steered her into a crowded bar off Wardour Street and installed her at a small table while he went up to order a Budvar for himself and a kriek, the Belgian cherry beer, for her.

Nina looked round, wondering how many of the punters were going on to a strip show at the end of the night's drinking. She told Andrew her thought.

'That crowd over there, almost certainly,' he said, pointing at a group of middle-aged men obviously in town for a good time. 'But not the same sort of show we're going to. They'll be rushed for an entrance fee, sold fake champagne at fifty quid a bottle and see absolutely nothing because they'll be too busy talking to a hooker who'll make them pay a fortune for a blow job. Not that there will be much to see on stage anyway. Whereas we will be close to the stage, have a proper drink, and see a selection of really erotic acts, not a couple of girls skipping around a bit and taking their clothes off with as much interest as if they were on the checkout at the supermarket.'

'So how come they won't go to our club?'

Andrew raised his eyebrows. 'That's the great thing about living in the city. You know where to go. The other half of the punters in town tonight haven't got a clue.'

She laughed. 'You make me feel as though I'm an innocent in my own town.'

'Well, not really. You know which bars, clubs and so on to go to. Many provincial girls wouldn't know how to find a strip club.' He knocked back his beer. 'Anyway, not just anyone would get into this place. Ready to be initiated?'

Nina savoured the last drop of the strong, fruity beer and they left the bar and hit the night once more. The sun was setting and the sky in the west was a fiery red as Andrew led her through the maze of Soho streets, past Chinese restaurants and burger stands until they turned into a quiet alley where they entered a shop doorway, above which a sign advertised 'Live Sex Show'. The man on the door began a spiel but Andrew murmured something to him and instead of ushering them down the steps to the basement club he opened the adjacent door and they went up a dimly lit flight of stairs.

Another closed door was opened to Andrew's knock by a muscled bruiser who would have had no trouble getting rid of any undesirable visitors. Finally they gained admission to the club. It was a small, brightly lit, smoky room almost full of customers sitting at wooden tables and chairs, making desultory conversation while a tape played blues music in the background. There was a small wooden stage no more than three feet high, and most of the punters were gathered in front of it. Apart from the lighting it could easily have passed for a jazz club.

It was a hip crowd, Nina noticed with surprise. There was a young, eccentrically dressed group who looked like art students and a gang of impossibly thin, attractive women who could have been models. A party of Latino men wearing skin-tight trousers and open shirts were jammed round one table, smoking and talking energetically.

And sitting right in the middle of the room was Costas with several other people.

'Hey, Andrew! Nina!'

Chairs had been saved for them, and Nina sat down, feeling at once that she wasn't dressed for the part at all. Introductions were made. There was an older woman who Nina realised was also Greek, her name Ariadne. She was about 50, her dark hair threaded with grey and swept upwards, her features strong and handsome. Her black dress was probably Armani, her perfume definitely Chanel. She inclined her head regally towards Nina, while Andrew bent down to kiss her cheek.

Next to her was a tall peroxide blonde with short hair and a pale face, made up sixties-style with sooty lashes, eyeshadow and lots of mascara, full lips emphasised by beige lipstick. She was dressed in a black leather basque top which made Nina wish she'd worn her own black leather outfit, showing off a full cleavage, wide shoulders and muscular arms. She stood up to shake hands with Nina, smiling openly.

'Hiya! I'm Beverley.'

She was wearing a minuscule black leather skirt on top of the basque. Nina felt slightly less overwhelmed by the girl's obvious friendliness.

The third woman was introduced as Katya. She too was dressed in black, with dark hair slicked back from her face. She nodded curtly at both Nina and Andrew, seeming bored with the company, smoking and staring into space.

Nina sat down between Beverley and Andrew. There were bottles of vodka and brandy on the table and Nina accepted a vodka, diluting it with orange juice.

'This place is fantastic,' the blonde said to Nina. 'Just look at some of the outfits.' She pointed out a woman in a black chiffon dress standing right at the front with other glamorous companions. High necked, long sleeved and knee length, the dress would have been the height of impeccable chic, were it not transparent. The woman wore no bra, her firm breasts outlined by the tight chiffon. Her only concession to modesty was a black G-string. She had wavy dark hair cascading down her back, and her face was dominated by lips painted a brilliant red. As she was talking she gesticulated imperiously, lipstick-stained cigarette in her hand.

'She looks like she's auditioning for *Carmen*,' observed Nina.

Beverley looked around the room. 'And how about the redhead?' She indicated a woman with brilliant red hair and a deadly pale face, whose shimmery silver dress was just like a longer version of Nina's camisole, with tiny straps and a low neck, close fitting, but ending just below her crotch. She turned quickly as someone spoke, revealing pants matching the silvery material of the dress.

'Are they strippers?' Nina asked Beverley.

She shrugged and smiled teasingly. 'In this place you just don't know till the action starts,' she said. 'Won't be long now, anyway. Ever been to a strip show before?'

'Just a really tacky hen night a few years ago, before you started getting loads of Full Monty shows. You know, a couple of Tom Jones lookalikes who got members of the audience on stage to undress them, then at the end one rubbed his cock all over my friend's head – it made me feel sick.'

Beverley laughed. 'Yeah, real suburban sleaze. This is really cool compared to that crap.'

She leaned closer to Nina. 'Are you bi?'

Nina blushed. 'God, no. I mean, I've never done it with a woman.' Apart from the other night with Angie, her inner voice murmured. That doesn't count, her conscious mind retorted. You didn't really do anything.

She looked curiously at Beverley. 'How about you?'

'Well, I don't really like labels, though I suppose most people would call me bisexual. I've been with Ariadne for about three years now. She's probably ninety-five per cent gay, I suppose. She's the only constant in my life. I can't imagine life without her.'

'Do you live with her?' asked Nina.

Beverley laughed. 'God, no! She's a massively high-powered businesswoman. For one thing, she spends as much time abroad as she does in London, and for another, I like my independence.' She chuckled meditatively. 'My men, and other girls – not that I keep anything a secret from Ariadne. She loves to hear about my other girls.'

She put a hand on Nina's shoulder. 'Do you want to be one?'

Before Nina could react, the lights dimmed and a short man climbed on to the stage and stood in the spotlight. The music changed, bizarrely, to *The Nutcracker Suite*, and with no preliminaries he announced the first act as the Ballet Russe. Nina was bemused as a ballerina danced across the stage. She wore a white tutu and pointed shoes, her dark hair pulled up into a bun in the classical style.

The ballerina continued to dance for a couple of minutes, as accomplished as a professional dancer, as far as Nina could tell. Then a man dressed in black with a cloak hanging from his shoulders leapt into the centre of the stage. He too was obviously a real dancer, his tights displaying his bulging leg muscles. He carried a cane and pointed at the ballerina's breasts as she spun round. Without missing a beat her hands pulled at the top of her tutu and Nina heard the sound of velcro ripping as it came apart. She held it aloft as she continued to spin topless, her small firm breasts free. There were murmurs of appreciation from the audience. Then the man pointed the cane at her crotch and she dropped the top and put her hands under the flare of the skirt. Again there was the tearing noise and the bottom of the tutu was ripped away.

The ballerina continued to dance as before, naked apart from the ruff of the tutu around her hips. Nina's pulse shifted up a gear as with the rest of the audience she fixed her eyes on the dark thatch of hair and the tight, muscled buttocks as the dancer continued, as though oblivious to her nudity.

Next the man patted her thigh with his cane and she raised one foot with her hand and held it up, pirouetting on one foot, her vagina exposed and open. At the end of every pirouette she paused, facing the audience, and the man tapped her inner thigh with his cane as though commanding her to twirl round again.

She stopped and the man took one of her hands and pulled her around him so that she had her back to the audience. As she raised one of her legs in an arabesque, he kneaded her buttocks, pulling them apart so they caught a glimpse of the deep rosy entrance to her arse. Then he turned her round and while she raised her arms gracefully above her head and bent her legs in the pliée position, he rubbed the cane from behind along the length of her pussy. She stood in position while the cane pushed backwards and forwards several times.

The obscene gesture raised another collective gasp

from the crowd. Nina wished it was her own pussy being pressed by the cane. The ballerina was sweating but the moisture that started to bead the stick wasn't sweat, Nina knew.

Abruptly the man stopped and so did the music, and the woman curtsied while the man retrieved her discarded clothing. They left the stage.

'You see, Nina, when I wanted you to dance for me as you stripped, I was expecting something a bit more classical,' joked Andrew.

He'd barely lowered his voice and Nina flushed as she felt rather than saw the smiles on the faces of Ariadne and Katya. Beverley, however, pressed her arm and changed the subject.

'That's got me hot already,' she announced generally. 'How are they going to follow that?'

She was quickly answered as the MC announced the next act as Barbara. A blowsy blonde skipped on to the stage and started to perform a standard striptease. Beverley turned to Nina again.

'Did that turn you on?'

'God, I wouldn't be human if it didn't,' replied Nina. 'Have you seen that before?'

'No, that's the great thing, they keep changing the acts here. But you always have a fair portion of this sort of thing.' She waved a dismissive hand at the stripper on stage, who was now down to a bra, G-string and hold-up stockings.

'She must be forty, and she's too fat – though some men like that. And she'll put out in the back afterwards.'

Nina watched in fascination as the stripper removed the bra. Her breasts were massive and swung happily after being released.

'Mind you, I like big tits,' said Beverley teasingly. 'You look like you've got a nice pair, Nina.'

Nina blushed again. 'Well, if I'd known exactly what

sort of entertainment was being laid on I might have made a bit more of them.'

In a flash the other girl put her hand out and cupped one of Nina's breasts, weighing it in her hand. Nina gasped and pushed the hand away. Andrew laughed.

'Approve, Beverley?'

'Oh yes. If you don't mind.'

'What about if I mind?' said Nina fiercely.

Beverley patted her arm. 'You only mind because the others are watching.'

Nina wanted to keep feeling angry, but had to laugh and admit that Beverley was right.

Andrew kissed Nina on the cheek.

'You want her, don't you?' he whispered. 'Wait till later.'

She still felt annoyed with him for announcing to the table in general that she'd stripped for him, and gave him a cool glance.

'That's up to me, isn't it?'

Andrew's eyes took on an opaque look. 'Everything you do is up to you,' he said flatly. Nina felt inexplicably as though she'd lost an argument.

The woman left the stage, naked by now, but there wasn't a great deal of interest from the audience. The next stripper came on bouncing a large rubber ball, her hair in pigtails and dressed like a schoolgirl on games practice in a crop top and tennis skirt. She was small and pretty and made a show of being oblivious to the audience while she did a couple of cartwheels and back flips before stripping off and bouncing on top of the ball and grinding against it as though she meant it.

The lights went up again after she had left the stage and Andrew poured Nina another drink and excused himself. Costas, Ariadne and Katya were talking intently and Nina was once more thrown together with Beverley.

'You'll want me after the next act,' the blonde told her matter-of-factly. Nina laughed at her cheek.

'How do you know?'

'Because it's me!'

Nina looked at her in astonishment. 'What do you mean, it's you?'

'The next act is me. If I turn you on, will you come upstairs with me?'

'What are you doing an act for?'

'Ariadne thought of it. She loves watching me, and I thought it'd be a real turn-on. Even more so now you're here. So will you come upstairs with me after?'

Nina shook her head quickly, as though to clear her brain. 'Wait a minute. What is upstairs? Is it a knocking shop?'

Beverley shrugged. 'Well, the performers make a few quid afterwards if they want. I wouldn't, but I'm only doing it for fun.'

'For God's sake. Is this just a front for a brothel?'

Beverley laughed. 'Don't be so po-faced! Of course it's not a brothel. But let's face it, the idea of a strip show is to turn the punters on. It makes sense to make the most of it afterwards.'

She stood up. 'Better get ready. Katya?'

The unsmiling woman nodded and rose and left with Beverley, who rubbed her hand across Ariadne's cheek before leaving.

Costas turned to Nina. 'Are you enjoying the show, Nina? What was your favourite act?'

'It had to be the ballet,' she told him.

He smiled. 'For me too. Though I think Andrew appreciated the games lesson most.'

Nina looked at him uncomprehendingly. Then it hit her that Andrew had been away for longer than it would take to use the toilet. 'Oh, please,' she said quietly. Presumably he was upstairs with the schoolgirl.

Costas laughed. 'You're not a jealous person, are you?' he asked. 'After all you did on Monday, Andrew probably feels as though it's his turn.'

Ariadne was looking on, obviously amused.

'Don't listen to him, Nina,' she said softly. 'Costas enjoys winding people up. His imagination's overactive, too.'

'Yes, I've had experience of that,' said Nina tartly.

The old man laughed.

'I'm glad you've still got your sense of humour,' he said, his eyes glinting malignantly. As she had the last time she met him, Nina got a strong sense of power and ruthlessness behind the facade of the genial old man.

Andrew returned just as the lights went down again. Costas said something to him that Nina didn't hear, and Andrew laughed and patted Nina's arm.

'He's talking rubbish,' he whispered to her. But she pulled away from him, sure she could smell sex on him. She thought of leaving, but then forgot it as Katya led Beverley on stage.

She was still wearing the leather basque, though it looked as though it had been laced more tightly, pulling her waist in and pushing her breasts up and out. The skirt had been discarded to reveal that the basque flared out from the tight waist to end just above a silky shock of impossibly blonde pubic hair. Suspenders, black stockings and high-heeled shoes completed the outfit.

More excitingly, there was a thick leather choker around her neck. Attached to it was a chain, which Katya, now dressed in a black catsuit and thigh-high boots, was holding.

There was a rumble of comment and appreciative gasps, which were drowned out as the music increased in volume and changed to the sound of rhythmic, insistent drumming. Andrew was watching Nina's face.

'Isn't this the stuff of one of your fantasies, Nina?' he asked.

Nina felt uncertain. She certainly had fantasised of being in such situations. But now, confronted with it, she felt indignant on Beverley's behalf, led by the chain like a dog, dressed up to titillate, and she was worried about what was going to happen next.

Beverley was not, however, looking at all ill at ease. She appeared to have assumed the role she wanted to play; having shed her friendly and open manner and gazing around the room almost arrogantly, as though she were in control of the situation rather than the one being controlled. She inclined her head slowly at their table with an enigmatic smile, and then again stood straight upright.

Katya clapped her hands and two uniformed men appeared. One took the neck chain and fastened it to the wall behind while the other bent down and put cuffs around her ankles and chained them far apart. She stood there, her sex exposed, still looking confidently into the crowd.

Nina felt a deep thrill. Although she had had doubts about what was going to happen, she knew that Beverley had chosen this herself. By her enthusiasm before the performance it was obvious that she wasn't doing it under duress. She wriggled a little in her chair, clenching the muscles of her sex to feel the throb of pleasure and anticipation inside. Andrew was watching her and put his hand on her thigh under the table. Although she was still annoyed with him, she let it rest there.

Katya picked up a whip, which she cracked experimentally in the air.

Although the crowd had been excited by the erotic cabaret that had preceded Beverley's act, for the first time there was a palpable charge of sexual energy in the atmosphere. Unlike during the other acts there were no remarks about the performers. Everyone was watching the stage as Katya raised the whip and brought it down on Beverley's thighs. There was a collective gasp as Katya struck again and again.

In contrast, Beverley had not uttered a sound. Already her thighs were marked, but the only other sign she gave of the pain was a heightened colour in her still impassive face. Stroke succeeded stroke but her eyes still gazed out challengingly into the room. When Katya lay down the whip, Nina sighed with relief; but only to see her pick up a riding crop.

The blonde shuddered in anticipation, and so did the audience. The relentless drum beat of the music echoed the throbbing of Nina's pulse. She knew everyone in the audience was as aroused as she was.

This time, though, they did not see the blows strike home, for Katya brought the crop down on Beverley's backside. Still she did not cry out; but with the first blow her eyes closed, and with every following blow her head drooped a little further, until it was almost facing the floor, which was as far as the chain would allow it to droop. As her head fell forward, Nina felt almost a shock of identification with her and a surge of electric excitement. As though he sensed it, Andrew's hand moved from her thigh to her heated cunt, feeling the slipperiness of her under the silk as he traced a line up to her clit. But Nina shook her head impatiently, and Andrew moved his hand. It wasn't him she wanted.

Finally, Beverley moaned. As though this was the signal, Katya stopped and lay down the crop. She went over to the blonde and raised her head. Nina could see her smile wanly. Then the severe Katya took Beverley's face between her two hands and kissed her.

She was unshackled and turned round to show the marks of the crop, which were deep and red. As she turned back to face the room, the dominatrix dropped to her knees and buried her face in the blonde pubic hair. Nina thought she could see Katya's tongue delve and probe around Beverley's clitoris, but wondered if she was imagining it. The blonde stood impassive and still as the woman's head worked from side to side, only suddenly grasping her shoulders and then closing her eyes. She was coming, Nina knew, and so did everyone else. The room was silent apart from the continued beat of the drum music as the audience watched the blonde pubic mound pushing forward into the face of the other woman. When Beverley had stopped her convulsive movements, Katya stood up and once again kissed her full on the mouth. She picked up the chain and they left the stage as unobtrusively as they had entered it.

Nina felt shell-shocked. She had almost felt Beverley climaxing and knew that just a touch on her own swollen sex could make her come. And Beverley wanted her to go upstairs with her.

'I think you could call that art, don't you, Nina?' asked Andrew.

She looked at Ariadne. 'I would think so. Would you, Ariadne?'

The older woman regarded her with narrowed eyes.

'To me everything to do with Beverley is art. She is as far as I am concerned the most beautiful thing to look at. The execution of the piece, that I believe she thought to be artistic. It was important to her. But the whipping, the sex, was for our pleasure. At least, the enactment of it in a public place was for my pleasure – and I believe for hers as well.'

'And did it give you pleasure?' asked Nina. Ariadne's gaze softened.

'Oh yes. Especially when she came. You too found it pleasing. I can tell.'

Nina blushed but Beverley and Katya's return saved her from Ariadne's probing regard. Katya had changed but Beverley had merely put a pair of black knickers on. Ariadne exclaimed over the wounds she had sustained from the whip and crop.

'That's why I couldn't put my skirt back on,' Beverley explained. 'It's too tight. God knows how I'll get out the front door. Did you like it?'

She looked at Ariadne intently. Nina felt like a voyeur, watching them gaze at each other. The older woman smoothed Beverley's hair with a tender gesture.

'I was just telling Nina how much I enjoyed it. Especially when you came. And she agreed that was the most exciting moment.'

'How painful was it?' Andrew interrupted.

Beverley grimaced. 'More than I expected. It'll probably get worse later as well. But I had to try it some time, and what better way! It was a real turn-on, everyone looking at me. Though I wouldn't have wanted it to go on any longer.'

She turned to Nina and smiled widely, light years away from the wan smile she had managed to raise after her whipping.

'Did it turn you on, Nina?'

She grinned as Nina nodded, blushing.

'We had a deal, right?'

'What sort of deal?' Andrew asked, a smile playing at the corners of his mouth.

'Our business,' retorted Beverley. 'Watch the next act.'

With a start Nina turned towards the stage. She'd been so engrossed by Beverley she hadn't noticed that the Spanish-looking woman in the transparent dress they had discussed earlier was lying at the edge of the stage. She had made no attempt at a striptease act. Her G-string was gone and her chiffon skirt was around her waist as she pulled her labia apart to give the audience the best possible view of herself. She pushed one finger inside herself and brought it out, obviously wet, and stroked her clitoris with it.

'Oh, man,' said Andrew.

Nina's attention was diverted by a squeeze on her shoulder from Beverley.

'I can't sit down, it's too painful. Come upstairs with me,' she whispered.

Nina reckoned she would prefer a lesbian scene with a beautiful blonde to sitting next to her boyfriend while he watched another woman wank, and followed.

Although the club was marginally on the right side of seedy, the back stairs were definitely not. Bare bulbs cast a dingy light and the worn stair carpet smelt of grease and piss, the smell not helped by the toilets on the mezzanine floor. 'Changing room,' Beverley said as they passed, indicating the ladies' with her thumb. There were two closed doors on the first floor, which Beverley led them straight past, and on the second floor another three, two of which were closed. They entered the room with the open door, which had a torn 'Private' sign pasted on it.

Nina didn't care to think about what was happening behind the other doors.

The room they entered was not as bad as she had feared. The cord carpet was also worn but serviceable, and a lampshade covered the lightbulb. A small wash-basin was clean with a bar of soap on it, and the paint on the woodchip-papered walls was reasonably white.

Although the only furniture was a divan bed and a chair, at least the bed was covered with a clean-looking bedspread. There were a pair of decent flower prints on each of the side walls, and a mirror behind the bed.

Beverley lowered herself gingerly on to the bed. 'Ow! Actually it's not too bad. Perhaps I'll try my front.' She rolled over, exposing her wounded arse to Nina. 'What does it look like?'

The skin was broken and blood had already started to coagulate along the scars.

'Not bad. But will you be scarred for life?'

Beverley looked round. 'Shit, I never thought of that. I don't suppose so ... although I suppose it wouldn't matter too much.' She twisted further round and looked at Nina. 'Come closer.'

Nina walked to the edge of the bed, not sure what the first move should be, but she didn't have to make it. Quickly the blonde's hand snaked up under her skirt and touched the crotch of her knickers.

'Yeah! I did turn you on!' she teased.

Nina could hardly deny it. She knew how wet she was and that Beverley would have no trouble finding out either through the thin silk.

'I'd like to see your silk undies,' whispered Beverley. 'Why don't you do a strip for me?'

Nina backed away. 'Look, I feel really awkward now. I haven't done this before, I mean, I've never been with another girl.'

'Never even kissed a woman before?'

'Well, yes, I've done that.'

Beverley got off the bed and put her arms round Nina's shoulders.

'So this won't feel too strange.'

You can't imagine how strange it is to find myself kissing a woman dressed in black leather underwear for the second time in three days, thought Nina. Or how exciting.

Too exciting even to compare the two female mouths she'd kissed. It registered that Beverley's breath had the scent of the orange juice they'd mixed with the vodka, compared to Angie's wine-stained mouth. And that Beverley was taller than she was and she was reaching up to her mouth, which was nice, like kissing a tall man. But just as when she'd kissed Angie, her

94

cunt took over and ground itself against Beverley's pubic bone.

'Come on, strip for me,' whispered Beverley.

Inexplicably, Nina felt less self-conscious than when Andrew had made her strip for him. She didn't feel she had to dance or sway, but kept her eyes avidly on the other girl's breasts and pale face still brought into relief by the black leather choker as she loosened the drawstring top and undid the front buttons. As she removed it her breasts revealed themselves full and hard-nippled under the blue silk. Beverley made a small pout of appreciation and Nina undid the skirt, let it drop to the floor and stepped out of it.

'Oh, nice one,' said Beverley, reaching out and touching the buttons on the little shorts. 'Will I be the first person to undo those buttons?'

'You're going to be the first person to do quite a lot of things, I would think,' Nina answered, her voice husky as her mouth suddenly dried up.

As the other girl touched one of her nipples, she closed her eyes so as to concentrate more fully on the sensation of touch. Her breasts felt super-sensitive as Beverley rubbed across the nipples through the silk and then mashed them together.

'Open your eyes and talk to me,' ordered Beverley. 'Are you enjoying this?'

'Yes, of course I am.' Nina felt guilty, as though she ought to be participating more. The story of my life, she thought. She brought her hands up to touch Beverley's nipples through the black leather, but the other girl shook her head.

'I want to seduce you first,' she said. 'Lie down.'

Nina sat then lay across the bed, leaning back on her elbows. Beverley straddled her and as she started kissing again Nina relaxed and concentrated on kissing her back. Then the blonde's hands were everywhere, breasts and belly and thighs and then, thank God, cunt.

'Let's get these buttons undone,' she murmured. 'Oh, God, you're really wet.'

Nina felt she could come straight away as one of Beverley's cool fingers ran from her clitoris down past the wet mouth of her vagina to her arse and back again.

'I've been wanting to come since I saw you on stage,' she moaned. 'I can't wait.'

The finger moved faster in response and another two sneaked surely into her as the other girl laughed softly.

'Come on, then. I want to tongue you but that can wait. If that's all right with you? You can do it to me too if you want. I'll teach you to be as good as Katya.' She smiled down at Nina. 'You're coming now, aren't you?'

As easily as torched petrol bursts into flames, thought Nina as the liquid fire coursed through her and exploded.

Nina decided that if she'd met Beverley before Andrew, she would have thought that lesbian sex was the solution to her problems.

Beverley gave her full marks for cunnilingus. They agreed that it was easier to know how to satisfy a woman when you had exactly the same experience yourself. Although having come from Katya's mouth, Beverley made Nina bring her off with her hands – 'just for a change,' she quipped. They compared the taste and look of each other's juice. Nina's was clearer and sweeter, like peach juice, Beverley decided, while her own pearly translucent sap tasted exotic, like lychees, Nina told her.

As Nina fingered Beverley, she asked her what sex with Ariadne was like. The blonde laughed.

'Great. But she always needs something extra to turn her on. She doesn't just come round and say, "Hey, let's fuck." We dress up, you know, like this, or she makes me strip for her – that's why I wanted to watch you do it. And she really loves showing me off, especially to men.'

'What do you mean?' asked Nina curiously, not relaxing the rhythm of her fingers.

'She'll make me go out without underwear on, and then she'll let someone know about it. Like once, it was the first time she did it, we were in the lift in Liberty's or Dickins and Jones, I can't remember where it was, some big store where there's a lift attendant, and as we got out, I was first, and she just lifted up my skirt so he could see my arse . . . thank God he couldn't see my face, it was like a beetroot.'

Nina held her breath and waited, hoping for more.

'Then we'll be in a pub or somewhere, and she'll just put her hand out and stroke one of my nipples, if someone's watching. And once we went to the Tower of London, and there are all these cannons overlooking the river, and she'd made me go out without knickers and I was wearing a short pleated skirt, and she got me to straddle this cannon. My God, it was cold and hard, and she was taking photos of me and made me stay there ages pretending she couldn't get the camera working properly. Some American tourist came to help her with it, and she thanked him, then she asked him if he'd take one of us both together and she sat right behind me and put her arms on my waist. She started playing about with my skirt and just when he said, "Say cheese," she pulled the skirt back and it rode right up. He must have seen everything. Anyway, it was in the picture.

'After that she just wants to get somewhere in private and fuck. Well, fairly private – the car'll do if it's around. Or a public toilet.'

'Oh my God.'

'Yeah, we went into the toilet in the Tower of London after she'd flashed me at the tourist. There was a queue and she said, "Come on, Beverley, it'll be quicker if we go in together." She made me sit and pee while I brought her off with my fingers so no-one would know, then she peed and sucked my fingers. Of course I had to wait till we got home. I was desperate by then. But that made it really sweet. She always takes her time with me, you know. She loves teasing me and making me wait, though for herself she usually just wants a quick finger fuck when she's ready.'

Beverley's breath was getting faster and Nina felt that she could almost come again too, her imagination putting herself in the other's place and savouring the thought of the public display. Her fingers thrust harder into Beverley's cunt and she increased the pressure of her thumb on her clitoris. She knew her reminiscences had turned Beverley on as well, and in seconds Nina felt Beverley's hips convulse and knew she was starting her climax.

'You haven't forgotten that tonguing you promised me?' Nina asked a few minutes later.

Beverley sat up, her face still beatific from her orgasm.

'You liked my stories, didn't you?'

'I presume that was the intention,' said Nina, smiling. 'But don't tell me you didn't enjoy telling me. I could tell from the way you were moving.'

'Sure. Anyway, of course I haven't forgotten. But seeing as I had to have a whipping before I got mine, I think you should suffer first before you get your reward.'

Nina stared at her. 'You're not whipping me,' she announced flatly.

'With what?' The blonde gestured round the empty room. 'But I've had a good idea.' She undid the leather choker and told Nina to kneel on the bed, then fastened her wrists together with the choker. Facing the mirror, Nina moaned as Beverley lifted her bound wrists above her head, the girl who'd played the submissive role in front of the audience now turned into the leather-clad dominatrix. In the mirror Nina saw Beverley's other hand rise in the air and then come down swiftly with a stinging slap on her buttocks.

'That hurt!' she cried. Beverley laughed and smacked her again.

'Chastisement does. But it gets better.'

She delivered a few more slaps in quick succession. Nina's arse felt like it was on fire.

'Isn't it nice as well as painful?'

'Yes – I think so – but I don't know if I want too much of it.'

The blonde girl let go of Nina's wrists, and brought her hand round to cup her pubis. She pressed firmly and slapped again.

'How about that?'

'Oh yes,' breathed Nina. 'That's very nice.'

Beverley spanked her twice more, then pushed Nina back on the bed, raising her arms with their bound wrists above her head. Her hard tongue snaked inside her and then lapped up to her clitoris, which it caressed firmly, then moved back again.

The combination of Beverley's practised tongue, the spanking and the restraints of the black leather around her wrists meant that Nina had no way of resisting the orgasm which came all too quickly. She tried to hold back, wanting to feel that tongue work on her for longer.

Both girls sated, they lounged on the bed, talking about getting dressed and going back to the others, but lacking the energy to do so. The door opened, and Nina sat up indignantly, only to see Andrew standing there. He clapped his hands slowly and laughed mockingly.

'Lovely show, girls. Better than the ones downstairs.'

Nina glared at him and looked round at Beverley, who was looking embarrassed.

'Sorry, Nina. Two-way mirror.'

Nina felt as though her heart had stopped.

'You fucking cow.' She jumped up and pulled on her top and knickers. Someone came out of one of the rooms opposite and glanced casually inside the open doorway.

'Will you shut that sodding door!' she yelled at Andrew. He came inside and took her hand.

'Hey, don't be so mad. Haven't you fantasised about being watched? Anyway, you were happy when I watched you with Costas. And Costas watched you with the waiter.'

'Yes, while I knew you were watching. It's not the same as strangers watching you when you don't even know about it.' She snatched her hand away and put on the rest of her clothes.

'Look, it wasn't the whole club. Just me, Costas, Ariadne and Katya.'

'And you were excited when I told you that Ariadne exhibited me in public,' Beverley put in.

Nina hesitated. 'That's different.' She turned back to Andrew. 'Was it really only you lot?'

Andrew frowned. 'You might not think much of me at the moment, but give me a bit of credit. There's only a tiny room behind there anyway. What do you think, we charged admission?'

'How should I know? You might have a video link with the room downstairs for all I know.'

He laughed. 'That's not a bad idea. Oh, come on, Nina, chill out. Think about it. It was exciting. If you'd known, you'd have loved it.'

She considered.

'Yeah, if I'd known about it beforehand and agreed to it, I might well have loved it. So why didn't you tell me?'

'That's my fault,' confessed Beverley. 'I almost did. When you got turned on when I told you about Ariadne I felt a bit guilty – but it was too late then. I'm really sorry, Nina. Don't be mad.'

'OK.' She still felt as though she was in one of those dreams where she was walking down the street with no clothes on, ashamed and embarrassed.

Andrew stroked her hair. 'You were fantastic. Both of you!' he added, turning to Beverley. 'Two performances in one day, Bev. You should turn professional.'

'Very funny.'

He kissed Nina's cheek. 'Better? Sure?'

She nodded. 'I'll feel better if I can have a drink. A very large one.'

When they returned downstairs half the punters had left. Ariadne rose and kissed Nina on both cheeks.

'Thank you, Nina. From me and from Beverley. I hope we'll see you again.' She turned to her lover. 'Come on, let's go home. I need you.'

The whole party rose and took their leave. Costas gave Nina a smacking kiss on the mouth.

'You know I really thought you were a professional the other day. Forgive me if I seemed disrespectful.'

Nina made a disclaimer, but still something about the old man repelled her. The enigmatic Katya walked out of the club without any farewells, and somewhat abashed, Nina kissed Beverley goodbye and followed Andrew outside.

The streets were wet and the air cooler. She hadn't noticed the rain. It was as though while she'd been inside the club the whole world had been washed clean. Nina wished she felt the same.

Chapter Five

Consciousness stabbed at Nina. She tried to ignore it and snuggle drowsily into Andrew, whose body was wrapped round behind her, spoon fashion, his early-morning erection pressed against her. Still fast asleep, he pulled his arm more firmly around her and grunted indistinctly.

Suddenly the events of the previous night started replaying themselves in her memory and she woke up without any further prompting.

Beverley coming. Andrew standing in the doorway of the room. The ballerina. Costas implying Andrew was with the stripping schoolgirl. Beverley being whipped. Beverley making her come. Beverley volunteering the story of her and Ariadne.

A graphic artist, she had decided to go freelance, but things had been slow to get started. She'd almost given up and gone back to working for someone else. To cheer herself up she had treated herself to a day membership at an exclusive health club, and it was there she met Ariadne.

'We were in the swimming pool, this great pool in this really plush club, and we were the only two in it.

All the other women were lounging around between massages and facials and what not, and there we were ploughing up and down the pool. We came out at the same time and went into the sauna and started talking. I'd never been with a woman before but she was just so strong looking, that amazing face, and her body's terrific despite her age. She took me back to her flat and I had the best orgasm I'd ever had. We started seeing each other and mysteriously I started to get really busy.

'She knows a lot of people, you know, business people. If it was a coincidence that my company took off, well, I'd be amazed. That was three years ago. Now I've got more work that I can handle.'

Nina shuddered a little as she remembered Beverley's tale. Yes, these people were obviously powerful. But if they could make you, maybe they could break you too.

Andrew stirred again, as though her shudder had communicated itself to his body. He pulled her closer again, and kissed her randomly on the side of the head.

'Good morning, beautiful,' he murmured.

'Good morning.'

'Not still angry about last night?'

'I haven't decided yet,' said Nina, remembering the schoolgirl. 'How about you? You didn't have much fun.'

Andrew chuckled. 'Do you honestly think it wasn't fun watching two beautiful women, one of whom I adore, making love?'

'Adore?' Nina caught her breath.

'Of course. I've always adored Beverley.'

They laughed together.

'Yes, but weren't you turned on by watching us? I think if I'd been watching you through the mirror I'd have been desperate to rush home and fuck.'

'How do you know I didn't make love to Ariadne?'

'Well, I know she's ninety-five per cent gay ... but I don't think she used up her five per cent on you last night.'

'No, you're right. I couldn't have sex with Ariadne anyway, I know her too well. Anyway, she wouldn't let me.'

'That's more like it.'

'Maybe I just masturbated while I watched you.'

'No, you wouldn't do that either. If you couldn't have sex with her you couldn't wank in front of her either – nor in front of Costas. What about him? What was he going to do with himself? We all seemed to break up suddenly.'

Andrew shrugged. 'Don't worry about Costas. Watching you two was probably enough for him. Anyway, he knows how to get a girl if he wants.'

They had both been silent in the cab on the way back to Nina's flat. She certainly had had no intention of talking about the evening in front of a taxi driver, and Andrew had seemed preoccupied. Nina also wanted to think further about how she felt about her unwitting live sex show.

She had been tempted to ask Andrew if he had had sex with the schoolgirl stripper, but having calmed down after one outburst of righteous indignation she felt it was the wrong time to launch into another one.

He made no move towards her sexually. After a nightcap they went to bed and cuddled briefly, then Andrew was the one to instigate the good nights and they had gone to sleep. She had been both relieved and dismayed that he didn't want to make love; relieved because she'd really had enough, but dismayed because it seemed obvious that he must have fucked the stripper ...

'But you weren't turned on enough to want me when we got back.'

Andrew sighed.

'You were annoyed with me, remember? If you hadn't been annoyed with me in the first place you might not have gone upstairs with Beverley.'

Nina sat up. So he wanted to get it out into the open.

'OK, so was I right to be annoyed with you?'

Andrew's eyes were unreadable. 'No. And before you jump to conclusions, when I say no, I mean you have no rights of exclusivity over me, Nina. Not unless we both agree to go exclusive.'

'So you fucked the schoolgirl.'

His face remained expressionless. 'Actually, no. She doesn't fuck. But she gives great head.'

'You shit.'

'You had Beverley.'

'That was different. You were watching.'

He smiled patronisingly. 'Jesus, I didn't realise. You would have been welcome to watch me and Zandra. If only I'd thought of it.'

'Fuck off.'

Nina jumped out of bed and put on her towelling robe.

'Yeah, it'd have been great, she would have loved it. She doesn't mind an audience – well, I suppose you guessed that.'

She marched into the kitchen and put the kettle on, pulling orange juice out of the fridge and slamming the door so hard it bounced back towards her. She poured herself half a pint of juice and put it back in the fridge. He could get his own if he wanted any.

Zandra. He'd even found out her name. Or did he know her already?

As she ground the coffee beans, Nina imagined watching them. He'd probably gone up to the ladies' toilet knowing she'd be changing there. She hadn't used the toilet herself, but imagined it had the same pissy smell as the stairs. It probably wasn't very clean.

Had they gone inside a cubicle, or not bothered, not

caring if anyone walked in? She guessed the latter. The regular punters at the club were probably used to it. He would have fondled her, she would be wet from grinding herself against the ball. Maybe he'd made her come with his hands before she sucked him off. He would have been leaning back against the grubby wall, his jeans round his knees. And she'd have been kneeling on the floor, which would have been not very clean, and wet from where others had spilt water after washing. His hands would have held her head, her ridiculous pigtails, as he came. Did she spit or swallow?

What was so good about her blow jobs? Perhaps if she'd been watching she could have picked up some tips from the wonderful Zandra. Or Andrew could have given her a running commentary on what she did that was so great.

She was tempted to bunch her hair up into pigtails before going back into the bedroom.

With a sudden shock she realised that someone must have walked into the toilet. Beverley and Katya had gone off to get changed just a couple of minutes after Andrew had disappeared.

Not only had Beverley betrayed her with the one-way mirror, she had known that Andrew had betrayed her already.

Andrew watched Nina carefully as she came back with a tray of coffee. He was afraid he'd pushed her too far.

He guessed it was time to take it easy. She'd had a pretty amazing week of it, and all things considered was handling things really well. But he had to let her know that there was no way he was going to let her call the shots. He liked life to be seedy from time to time. He got a thrill from having a pigtailed stripper give him head on the dirty back stairs of a strip club.

He'd got her to sit on her ball again while she sucked him, and afterwards he'd watched her bring herself off.

She had put her tongue right out and licked her fingers like a lollipop before moving her hands down to her pussy, still playing the schoolgirl.

Beverley and Katya had come up to get changed while Zandra was lapping at his cock. They had smiled and Katya had lingered, watching them with an appraising glance, while Beverley had gone into the ladies'. He didn't mind. She stayed till he came then went in to change.

He wasn't going to give up other women, and there was no way he was going to do without the sleazy side of sex. But maybe he'd have to separate Nina from it.

She was a different person from the one he'd first gone out with. If he had told her on their first date what she would be doing by now, she'd probably have slapped his face and never seen him again. Although her cool confidence indicated she could be frigid, something told him to persevere – and he was glad he had.

He really did want to make all her fantasies come true. He got as much enjoyment from her pleasure in a new experience as she did, and the voyeur in him was having a ball. And although their relationship was primarily based around sex, he had grown very fond of her.

Even so, part of him wanted to degrade her, to make her abase herself for him. But he wasn't going to feel bad about it; after all, he knew that her fantasies encompassed humiliation and subjugation.

This morning, though, he thought it would be better to play the contrite lover.

'Sorry,' he said, before she could get in first. 'You're right. I'm a shit. I don't deserve you. And you've even made me coffee.'

'I've made myself some coffee. But I thought I might as well bring you some too.'

She smiled and he knew it was going to be all right.

'I don't suppose anyone was ever initiated into the

more unusual aspects of erotic practices by a perfect gentleman,' she continued. 'I'm probably a bit oversensitive.'

'Hell, no, I'm a shit, you're right,' he insisted, taking the coffee she handed to him. 'I know I'm a bit sarcastic sometimes – I'm sorry.'

'OK, one sorry was enough,' said Nina drily. 'Anyway, I was just imagining you and the stripper – it really turned me on. Did Beverley walk in on you?'

He was unprepared for that question, but thought he might as well tell the truth.

'Not exactly walk in. We were on the stairs just by the toilets,' he explained.

'Oh God. I'd pictured you in the toilet. So they couldn't help seeing you.'

'Yes. Katya stayed to watch for a bit.'

'Right. So Beverley knew when she took me upstairs.'

He shrugged. 'Does that make a difference?'

'I don't suppose so. Anyway, I'd already said I'd go with her if her act turned me on. Which it did.'

'Yeah, well, there would have to be something wrong with you if that hadn't turned you on.'

They both laughed.

'And I was pissed off with you because your eyes were glued to Carmen at the time.'

'Carmen?' He backtracked. 'Oh wow, now, she was something.'

'Don't start again!'

Andrew's morning erection had subsided but remembering the masturbating woman made his prick jerk to attention again. That was really cool. No act, no pretence at skipping round the stage, dancing or anything like that. She just wanted to wank in front of the audience. He suspected there was someone in particular she was doing it for, in the way that Beverley had put her act on for Ariadne, but no matter. He almost wished he hadn't followed Zandra upstairs. It would have been fantastic to have had that red mouth around his cock.

Better not to think about her now. After all, he was bound to run into her again sometime.

'What other acts were there after her?'

He laughed. 'Do you really think I wanted to watch any more when I knew you and Beverley were upstairs?'

'I suppose. How did you know we'd be in the room with the two-way mirror?'

'Because I reserved it.'

He answered without thinking and then winced. 'Shouldn't have told you that, I suppose.'

She was looking at him steadily. 'So I did exactly what you wanted me to?'

'Yes. Thanks.'

Nina put her coffee down and flopped down on to her back.

'Why do I feel that you're pulling my strings?'

'You wanted me to give you experiences,' he reasoned, stroking her hair. 'We talked about you having a woman. Beverley was the obvious choice. And it was good, wasn't it?'

Her lips twitched. 'Yes, it was good.'

'So thank me!'

Nina laughed. 'I said it turned me on thinking about you and the stripper – perhaps I could thank you this way.' Her hand reached out to his erection. 'I think this needs some attention.'

He sighed as she stroked his cock, now fully hard. It crossed his mind briefly that they'd both turned themselves on with thoughts of other women. But it wasn't the moment to talk about it.

Nina needed to make love this morning, rather than have sex. He felt that before she could move on to her next adventure she needed to feel more secure about their relationship.

He turned to face her.

'Nina, you really are beautiful.'

Still stroking her glossy hair, he kissed her face tenderly.

'I want to make love to you. Not just fuck you.'

He moved his hands down to her breasts and caressed them as their mouths met and melted into each other's. He kissed her softly at first, and then his tongue was moving insistently in her mouth and she was responding ardently. His hands grabbed her breasts harder, his thumbs rubbing her hard nipples. The image of the woman in the black dress came into his mind and made him grunt as he moved his hand down her body, wanting only to get inside her and come. But satisfying his desire wasn't his main motive.

He knelt with his legs on either side of her.

'You're a goddess. You are beautiful, you're so beautiful,' he repeated, like a mantra. He sucked at her nipples and she sighed as he gently pulled her thighs apart and stroked upward to the satin-soft creamy skin just at the top.

'You're so beautiful,' he murmured again, then his head moved down to the bright chestnut mound of hair. He pulled her thighs further apart, and Nina whimpered as he ran his finger gently down from her clitoris to her pussy lips.

'So beautiful,' he repeated, and then his head moved down further.

She was wet, and as he tongued her he wondered whether thinking about him and Zandra was responsible for it. It occurred to him that they hadn't showered before falling into bed the night before, and that his tongue was following Beverley's. And that his cock was unwashed since he'd come in Zandra's mouth. Another time he would have told Nina about that and how exciting he found it – but not now.

He wondered briefly if he should finish her off with

his tongue, but didn't feel quite that unselfish. He lapped gently at her clitoris, feeling it was better to prolong their lovemaking. Nina was moaning as he pushed two fingers inside her. Oh man, her pussy was wet.

Pulling himself up the bed he kissed Nina with a mouth smeared with her own slippery juices. He kissed her with a passion he couldn't resist any longer, and she responded just as strongly.

Andrew realised he didn't need to pretend. Although he couldn't call it love, he really did have feelings for Nina. His prick reared up, blindly seeking her cunt, and she was responding instinctively too. Without need for further communication he knew she wanted him inside her, and as he pushed gently into her she raised her legs and wrapped them round his back.

They moved together, slowly but purposefully. Her eyes looked into his and he felt that it was an almost perfect moment; that if he were ever to fall in love that it would be like this.

'No rush,' he whispered, moving with gentle strokes in and out of her. 'Take your time, beautiful.'

'I don't know if I can wait too long,' she answered breathily.

Her hips bucked under him.

'Nina. Oh, baby,' he murmured, not taking his eyes from hers. 'Are you coming now?'

'Yes, you know, don't you – Andrew –'

In the second before his orgasm shook him, he felt her cunt grip his cock as she came.

They lay entwined on the bed, breathless and silent. Andrew felt Nina's eyes blinking and looked down.

'OK?'

She nodded, but he noticed tears trembling on her eyelashes.

'I hope that's post-coital tristesse, and not disappointment,' he teased.

Nina smiled but her voice broke.

'Of course it's not disappointment!' she cried, her tears coming faster. 'I don't know what's the matter with me. I've never had it before.'

Andrew pulled her closer. 'Maybe you've never made love like that before,' he said simply. 'That was pretty intense.'

Perhaps I shouldn't have said 'made love', he wondered. He hoped she wouldn't read too much into it.

She wiped her eyes. 'I'd heard of this, but it's never happened before. I don't know whether I altogether approve!' she managed to add, half humorously, and Andrew chuckled fondly.

'Well, it's another experience you've got under your belt, although I don't really think I can take the credit for it – or the blame,' he said.

'I'm sorry. My emotions are all over the place. I've been a bit mixed up lately,' she admitted. 'All of a sudden men are looking at me all the time. My friend Angie said that because I've got a great sex life all of a sudden I'm giving out sex signals, but while I like having the great sex life I don't want complete strangers to think I'm begging for it.'

Andrew grinned at her. 'You really are an innocent,' he said, hugging her. 'Haven't you ever noticed men looking at other women?'

'Of course –'

'And when you have, has it occurred to you that it's because those women are begging for it?'

'No!'

'No. They're just sexy women, and men can't help noticing them. You might very well be giving out sexy woman signals, but that doesn't diminish you in any way.'

He looked at her steadily. 'Do you know what signals you used to give out when I first met you?'

'Well, none, I suppose. I was just doing my job,' she replied indignantly.

'Wrong! You were saying, "Don't touch, don't go too far with me, I don't want to be your friend."'

'Oh come on! How did you ever ask me out if I was that forbidding?'

'Because once we'd started talking and broken the ice you changed, you were much warmer,' he continued patiently. 'And now you don't walk into a room with that old "don't touch" attitude. What did they call you at work – the Ice Queen? I bet they've forgotten all about that.'

'Yes. Now Max keeps asking me out for a drink after work.'

'You mean he didn't before?'

'Well, I suppose so. But then he was asking me about what I do outside work, and about you. Well, not you. But he guessed I had a new boyfriend.'

'Because you're not as uptight as you were. Isn't that good?'

'But I don't want to be the me you know when I'm at work – if that makes sense,' said Nina in a small voice. 'I want to be the same as I always was.'

'You can only be what you are,' he said philosophically. 'And what you are now is a fulfilled woman – or at least I hope so.'

She looked at him with a small smile. 'Of course. You must think I'm really stupid!'

Andrew sighed. 'Only when you say things like that. Now let's get up. I think what you need is a break from this sexual fervour. How about we drive out to a country pub for lunch? I'll get a cab home and pick up the car and see you back here in a couple of hours.'

'Mmm – or you could stay here, and I could make us a late breakfast. Then we wouldn't have to get up.'

He laughed. 'No, my idea's best. It's going to be another brilliant day. We'll get the wind in our hair driving down to the country, and find a nice pub with roses round the door, rustic furniture and home-cooked food.'

Andrew dressed as he spoke, and though he suspected Nina really wanted him to stay, he wanted to get back to his own flat – and think about the afternoon's entertainment.

He pulled up outside Nina's flat two hours later feeling fantastic. After leaving her he had got a cab straight away and within half an hour was showered and changed into a grey short-sleeved V-neck and jeans. Picking up the papers on the way, he'd spent an hour reading in his local café with a couple of espressos and croissants to stave off the hunger pangs until lunch.

'Looking good,' he said, as Nina opened the door. She was wearing a short flirty cream skirt and a matching sleeveless top buttoned down the front.

'And you,' she returned, looking him up and down.

Andrew manoeuvred the car as quickly as he could through London. They weren't the only city dwellers heading for the countryside or the coast and the traffic was fairly heavy. However, they managed to keep moving along the A3 and the A24, and finally pulled off the main road at around half past one.

'Right, let's find that country pub,' said Andrew, turning down a quiet road lined with feathery cow parsley.

'Do I have a strange feeling that you're not just turning down here on the off-chance?' challenged Nina, smiling. 'I bet it won't be long before we come across a pub with roses round the door and, what was it, rustic furniture and good food?'

He laughed. 'Am I that transparent?'

After another ten minutes' drive along country lanes, the pub sign came into view, with several cars parked in front, and deep pink roses tumbling over the old wooden lintel.

'Rustic furniture?' asked Nina facetiously as she got out of the car. Andrew pointed to a sign that said 'Beer Garden'.

'I think you'll find it's just through there.'

Until he'd found the Horse and Farrier in Throssington, Andrew had thought that the ideal village inn didn't exist. They had either been spoiled by local yobs playing pool or noisy computer games, or the locals were so unwelcoming that strangers wished they hadn't bothered.

But the Horse and Farrier was so perfect it was like a film set. The interior was cool with stone flagged floors and low wooden beams, and the only noise was the lively chatter of conversation. It was full but not uncomfortably so. There was a selection of real ales and a good though short wine list, while the menu ranged from home-made steak and kidney pie to sundried tomato and Roquefort salad with French country bread.

'I'm going to be a stereotypical male and have the steak and kidney pie,' he said. 'Let me guess – you're going to have a salad.'

'Don't tell me what I want!' she said indignantly. 'Actually, I'll have the carpaccio of beef with mustard dressing.'

'Comes with salad as well, though,' he said, laughing. 'Drink? Wine or beer?'

'Well, with beef I'd really like some red wine, though if we're sitting out in the sun I'll probably regret it.'

Andrew ordered the food and a glass of red wine for Nina and a pint of bitter for himself. They took their drinks out to the garden. Even there, with children and a couple of dogs running round, nothing spoiled the perfection of the setting. There were rough-hewn wooden benches and tables, a couple of apple trees seemingly planted at random in the grass, and borders in which a profusion of early summer flowers fought for space.

'This is perfect,' said Nina as they sat at a table under one of the trees to shelter from the early afternoon sun. 'How did you find it?'

'Just driving around,' he told her. 'I think you only ever find places like this by accident. If someone else tells you about them, they're already too popular.'

'I don't really get out of town much, except to visit my parents, and then I spend most of the time vegging out in front of the TV. Which I suppose is what I used to do when I lived there,' she said laughing. 'I suppose we're all the same. How about your parents? Where do they live?'

He frowned. It always had to come up sooner or later.

'They died when I was twelve. In a car crash.'

'Oh God, Andrew, I'm sorry!'

He shook his head. 'Don't be. I've had nearly thirty years to get used to it.'

'But I thought your father started your business – so what happened to it until you were old enough to take over?'

'Costas looked after it,' he told her. 'He was one of Dad's best friends. He was always Uncle Costas to me till Dad died – then he became more like a father.

'He left his own business and moved to London for six months to make sure everything was running all right, and after that he came back every couple of months to keep an eye on things. I owe him.'

He noticed with irritation the pity in her eyes.

'Don't feel sorry for me, Nina. It's one thing that really pisses me off. I had a brilliant childhood, thanks to Costas and his family. I went to boarding school here and went to stay with them in Greece in the holidays.'

'So that's how you speak fluent Greek.'

He nodded. 'Yeah. Of course, it was hard to start

with. But Costas has a lot of family, so holidays were fantastic. All the family looked after me, especially Costas and Ariadne.'

He watched, amused, as Nina almost choked. 'Where does Ariadne fit in?'

'She's Costas's niece. Her family lived in Crete. I used to stay with them in the summer holidays.'

'And Ariadne would be – what – about twelve years older than you?'

'That's right. She'd just finished university when I first stayed with them. I was still miserable and she really looked after me.'

Not as well as she looked after me when I got older, he said to himself. But that was none of Nina's business.

Their food arrived. Andrew's pie came with a mountain of golden chips while Nina's rosy beef glistened with dressing, beside a pile of peppery rocket and two slices of French bread, blistered from the grill.

Andrew was glad to stop talking about his childhood. He'd had his fill of pity over the years and rarely told anyone about the loss of his parents. Although he'd been happy with his Greek 'family' during the holidays, he'd not liked school. He had felt alienated from the other boys by his foreign family and his lack of real parents, and he knew the teachers made matters worse by making allowances for him when he was bad or lazy because they felt sorry for him. He knew they meant well, but he always felt that they composed their faces into a sympathetic expression every time they saw him for the first couple of years.

He lived for the holidays, when he would run around the beaches with his new Greek cousins. He quickly picked up the language and with his dark hair and fast-tanning skin it would have been hard for anyone to tell that one of the children was English. As they got older he learned with his cousins how to sail and surf, and later on how to smoke strong Greek cigarettes. Then one summer he learned how to make love.

It was the best holiday of his life, the one after he'd finally and thankfully left school. Barely eighteen, he was off to university at Costas's insistence. Andrew had fought to be allowed to start work as soon as possible, but his guardian had proved inflexible in his desire to put him through university. Sulking hadn't helped, and he had had to give in, respecting Costas's strength.

So the summer had not started off well. That year there were ten children and teenagers staying at the Saphianos holiday house in Crete. As usual Andrew spent most of his time hanging out with Nikos and Vassili, but this year there was a difference between him and them.

They were both older and already at university, where they had discovered girls. Andrew had always assumed that all Greek girls were virgins until they married, but they boasted otherwise.

He felt like a child as they compared notes about their conquests. For the first time since he had started spending his summers in Greece he felt an outsider in his adopted family, as well as one at school.

Ariadne had saved him. Now forging a career in public relations, she came home for the holidays and noticed he was left out. One day he came stomping back from the beach after the other guys had teased him mercilessly. They had started talking about blow jobs they'd had, and not wanting to be left out he had made up a story about being sucked off by the school matron. It was so obviously fabricated Nikos and Vassili had been in stitches.

She was reading in the garden when he went in. Everyone else was at the beach, and the house was otherwise deserted. He had made to walk past her up

118

to his room, but she had stopped him and demanded to know what his problem was.

He refused to tell her but she had already put two and two together and eventually he let her drag it out of him.

'I'm fed up being the odd one out. I'm fed up being a virgin. I'm fed up with everything,' he told her. 'I'm the odd one out in school and now I'm going to university I'll probably be the odd one out there as well.'

'You poor thing,' said Ariadne, stroking his head. 'I won't let you be the odd one out again.'

She had risen and taken his hand and led him to her room, where to his delight he had found out exactly what a blow job was like. Sworn to secrecy, he crept into her room several times over the next week and she had taught him everything he needed to know about sex.

'Now you're a man, Andrew,' she had said to him on their last night together before she went back to work in Athens. 'This is the last time for us, not just this summer, but for ever. We may not be cousins by birth but in every other way we are family, and members of a family don't fuck each other. So forget this, OK?'

She had kissed him. 'Go back to England and practise what I've taught you. Then next holidays you can tell me all about your girls. I like to hear about other girls.'

That meant nothing to him at the time, but over the years he had come to understand what made Ariadne tick.

When he got to university he took her injunction seriously and took up practising sex with more fervour than he took up his studies. The reactions he got from his prowess made him realise just what a good teacher she had been, and how much he owed her.

He changed the subject to the food, the pub, the other

customers. He knew that he had succeeded in making Nina feel more relaxed and secure. Maybe too secure, he wondered, as she sighed contentedly after she'd finished eating and he'd brought more drinks.

'This is the life. Imagine living near here, and having this as your weekend local,' she said.

He raised his eyebrows. 'Yes, and spending hours commuting to work. And living in a little village where everyone knows everyone else's business.'

She giggled. 'Well, I can see that'd be a bit inconvenient with our lifestyle at the moment. But if we were a normal couple . . .'

He tutted and shook his head. 'We're not. And we won't be.' He leaned over the table towards her. 'You see all these happy families, and you think that's what you want. Husband, two kids, country house, garden, au pair. It's what everyone wants, isn't it?'

She backed away slightly. 'Well, it doesn't seem such a bad life to me.'

'How many of these men do you think are having affairs with their secretaries? How many of the women do you think hit the sherry bottle at elevenses time? How many of the kids wet the bed?'

'God, you're cynical.'

'You bet. Happy families don't exist, Nina.'

'You said just a few minutes ago that when you were a child you had brilliant holidays in Greece with Costas and his big family!'

Andrew laughed. 'Yeah. I was a kid and I had a fantastic time. Especially with Costas's grandchildren. He had a lot of those because he had six children from his three marriages. Out of his six children only one of them didn't marry more than once. And that's because he was gay.'

He leaned back again and smiled cynically at her. 'OK, let's pretend you could have a happy family with all the trimmings. Don't you think you'd get bored?

You might just once in a while feel like going up to town to fuck Beverley. How would you explain that to your little hubby?'

'If he was like you it would be easy.'

'Husbands aren't like me, don't kid yourself about that. You've only just started to explore your sexuality. Don't think you're going to get back to a little suburban lifestyle after this, Nina. It won't work for you.'

He saw her flinch and took the hand which was lying on the table.

'You know how to live now. It isn't a rehearsal. Don't think you can go back to fish fingers now you've tried carpaccio.'

'Neat metaphor.' She laughed, a bit uncertainly. He stroked her hand again.

'It's true. You can try if you like. Stop seeing me, try to play the Ice Queen again. But it won't work. Once ice melts it's gone for ever.' He finished his beer. 'Another drink?'

'I think I've probably had enough.' She caught him looking at her derisively and laughed shamefacedly. 'Oh sod it, go on, then. Don't tell me – it's not a rehearsal. Are you trying to get me drunk?'

He smiled. 'Just a bit tipsy.'

Andrew didn't have another himself. One pint when he was driving was enough. Nina protested when he came back with just the glass of wine that she certainly wouldn't have had if she'd known he wasn't.

'I like you when you've had a few drinks. Your face flushes a bit, and you lose some of those old inhibitions.'

'Oh, do I?'

He leaned across the table and rubbed her nipple through her linen top.

'No bra. Nice one.'

She frowned and moved his hand quickly.

121

'You're wrong. I haven't lost any inhibitions. I don't like you doing that in public.'

'Any more than you liked Beverley doing it last night?'

'That's right.'

'Nobody's looking.' He moved restlessly. 'I'd like to see your tits.'

She giggled, taking another sip of the wine. 'Not here, mate.'

'In the car?'

'Probably.'

'So hurry up and drink that.'

'You shouldn't have got it!' But she drank again. Andrew watched impatiently, and as soon as she'd finished they left.

I knew red wine was a mistake in this heat, thought Nina lazily as Andrew drove back down the country lane. But what the hell, she was feeling pleasantly mellow and nestled down in the seat as he turned the stereo up.

'Where are we going?'

'We're just driving. I want to see your tits. Undo your top.'

She sat up, shocked. 'Not while we're driving along the road. Anyone can see!'

'Who's anyone? It's not going to be anyone you know, so what's the harm?'

Nina giggled. He was right. What was more, the thought of a stranger seeing her breasts flash past excited her.

'Go on,' he said patiently. 'Undo your buttons and pull your top out of the way.'

Teasingly she undid one button after the other, slowly, pleased to see the lines down his face deepen as he smiled. The buttons undone, she pulled the top either side of her breasts so the seat belt was the only thing in the way and turned to him.

'Nice one,' he said appreciatively. 'Play with them for me.'

'Andrew! I can't!'

He sighed. 'Nina. You will do what I say, you really will. So you might as well do it now rather than pretend to be so prissy.'

She pouted. Of course he was right, she was going to obey his instructions. But she pretended reluctance as she raised her fingers.

Tweaking and twirling soon hardened her nipples, and she made a show of circling them and scuffing them with her thumbs and then mashing her breasts together. Not only was she turning herself on but Andrew's sidelong glances were making her cunt miss a beat.

'Getting you going?' he asked. 'Take your pants off, and before you say, "Oh Andrew, I can't," just don't.'

He grinned, obviously pleased with himself. She didn't move for a few seconds, wanting him to think this time she really was going to defy him, but the thought of it was sending her muscles into overdrive. Lifting her hips she hooked her thumbs into the elastic and slid her knickers down her thighs and kicked them off.

'Great. Lift your skirt up, *without saying anything*, and let me see your pussy.'

Her eyes closed involuntarily as a shiver ran through her at his command for silence. Slowly she lifted her skirt, tantalising herself as she pulled it up her thighs and brushed it over her pubic hair.

'Is it wet?'

'Andrew!'

'The not saying anything rule still applies, except in answer to my questions. Is it?'

'Yes!'

'How do you know?'

'Of course I know!'

'Touch it, for God's sake. I want to see the wetness on your fingers.'

Holding her skirt up with her left hand, she obediently pushed two fingers inside herself. They felt good, and she wished she could thrust them in again, but she did as she was told and raised them to his eyes.

'Good. Rub it into your nipples.'

Suddenly Andrew veered into a layby and stopped the car.

'Walk in the woods?' he suggested.

Nina nodded.

'You can do your buttons up apart from the top two. But I don't think you'll need your knickers.'

'Oh God,' she whispered, looking at him as she buttoned. 'I'm feeling horny again.'

Andrew put his hand under her chin. 'Coincidence! Me too!'

He obviously knew his way around the area. There was a clear though narrow path leading into the woods and she followed him along it, ducking under the overgrown branches he lifted out of her way. Soon, however, the path widened and they were able to walk comfortably. The trees smelt fresh and cool, compared to the heat of the beer garden. The purple trumpets of foxgloves were everywhere.

'This is beautiful!' exclaimed Nina. Andrew walked slightly ahead, concentrating on the path.

'There's a clearing not far away,' he muttered. 'At least I think it's here.'

Sure enough they soon came across a perfect clearing in the woods, studded with the stumps of felled trees. A shaft of sunlight made its way through the tree tops into the clearing.

'It's like a magic place,' said Nina. 'I almost expect to see a group of fairies dancing round that tree stump.'

'I'm going to see something better than that,' said Andrew. 'I want to see you show me your pussy on that tree stump.'

'Oh God,' moaned Nina. 'What if someone comes along?'

'There's nobody about. Listen.'

They stood for a moment but all they could hear was birdsong.

Andrew sat Nina down. She felt helpless, as though there really was magic in the air and she was under a spell, and without moving let him undo the buttons of her top again and lift her skirt. He pushed her top out of the way of her breasts again, pausing to lick her nipples where she'd rubbed her juice on them. She moaned again and her head fell back.

'Put your arms on the grass behind you,' he ordered. Nina did so, opening her eyes and looking at him steadily.

'I feel as though you're choreographing my movements for a porn film,' she said. 'It's like when Costas was making me get in the right position with that waiter.'

Andrew laughed. 'Do you want to be in a film?'

'I suppose you could arrange that as well,' she retorted.

'Of course,' he said. 'That would be a good opening shot. Girl gives herself to abandonment in the woods, thinking there's no one about. Starts fingering herself. Well, go on!'

'You told me to put my arms on the grass,' she replied, giggling, but obeying him. Her fingers started moving on her grateful clitoris. 'What happens next? A handsome prince walks into the clearing?'

'Too corny. How about a gang of lesbian kick-boxers appear and take her one after the other?'

She upped the speed of her fingers.

'Oh yes. It seems OK to fantasise about lesbian gang rape.'

'But you must have fantasised about men raping you.'

'Yes. But I don't want to talk about it. Especially as my fantasies seem to be coming true at the moment. Which reminds me, my bum's hurting on the tree stump after my spanking last night.'

'Did that excite you?'

'Of course – but I'm not sure I could really get into pain.'

'So what next?'

'I'd like to get off the tree stump.'

'Tough. What fantasy shall we make come true next? Covering you with whipped cream and having the whole restaurant dine off you?'

'How did you know?' she asked accusingly. 'It's not quite right, but pretty close.'

Andrew raised his eyes to heaven. 'Please don't think for a moment that anyone's fantasies are that exclusive. Anyway, that'll take a bit more planning. What about being fucked at work while you're on a really important phone call without letting on? What's his name, Max, will probably oblige. He fancies you.'

Nina felt herself blush, and her fingers faltered.

'Keep stroking, but not too hard. You're not to come.'

'Well, I won't if we're talking about Max. He's just a colleague.'

'So you say. Give him half the chance though and he'll be in there. Won't he? I bet he's tried.'

'Yes. But I'm not interested.'

'Maybe I should phone you at work and talk really dirty to you so you get so hot you'd fuck anyone.'

'Oh please. I'd never get so desperate that I'd fuck just anyone.'

'You probably would have said that about Costas. Not to mention the waiter.'

126

He moved towards the trees. 'I've got to pee. Keep touching yourself. I'll be watching you. Don't dare stop.'

Andrew moved into the trees till he was sure he was invisible from where Nina sat. He pulled his cock out and pissed into the undergrowth, then ran his fingers meditatively along the shaft while watching Nina. He felt a sudden tenderness for her. She looked so wanton with her tits out, her skirt up and her fingers on her cunt, but knowing that she was being so sweetly obedient made him contemplate going up to her and giving her a really loving kiss.

No, she'd had the tender loving bit that morning. He wasn't going to spoil her. What did he really want her to do for him now?

As he watched her, stroking his now-hard cock, he saw her look round quickly and stop touching herself. She lowered her skirt and started to do up her top. At the same time he heard voices coming from the far side of the clearing.

Obviously not knowing what to do, Nina stood up, still doing up her buttons, and looked round for him. 'Andrew!' she called urgently. He watched amused as she took a few steps towards his hiding place, but before she could reach him a middle-aged couple dressed in shorts with rucksacks on their backs walked into the clearing.

'Hello there!' trumpeted the woman, simultaneously with the man's 'Good afternoon!'

'Lovely day!' he added.

'Yes, isn't it,' Andrew heard Nina say hesitantly, turning to face the couple.

'You're obviously not walking the Southern Green Way,' the woman said jovially to Nina.

'No, I don't know anything about it – we just walked

off the road. I'm with my boyfriend, but I seem to have lost him.'

The couple laughed. 'Can't be too far away!' And they made their goodbyes and walked off within two yards of Andrew.

'Nina!' he called her after they'd passed him. 'Nina, over here!'

She walked towards him, her face scarlet. 'For God's sake, fancy just leaving me there talking to that couple!'

'What's wrong with that?'

'For one thing I must smell of sex. God knows what they thought I was doing in that clearing on my own!'

'And what difference does it make to anyone what they might think? I presume they don't work in your firm or live in your street. Who the hell cares?'

He pulled her towards him and his hard cock pushed against her. He lifted her skirt and rubbed against her.

'You've probably had enough fingering, anyway. You don't want to get sore. It must be my turn – I think I'd like a mouth round my dick,'

'Any mouth? Or will mine do, seeing as the wonderful Zandra's not here?' she said sarcastically, still rattled.

He laughed. 'Definitely yours. I want you over me in a sixty-nine position.' He lay on his back, his cock ready for attention, his head by her feet. 'The thing is, I really do like to see you on all fours. I suppose it's because it brings you back to the animal you really are.'

'Oh God,' moaned Nina, dropping down on to her hands and knees. 'You are a shit.'

'Yes. And now you can stop talking and see if you can do as good a job as Zandra.'

God, I am a shit, he said to himself as she took his stiff cock into her mouth. But she loves it.

'When female monkeys are in heat they stick their arses up in the air, presenting themselves for sex. Did you know that?'

128

Obviously she couldn't answer. She wasn't doing a bad job, he thought, although it was always more satisfactory when the woman was the other way up.

'I like you like this because someone else could come up and fuck you from behind while you're sucking me,' he continued. 'That'd be a real turn-on, because I could see his cock driving in and out of your pussy. I bet you'd love that, wouldn't you? God, I bet you're wet.'

He lifted a finger and pushed it slowly in and out of her cunt. It was indeed wet.

'Or of course,' he added, 'they could fuck you up the arse. That's something we haven't talked about, isn't it?'

Her mouth swiftly pulled away from his cock.

'And that's something we won't be talking about –'

'Shut it! Get your mouth back round my dick or your precious little arse'll get it straight up, hard and dry!'

Nina shivered with fear, wondering if he would really put his threat into action. She wondered if she would ever trust him completely, and thought she probably didn't want to. She recognised by now the thrill that the fear and uncertainty he inspired in her gave. She lapped her tongue around the head of his cock, then closed her mouth around it and sucked it gently.

She heard a sigh escape him and then blissfully his finger pushed inside her again. Not for long, though. He trailed the slippery finger upwards and stroked gently around her arse with it.

Apart from her mouth, she was very still as she felt two fingers being inserted inside her and then withdrawn to lubricate around the tight hole. As he stroked around it she wriggled with pleasure, surprising herself.

Again a finger pushed inside her and then pushed lightly but more persistently at her arse.

'This is just my little finger. It's not really inside you. It feels nice, doesn't it?'

She was in a catch-22 situation. If she answered she ran the risk that he would carry out his threat and forcibly fuck her up the arse. If she didn't he could take it for acquiescence.

Anyway, it did feel nice. She couldn't help moving her hips against his finger. He moved it away from her arse again and into her pussy, then back again. This time he really pushed it into her.

She gasped as she felt the ring of muscle tense against his finger, only to relax and allow it in. He moved it gently backwards and forwards and she found herself moving her arse back to meet his finger, rather than away from it.

'It's amazing what you like when you try,' he said drily, continuing his tiny in-and-out movements. 'The Greeks love it up the arse. I really do recommend it, Nina.'

Briefly she wondered if he had ever been fucked up the arse. The thought of another man's cock ploughing into his narrow hole heated her even more.

She felt his hands grab her buttocks more tightly.

'OK, that was my little finger. Guess what this is.'

Shock waves went through her as she felt his warm breath on her bottom and then his tongue was lapping around the tight hole. She was barely able to concentrate on his cock as she felt his tongue, hard now, pushing against her rim as though he was trying to penetrate it, then again licking around it.

Every tendon in her body was strained to fever pitch and she knew that the slightest touch on her clit would made her come. Obviously, though, he wasn't going to let that happen yet.

'You see, you do like it! Tastes all right, you'll be relieved to hear. Talcum powder, I guess. Now how about this?'

His first finger snaked into her. She moaned with pleasure but before she could even settle on to it he quickly withdrew it with its slick wetness and slowly but steadily pushed it into her arse. As with his little finger, he sawed backward and forward and again she moved against him.

'Bet you'll be begging me to bugger you before long,' he said with amusement in his voice. 'But it'll take a while to get you ready. Still, you're enjoying the preparation, aren't you? Next time I'll bring some lube and we'll see how far you can go. After all, we want everything to be available for your guests by the time you become the dinner table, don't we?'

Suddenly she became aware of voices coming from the same direction as the previous couple. She released his cock and made to get up, but he quickly grabbed her head with both hands.

'No you don't,' he said softly and threateningly. 'They're bound to be going the same way as the other people. They won't see us. If you don't keep sucking I swear I'll hold you down and stick it right up your arse.'

The voices got closer. It was two men, also obviously walking the Southern Green Way. Their voices stopped moving and she guessed they had stopped to sit in the clearing.

'Brilliant day, couldn't have been better,' one said.

'Yes, and we've only got about five miles to go to the pub,' the other answered.

She guessed they were undoing their rucksacks. There was a sound of a screw top being turned and then water settling back into a container.

'That should do till we get a pint. I'm really looking foward to that.'

Although she was still lapping around Andrew's cock, the intrusion had made Nina lose her concen-

131

tration. He literally shook her back to business and she resumed her sucking obediently.

It obviously wasn't enough for him. Rudely he started to thrust in and out of her mouth, one hand on top of her head to hold her still. She struggled a little and then gave up as he started once again to finger fuck her arse. The thought that the walkers could stumble upon them while his cock was in her mouth and his finger up her arse sent her adrenalin rising to danger level. She was desperate to come but he was obviously not interested in touching her anywhere but her arse.

Maybe she wasn't going to be allowed to come, but as he pushed his cock harder and more brutally into his mouth she guessed he wasn't far off, and then suddenly his come spurted into the back of her throat.

Like the previous couple, the walkers passed just two yards away, exactly at the moment that Nina turned to spit out his semen.

She sank on to her side next to him. 'Fucking my mouth wasn't one of your better ideas.'

'I'm sorry.' He did really sound contrite. 'I desperately wanted to come, and I couldn't tell you to up the rhythm or those guys would have heard – I presume that would have been an even worse idea.'

She looked at him flatly. 'Too right. And what about me?'

'You liked me probing your arse.'

'Yes. Probing. Not actually fucking it. Bear that in mind. I think it's my turn to come, don't you?'

'Sure, don't let me stop you.'

She sat up in indignation. 'You mean you're not going to do it for me?'

Andrew shrugged. 'Well, I've just come, so I can't fuck you. And I think my tongue's had its share for now, don't you? So really you might as well bring yourself off with your hands rather than mine.'

'Don't be a prick. You've been teasing me ever since we left the pub –'

'As far as I can remember most of the action has been by your hands, so carry on.'

'And you knew bloody well this is on some walking path and people would be going past –'

'How was I to know that was going to turn you on so much? Jesus, Nina, seeing a woman so desperate for it really isn't a pretty sight.'

'You bastard.' She raised her hand but he caught it.

'You weren't really going to hit me, were you?' he asked, amused.

'I don't know.' Aghast, she stared at him. 'Oh God, what's happening to me? Look, I think I'd like to go home.'

He laughed triumphantly. 'Defeated? Never mind. Go back to your vibrator.'

'I haven't got a fucking vibrator,' she said fiercely.

Still laughing, Andrew rose and held his hand out to help Nina to her feet.

'I've got to wee,' she said grumpily.

'Why didn't you say so before? I'd rather have had a golden shower than a blow job,' he chuckled. She snatched her hand away and retreated further into the undergrowth. Andrew followed her.

'If you really can't pee in front of me after all we've been doing together, I really despair of you.'

She turned back towards him and laughed defiantly. 'You want to watch me? Be my guest.'

Raising her skirt, she squatted down and let the golden liquid spurt on to the dry undergrowth.

'You must want me to watch you, as you didn't really need to lift that skirt at all,' he observed. 'I don't know why, because I think it's probably turning you on even more, and I'm not changing my mind.'

She blushed as he read her thoughts and shook

herself to get rid of the last drops, ignoring his sugges-
tion that she wipe herself with her hand.

Andrew put his arm around Nina as they walked
back to the car but she was still cross with him and
shook it off. He shrugged and whistled, presumably
pleased with himself. I expect he's really pleased that
he's left me still dying for it, she thought furiously.

They drove home in silence but as they approached
Clapham he suddenly turned up Victoria Rise towards
Chelsea Bridge and the West End instead of going
straight on to her flat.

'I sort of thought it was home time,' said Nina
crossly.

'Errand first, if you don't mind,' he said non-
committally. The streets were quiet and before too long
they were in Tottenham Court Road. He turned down
by The Albert pub and parked, telling Nina to watch
out for traffic wardens.

Ten minutes later he was back with a gift-wrapped
box.

'OK, it wasn't all great for you today. Present.'

She felt tears spring to her eyes.

'Oh, shit. I feel like a real cow now. You didn't have
to buy me a present.'

'Don't get too excited,' he advised. 'It's not a ruby
necklace.'

She tore open the wrapping and opened the box. It
was a vibrator.

Almost despite herself, she had to laugh.

'About time I had one of these. Aren't you afraid I'll
prefer it to you?'

He kissed her cheek before pulling out into the main
road. 'You win some, you lose some,' he teased.

Chapter Six

'He's won again, Ange. Whatever I do I just don't seem to be able to be in control of what's going on.'

'So what did go on?'

'I can't tell you now. Max will be coming back any minute. Except that I did what we nearly did the other night.'

'You mean you're a certified bisexual?'

'We don't like labels,' laughed Nina. 'Well, if you like. I thought I was in charge then. But,' she lowered her voice even though she was alone in the office, 'he and three others were watching through a two-way mirror,'

'Nightmare!'

'You bet. Though thinking about it afterwards, it was sort of exciting. And you should have seen these acts! God, I kept getting worried the place'd be raided, but it turns out it's a private club, so they can get away with anything apart from children and animals, or something like that.'

'I thought that was W.C. Fields.'

'Yeah, yeah. But I feel a bit down about letting

him call the shots all the time. Anyway, I'll have to go.'

Max had come in.

'How about clubbing it next Friday?'

'Brilliant! Perhaps I'll pull. I've got a feeling my luck's going to change. Anyway, if it doesn't at least I'll have your latest stories to think about when I'm wanking.'

'Very funny. I hope there's no one listening to you.'

Max turned to her as she put the phone down.

'Clubbing on Friday? With your mate Angie?'

'Yep. Jealous?'

'Two ways jealous. You're both gorgeous. Are you coming for a drink?'

'Max, just because I gave in once doesn't mean I'm going to drink with you every night.'

He laughed. '"Gave in?" You really know how to make a bloke feel good. Anyway it must be a week since we had that drink. You're hardly going to get a reputation. Don't tell me you're going to do any more work now, and it's too early to get on the tube, it'll be murder.'

Nina nodded. 'OK. Tell me about your hip and trendy weekend.'

'Fantastic. Drinking on Friday night. Drinking on Saturday night. Drinking on Sunday lunchtime. Drinking on Sunday night.'

'At least you're consistent, if a little boring.'

'I never have boring weekends. So what did you do?'

Strip show on Friday night. Lesbian sex on Friday night. Boyfriend sex on Saturday morning. Flashed my tits and gave near-public blow job on Saturday afternoon. Played with new vibrator all day Sunday. She was almost tempted to say it out loud just to see Max's face, and then say, 'Only joking!'

It was easy to revise it to clubbing on Friday, country pub and walk on Saturday, and chilling out on Sunday,

136

as they pushed their way against the throng of office workers hurrying to the tube, and made it to the wine bar, where Max got them both large spritzers.

'Is Angie dating anyone?'

'No. Want me to put in a good word?'

'Is the Pope Catholic? Nina, I'd love you even more if you fix me up with Angie.'

'I didn't realise you fancied her. Actually, I thought it was me you were after. Still, I suppose it'd get you off my back if you were going out with Angie.'

Max lit up a Marlboro. 'Not necessarily. I could manage both of you, but I suppose you're still going strong with the new bloke.'

'Yeah. Look, Max, I'd better tell you this. It's Andrew Marnington.'

She had never seen Max so surprised.

'You are joking, aren't you? Not Andrew Marnington, Nina. Not Mr Sleaze.'

Nina frowned at him. 'Actually, one of the reasons I'm telling you is that I don't like you calling him Mr Sleaze.'

'Jesus.'

Max smoked in silence for a minute, then swallowed half of his spritzer.

'He's dodgy, Nina. I can't really say anything – well, I don't really know anything. But he's definitely up to something with Limanos Hellas. It's not just the invoices. I've got a friend who mentioned something when I said we were auditing their accounts.'

She let her irritation show in her voice. 'This is pure fantasy, Max. I know you don't like him but this is ridiculous. I mean, what sort of thing? I hope you're not talking drugs.'

'No. Sex.'

Nina almost choked on her drink. 'Oh, great. You mean he really runs a fleet of strip clubs instead of ships?'

'Yeah, maybe. I don't know. I shouldn't really have said anything, it's not my story. I just don't want you to get hurt.'

It wasn't possible – was it? But maybe Andrew and Costas did own the club. And maybe there were others. But so what? It wasn't such a big deal.

Except for the upstairs rooms, of course.

Nina brushed the thoughts from her mind. It was too ridiculous.

'We can change the subject or I'm going.'

'Right. There might be nothing in it. Or it might not be so sleazy. Sorry,' he added, seeing her frown as he used the S-word again. 'Let's go back to talking about Angie. Do you think I might be in with a chance?'

He looked as eager as a puppy as his eyes lit up with the thought of dating her friend. Nina had to admit to herself that she was quite fond of him.

'If you behave yourself. After all, without me to set you up with her you've got no chance at all.'

He stood up. 'Let me get you another drink, dear Nina.'

'My round, dickhead,' she laughed, rising at the same time. 'You're not going to buy a date with Angie with spritzers.' She pushed him back into his seat. 'Sit and stay. Good dog.'

'Sure. I'll sit up and beg if you like.'

Nina smiled as she went to the bar. The thought of Max begging gave her a warm glow. It certainly made a refreshing contrast to the image of her crawling about on all fours waiting in vain for Andrew to deign to service her.

'There was a rumour going round the office that you and Angie were an item,' said Max slyly as she got back with the drinks.

'Oh, was there! And how did that start?' she asked tartly.

'Well, you brought her to the Christmas party and

then to Joan Daker's leaving do. You never had a bloke. No one ever knew you to go out with anyone.'

'And I suppose that's why John Daly and Mike Thatcher started spreading rumours.'

Max shrugged with a smile playing at his lips.

'Yeah, well, big male fantasy, two beautiful girls having it off with each other,' he said with an exaggerated leer. 'Especially if you're invited to join in.'

'If we were dykes we wouldn't be inviting anyone male to join in.'

'Yes, but you're not, are you? Or you wouldn't be going out with Mr – Mr Marnington.'

'Touché,' laughed Nina. 'So you want to come out with me and Angie on Friday?'

'Want to? Are you kidding? Shall I get on my knees and beg?'

The muscles in her vagina contracted powerfully as he mentioned that word again. She imagined herself dressed in black wielding a whip, like Katya, and making Max beg her to let him touch her, imploring her to let him make her come.

Shut it, Nina. That's enough. She shook her head to clear her mind and the look she'd felt in her eyes, and hoped he hadn't seen it.

'Max, has anyone ever told you that you might have more luck with girls if you played it cool?'

He shook his head. 'Done that, seen the film and worn the T-shirt, then I realised that you never get laid by standing up at a bar wearing shades and smoking with attitude. Life's really looked up in the last couple of years.'

She couldn't help laughing at him. 'So why do you keep hitting on me if your sex life's so great?'

He lifted his hands. 'Because that's how it carries on being great! So can I come out with you two?'

'I was joking. Look, it's a girlie night. We've got girlie things to talk about.'

He nodded. 'Like your sex life with Mr M. I understand that. But I could meet you afterwards, maybe make sure Angie gets home safely.'

They both laughed. 'Enough, Maxie. I'm off home.'

'Out with him tonight?'

'No, staying in with my vibrator.'

He laughed, little guessing that it was the truth. Nina couldn't understand why she'd lived without one for so long, especially before she had met Andrew. Too uptight to go in a sex shop, of course, she told herself.

Life's really looked up in the last couple of weeks, she thought, paraphrasing Max, and it wasn't just the sex. Her relationship with Max had improved a thousand per cent since she'd stopped getting paranoid every time he asked her out for a drink. Although she'd always enjoyed her job, she really looked forward to going in now they had such an easy, bantering relationship.

She really didn't fancy him, she told herself. But as she sat on the Northern Line it didn't do any harm to let her mind drift over the possibility of having Max eager to fulfil her every whim. And just maybe rewarding him once in a while with a few caresses, maybe letting him come once in a blue moon – as long as he realised what a big favour it was and was suitably grateful . . .

As long as she didn't confuse the fantasy Max with the real one, it was something rather nice to think about. Nina decided it wouldn't do any harm to continue thinking about it later. She might even get the vibrator out again.

Anyway, there was nothing on TV.

'I've led a sheltered life,' Nina explained acidly. 'I've never been in a tattoo parlour before.'

The big man standing before her had a shaved head and a tattoo on the back of his skull, but despite the threatening appearance his smile was friendly and his voice warm.

'Hey, man, just chill out,' he said easily in an American accent. 'No pressure. Just have a look through the book with your boyfriend. Come and have a look round, ask anything you like. If you want reassurance there's even a regular customer in the back I can take you in to. I know he'll be cool.'

'Cheers,' said Nina, picking up the book. 'I'm not sure this is a good idea, Andrew.' She leafed through the book illustrating various tattoo designs. 'I feel like I'm picking out new wallpaper.'

He laughed. 'Look, it's up to you.' He lowered his voice. 'You know I just like the thought of undressing you and seeing something that says me and you on your body.'

'But it's not as if we've decided to commit to each other, is it?'

Andrew shrugged. 'You said you wouldn't mind having a look. So here we are.'

'Yes, though I must say I preferred your first plan for tonight.'

Originally they had a date for dinner at the Mirabelle, which Nina would have died for. She had even bought a new outfit for the occasion, so Andrew's inexplicable switch from a Michelin-starred restaurant to a tattoo parlour had tried her patience more than a little. He had coaxed her into agreeing by telling her graphically on the phone while she was at the office how much the idea turned him on, leaving her unable to concentrate on the afternoon's work.

Nina had always been half tempted by the look of a tattoo but put off by the image it projected. Neither had she been able to think of the right kind of design she would like to decorate her body with. When everyone else was having butterflies and roses on their shoulders, she and Angie had decided it was tacky. But the thought of having a tattoo done for Andrew was exciting.

She'd already stipulated that she didn't want it to show at work, in the gym or in the swimming pool, which ruled out the very top of the inside of her thigh, which Andrew had suggested. She'd suspected as well that the tender skin there would make it extra painful. He was also keen on a buttock, but Nina pointed out she wasn't going through pain to have her body decorated where she couldn't see it herself. So she'd decided on the right side of her belly, inside the pelvic bone and just above the pubic hair. That way she could look down at it but it would be covered by her swimsuit and workout gear. It would show when she wore a bikini or undies, but since she wasn't planning to exhibit herself in either of those in front of anyone who knew Nina the auditor rather than Nina the firebrand, that was fine.

That was one problem solved. But what about the design?

Flowers were an obvious choice. But really, did she want a rose? There were other small stylised flowers in the book. Butterflies galore. And why did it have to be a flower? Flowers for girlies, dragons and snakes for men. She considered a little snake, his tongue pointing down to her vagina. Or an arrow pointing in the right direction. Maybe through a heart?

'This is silly,' she said. 'I don't really want any of these. I want something a bit different.'

The laidback guy had returned. 'Come and look at this guy out back,' he invited her. 'He said it's cool. You might get some ideas from him.'

They followed him into one of the back rooms. A masked and gloved woman tattooist was intently drawing with her needle on to the thigh of a tall, muscular man in his thirties, whose short hair was finished with a grungy plait down his neck. He nodded at them.

'Hi. Understand you want some inspiration from my body.'

Nina laughed. 'He said you don't mind.' She went closer and studied the man's back.

A large eagle was the centrepiece. It looked like it had been copied from a design on the back of a biker's jacket. Around it were snakes and spiders' webs, and two scrolls, one inscribed 'Jim' and one 'Mary'.

'You must be Jim,' said Andrew. The man shook his head. 'Nope. Jim and Mary were my parents.'

'Adam,' read Nina on his left arm. 'Have you got Eve on the other arm?'

'No, my name's Adam,' he said patiently.

She studied the thigh that was being decorated. He already had a vine growing up from his knee and the tattoist was adding clouds and a moon above it.

Nina was starting to feel like a voyeur. She raised her gaze to the man's chest, and there it was.

A shower of stars cascaded from the man's shoulder down towards his left nipple.

'A meteor shower. That's what I want.'

'No problem there, ma'am,' said the tattooist.

'Will that be easy? I mean, not too painful?' she asked him.

'Hell, no. You want it just like that?'

'Smaller,' she said hastily. 'Is that OK? Can you do tiny?'

She made a crescent shape about five inches by one inch with her fingers and thumbs.

'Yup, can do. Step just this way, little lady.'

Nina was starting to feel that John Wayne was going to draw on her body. 'Are you coming?' she asked Andrew.

'Of course. I'm going to hold your hand.'

'Do you like the stars?'

He nodded. 'Not what I'd have chosen. I suppose I'd have gone for flowers – but it'll be pretty.'

In the small cubbyhole, Nina took her sandals and skirt off and lay down on a couch, feeling rather like she was in a doctor's surgery. The tattooist disappeared for a couple of minutes, then returned with a stencil of a star shower.

'Now, where exactly do you want it?' he asked.

Embarrassed, Nina indicated the chosen spot. She'd taken the precaution of wearing a G-string instead of knickers so that nothing would get in the way, but it left her feeling exposed in front of the stranger. Still, she reminded herself, he's a professional.

'OK, ma'am. Now just remember when you go to eat another piece of pie that if your belly gets fatter, so will your tattoo.'

'I think it might be a good deterrent to eating too much,' she agreed gravely.

He marked her skin with the stencil and asked her to approve it before he started. She stood and looked at it in the mirror.

It looked pretty good. Nina felt pleased with herself; standing there in only her vest top, G-string and tattoo.

'I must just remind you, ma'am, that once you have a tattoo it is not an easy job to remove it. I must ask you if you have thought seriously as to whether you want this permanent mark on your body.'

He quoted the phrases as though he were a policeman perfunctorily reading her her rights. Nina smiled and nodded.

'Yes. Do it.'

It wasn't as painful as she'd expected. When they'd talked to Adam while he was having his clouds and moon tattooed on, she had assumed he was a real stoic, but once she'd stopped flinching away from the buzzing needle it wasn't too bad. Andrew stood behind her head, stroking her hair and talking to her. She knew he was doing it to keep her calm, but couldn't dismiss the feeling that it was like he was overseeing work done on his property.

She wondered too if he liked her pain in having his mark branded on her, seeing the tiny teardrops of blood welling up along the lines of the design.

When it was over, the tattooist smoothed Vaseline on and covered it with gauze, warning her to keep it covered for a couple of hours.

'You didn't bleed much, so you won't have too many scabs. But don't pick them off!'

And that was it.

Out in the street, Andrew put his arms around her and hugged her close to him.

'You know what would make it look perfect, Nina?'

'What now? What's not perfect about it, anyway?'

'If you had your pubic hair shaved off.'

She stopped and looked steadily at him. 'Why?'

'Because it'll distract from the tattoo. And because it's sexy. I don't suppose you've ever done it.'

'You want to bet?' She laughed at the look on his face. 'No, of course I haven't. Why's it sexy?'

'Because you can see it all,' he whispered to her. 'You can see where the cleft starts and where the clitoris is. When you open your legs you can see the labia properly. It's turning me on just thinking about it.'

She looked at him suspiciously. 'Did you plan this?'

He smiled. 'I just happen to know a hairdresser round the corner.'

'Why can't I do it myself with a lady's razor?'

'You won't get it close enough. This guy'll really give you a close shave, and he'll be able to take care not to touch the tattoo. Then we'll go back to my place.'

He's done it again, she thought. For the last month she'd been dying to see Andrew's flat, but it was always more convenient for them to meet in town or for him to go to her place.

'Can't we just go to your place now and think about

shaving my pubes off? Or wouldn't it be quite exciting if you did it for me?'

'Sure. Except I don't know if my hand is steady enough. And I know this guy Charles.'

She sighed. 'You know, I think I might just as well have had "No Free Will" tattooed on my forehead.'

'At least no one could think of putting "No Sense of Humour" on it,' he laughed. 'So, are you up for it?'

'I've just had a permanent mark put on me. It doesn't seem such a big deal to let someone shave a bit of hair off.'

They rounded the corner and Nina remembered in the past seeing the old-fashioned gentlemen's barber. It looked like an expensive place and she felt vaguely comforted.

A short, plump little man with a rosy, unlined face and curly white hair bustled out from the back of the shop when the doorbell sounded as they went in.

'Mr Marnington! How nice to see you! Madam! Do come in!' he greeted them effusively. 'What a nice surprise! What can I do for either of you?'

'Hello, Charles,' said Andrew, patting the man's arm. 'Can you do a special shaving job on Nina for me?'

'Of course,' gushed Charles, beaming at her. 'Always a pleasure. Such a vast improvement, I feel. Have you had it done before, Nina?'

'No, this is a first for me,' she replied. 'But I've just had a tattoo done, so I'm a bit apprehensive about going through more body decoration.'

'Tattoo! Oh, you youngsters. Come into the back room and let me have a look at it. I'll tell you if it'll be a problem. And don't worry about the shave. It always gives pleasure, which I'm sure you deserve after all that pain.'

'Oh, it wasn't too bad,' she replied, following Charles, who she decided must be gay, into the back room, which looked just like another version of the

146

front barber shop with sumptuous beige leather chairs and gleaming chrome. There was also, however, a couch pushed across one of the walls. The smell of expensive shampoos and cologne filled the room and Nina felt quite comforted.

Charles busied himself pulling the couch out and covered it with an immaculate white sheet he got from a cupboard.

'Let's have a look at this tattoo,' he said, beaming. 'Take your skirt off, dear.'

Feeling much less self-conscious than in the tattoo parlour, Nina removed her skirt and showed Charles the gauze-covered patch.

'Hmm. What is it, dear? I can't see through the dressing.'

'Stars,' Nina explained.

He smiled benevolently. 'Very nice. Well, that's no problem. If you'd just like to get your shoes and undies off and hop up on to the couch, I'll have a look at these nasty hairs.'

Nina repressed a desire to laugh and slipped off her sandals and the G-string while Charles washed his hands thoroughly. She lay on a couch for the second time that evening.

'Lovely colour, dear, but rather coarse,' he said as he turned to her. 'Now the easiest thing is if I just cut off the excess with scissors and then shave you.' He grasped a handful of her hair as he spoke. 'Open your legs, dear, and let's have a proper look at how tricky this will be.'

Nina couldn't help feeling oddly excited as she raised her knees and spread her legs as though she was waiting for a smear test. The little man's fingers ran down either side of her vagina, pulling her apart slightly as he checked for hairs. He smelt strongly of aftershave.

'Not too much of a problem – just lift a bit more and

let's have a look at those nasty ones at the back.' She felt that his nose was practically touching her as his hands went under her buttocks and lifted her so he could inspect around her bottom.

'Right!' He beamed down at her. 'All off, Nina? Some girls like a little bit at the front, perhaps in a heart shape? I don't recommend it, because yours are a bit too coarse and curly. What do you think?'

'All off,' she decided.

'Lovely. Is that all right with you, Mr Marnington?'

'Yes, whatever Nina wants, Charles,' said Andrew, obviously amused. He had sat himself down in one of the leather chairs. Nina smiled at him.

'Right, let's just cut off what we can first.' Charles picked up a small, sharp pair of scissors and lifted a few clumps of Nina's pubes at a time and snipped. She was surprised how much noise it made and commented on it.

'Like cutting through copper wire, dear. Actually, that's just what your hair reminds me of,' added Charles.

Several more snips followed.

'Open wide, dear,' said the barber jovially. 'Press your knees out to the side, if it's not too uncomfortable.'

She felt the cold steel of the scissors against her warm flesh as he snipped down to remove as many of the long hairs as he could.

'That's a lot better already,' he said approvingly. 'Let's just get this hair out of the way.' He picked up a soft brush and carefully brushed the loose hairs downwards on to the sheet. The brush was like a thousand tiny silky strands stroking from the top of her pubic hair right down to her arse. Nina tried to ignore the thrill it gave her, but as he slowly brushed several times she was starting to feel decidedly heated.

He next lifted her legs and brushed the hairs off the

sheet on to the floor. Nina looked over the side of the couch at them. There seemed such a lot.

Charles was busy preparing hot water, shaving brush and soap, which he placed on a stand next to the couch.

'Now it's going to be a little bit tricky getting at the hairs just beneath that tattoo, dear, so please excuse me if I'm a bit clumsy. The main thing is not to hurt you.'

'That's fine,' she said as he lathered her pubic mound. As he picked up the razor she felt a slight tremor of alarm. What if he were a lunatic who was about to slice off her clitoris in a ritual circumcision?

Instead, the first thing she felt was a decided pressure on her pubic mound as he steadied his hand to shave off the hairs below the tattoo. Rather than fight it, she decided that, as when Andrew had been playing with her arse, she could relax and just enjoy it. She just hoped Charles couldn't feel the pulse that had started up in response to the pressure of his hand.

He didn't stop talking.

'This will be so much nicer, Nina. I guarantee you'll never grow back those ugly hairs again,' he said confidingly, pressing more firmly on her bone. 'What's the point of hiding your treasure under a helmet of hair?'

His hand moved and he started on the other side. Nina felt slightly cheated and grinned inwardly. You horny cow, she said to herself.

He stopped and looked down at her. 'Knees up and open this time, dear.'

His head disappeared from her line of vision, then bobbed back up again to look at her delightedly.

'What a lovely cunt you've got,' he said chattily. 'Beautiful lips! You wait till you see it without hair. You'll fall in love with it.'

Nina knew she'd gasped out loud, but she couldn't help it. While she thought of her cunt as just that, no one else had ever referred to it so colloquially.

'Oh, excuse me,' said Charles. 'I can't call it anything

else. All the other words seem so medical, don't you think so?'

'Yes,' said Nina weakly.

'Anyway, it's a long time since I've seen such a pretty cunt,' he continued, lathering his brush again and rubbing the soap in either side of her slowly liquefying slit. 'I bet it's nice and tight too. You won't have had any children, will you?'

'No,' croaked Nina. She had already been feeling mildly aroused by the pressure of Charles's hands and the stroking of the brush, but at his words her vaginal muscles had tensed deliciously.

'I almost feel jealous of you, Mr Marnington, having this lovely tight hole all to yourself,' he went on. 'Lovely rosy lips.'

As he picked up the razor again, his thumb moved deftly on to her clitoris. 'Not long now, dear. You'll be wanting to look at this all day. Do you look in the mirror a lot?'

'Not at my ... my cunt,' she answered.

'How strange!' said Charles. 'You just try it, dear. It's lovely to watch it when you masturbate.'

Was his thumb really rubbing her clitoris, or was she just imagining it? She closed her eyes and decided to let herself be carried into this surreal dream. He was definitely rubbing her. What was she going to do? Jump up indignantly and walk out half shaved? She could hardly pretend she wasn't turned on. Once the foam was washed away she knew she'd be revealed soaking wet.

'Have you got a vibrator?'

'Yes. It's new.'

'Do you like it?'

'Love it.'

She heard Andrew almost snigger, but he managed to turn it into a cough. She hadn't really planned to confess to him that she'd used it already. Several times.

150

'Well, you watch it going in and out of your shaved cunt, dear. That'll really get your juices flowing.'

She could have sworn his thumb slipped inside her for a second. It was all so bizarre she felt as if she'd been slipped an acid tab or a spiked drink – except that nothing had passed her lips since a coffee about four hours ago.

'Nearly finished. Now I hate to ask you to do this, dear, but I need you to turn over so I can finish off round your little bum hole.'

'That's OK,' said Nina. 'Though I don't want to put any weight on my tattoo.'

'Oh no, I need you on all fours with your bum in the air, dear. I'm sorry, it's not a very dignified position.'

It's one I'm quite used to, thought Nina drily, as she turned herself over and presented her arse like an orang-utan. Charles took hold of her thighs and pushed them further apart.

'That's lovely, dear. Sorry about this. Do you like being fucked up the bum? Hold still, now!'

With one hand he was spreading the cheeks of her arse wide apart and shaving with the other.

'No,' she muttered.

'Oh, what a shame,' he sympathised. 'Do try it. I'm sure Mr Marnington would oblige. However tight your cunt is, your arse will be even tighter.'

He moved to the sink and started to run some hot water, leaving Nina exposed, but soon returned with a warm flannel and started to rinse off the foam.

'Lovely! On your back again,' he said, giving her a playful smack on the bottom. Once more she spread her legs and he gave her a gentle but thorough rubbing with the warm flannel. Nina closed her eyes and surrendered to the sensation of the hot cloth. Then he dried her and put a tiny sprinkling of talcum powder on to the towel and patted her with it.

'That's beautiful, if I do say so myself,' he pronounced. 'Have a look, Mr Marnington.'

Nina lay there while both men looked appreciatively
at her shaved pubis.

'Look how her little clittie stands out,' said the barber, putting his finger right on it and fretting it.

'Great job, Charles,' said Andrew gravely. Nina could
hardly believe that he was watching the little man
finger her like that.

'And what nice lips! You can see them now.'

Charles ran his hands down and Nina felt the slick-
ness of her oozing on to his fingers. He gently pulled
aside her outer lips, allowing his fingers to slide a little
way up her wet pussy.

'Just a little arrangement, and you can see everything,' he said happily. 'So are you pleased, sir?'

'Oh, absolutely,' said Andrew. Charles's fingers were
inside her.

'Maybe we should show Nina,' Andrew suggested.
The barber raised his eyes to heaven.

'What was I thinking of! She should have looked
before you,' he cried, picking up an oval mirror. 'Nina,
don't tell me you don't like that.'

He held the mirror and Nina sat up and looked
down into it. She was startled to see how naked she
looked without pubic hair. And she was embarrassed
to see how obviously wet she was.

'It's amazing,' she said.

'May I take a photo?' asked Charles. 'It's just a little
tradition here. Just of the shaved area, my dear. Your
face won't be in it.'

'No way!'

Charles's face fell and she sighed.

'Well – if my face isn't in it, I suppose it doesn't
matter.'

'Lovely!'

He reached into a cupboard and took out a Polaroid

152

camera. Whisking away the mirror, he patted Nina's knees down on to the couch.

'One like that dear,' he said fussily, snapping her. 'Now while this takes its time, can you just put your hand down as though you were about to touch yourself?'

Nina closed her eyes and put her hand down in front of her clitoris.

'You can touch yourself if you want,' said Charles encouragingly. 'A lot of girls like to masturbate after their shave. Do you want to?'

She didn't know the answer. One thing was certain, she would have loved to rub that wet juice from her pussy all over her clit until she came. But there was no way she wanted Charles taking a photo of her doing it.

'Never mind,' he said, breaking the silence. 'Not compulsory. Here goes!' He took another shot of her with her hand poised over her clit.

'Now, if you could put both your hands over your pubic mound, dear – no, one over the other. Just move them down a bit. Now if I can just have you back on the all fours position, I'll take one of that lovely hairless little bottom,' he said. Nina felt helpless as she turned over and let him pull her thighs further apart, taking the chance to let his little finger slide inside her. She felt her newly exposed labia hanging down for his camera as he took his final shot.

'They will give me many hours of pleasure, Nina,' said Charles cheerily. 'Right, time to get dressed.'

She shuffled inelegantly off the table and put her G-string back on. Before she could get her skirt on he stopped her.

'Just look, dear,' he urged her, turning her round to face the mirror.

She had to admit she liked it. The G-string looked totally different without the hair poking out around it.

'Thanks,' she said to Charles, but she wasn't quite sure what she was thanking him for.

Chapter Seven

'*H*e's a pervert.'
'Well, you could say that. But he's a wonderful barber. Best shave in London.'

'Maybe. But he still made me shudder. He's a bit of a creep.

'No, he's not. When he looks at his photos he may like to imagine all kinds, but he's really harmless. Actually, he prefers men.'

'Rent boys, I bet.'

'Possibly.' Andrew was obviously amused. 'He does like to get women excited, though.'

'I couldn't believe it. If I'd had a drink, I'd have sworn you'd spiked it and I was tripping or something.'

'You were so wet.'

Nina blushed. 'I couldn't have been more exposed, could I?'

'And don't tell me that didn't turn you on as well.'

'You know it did.'

'And the photos?'

'Up to a point.'

The taxi turned right away from Regent's Park, which they'd been driving by, made a couple more turns and then stopped. Nina felt excited again at the thought of seeing Andrew's flat.

Inside the anonymous white-painted block the porter greeted him deferentially and summoned the lift. She noticed he pressed the top button.

'Penthouse?'

'Of course!'

The lift door opened to reveal a small wood-panelled hallway with a parquet floor. Either side of the front door was an occasional table adorned with vases of flowers. Andrew opened the door with a flourish.

'Welcome, Nina.' He took her hand. 'Not many women get this far, you know. I usually prefer to keep my home and my sex life apart.'

She looked into his hazel eyes, so often unfathomably closed, but now looking at her tenderly. She wondered how much to read into his remark. Sure, she was pleased to be accorded this special privilege. But did it mean anything more? Were they going to become a real couple?

The room they entered took her mind off everything. It was dark as they entered but Andrew pressed a switch and blinds swished as they were raised on three sides of the room. Suddenly the evening sun flooded the room with light and Regent's Park was spread before them.

'Oh, wow. This is fantastic, Andrew.'

He smiled. 'Good view, isn't it? As soon as I saw it I knew I had to have this flat.'

The room itself was large but minimally furnished with rich cream sofas and armchairs. Like the hallway, the floor was parquet and the one wall not glazed was wood panelled. The only other furnishings were a few low occasional tables and a large desk, both in bleached wood in art deco style. Large vases of cream flowers adorned the tables.

'It's incredible.' She went to the largest window,

which faced the park. It was hard to believe that they were in the middle of London, but the city spread westwards beyond the park, and both north and south were framed in the other two windows. It was like being in an oasis of green in the city concrete.

'Come and see the rest of the flat.' Andrew propelled her to a door that led directly into a dining room, the table set with eight chairs. From there another door led to the kitchen, which looked like something out of a design magazine, or maybe a modern restaurant. Everything was stainless steel and the floor was covered with industrial rubber. The only appliances on show were an Alessi kettle and an espresso machine. A small table and two chairs were at the window at one end.

Beyond the kitchen the small corridor led to an all-white bathroom and two guest rooms. Then they were in the main bedroom.

The bed was in the centre of the room. A four poster, but not a tacky metal curtain-framed one. The posts were obviously hand-carved and rose from the red-covered bed. The walls too were red and invited the touch; Nina realised they were covered in suede, almost tiled with the material. A huge mirror faced the bed, reflecting the view over north London from the window opposite. Pictures covered one wall and a black vase filled with exotic red flowers with little tongues like miniature penises in the centre of each one sat on the floor in front of the mirror.

'I've just had that suede done,' said Andrew, surveying it. 'I think it works. I wanted a sort of bordello effect – what do you think? Is it sexy?'

Nina laughed. 'You need me to tell you what's sexy? Yes, it is. Although after being teased with a shaving brush by a profane pervert, I'm not sure my judgement's totally reliable.'

Andrew pulled her close to him. 'You loved it. Are you still wet?' His hand reached under her skirt and one finger sneaked under the thin silk of her G-string. He laughed.

'Let's have the skirt off.' He undid her zip and she stepped out of it as it fell to the floor. 'Oh, pretty. You loved being photographed, didn't you?'

Nina nodded.

'Can I photograph you?'

She laughed. 'With my face in shot?'

'Definitely. How about a drink first, then I'll get the camera.'

'You'd better make it a large one.'

While Andrew was out of the room she wandered over to look at the pictures on the wall and felt a jolt of shock when she realised they were photographs of women, many naked, most posing provocatively. Most of them were of different women, not all pretty, she was surprised to see, although some women featured in two or three photos. There was one of two women together and even before examining it she knew instinctively one would be Beverley. She was naked apart from the slave collar and a masked woman in black leather stood behind her holding a whip. It wasn't Katya – it had to be Ariadne.

He returned while she was still in front of the picture of her female lover.

'So am I a good enough photographer for you to model for me?' he asked.

She had another shock. 'You took all these?'

He nodded, handing her a large glass of vodka and tonic. Taking his camera from round his neck, he raised his whisky glass to touch it against hers.

'To a good result,' he toasted, then took a big swallow of the drink. Picking up the camera, he gestured towards the bed. 'How about some shots with your vest and G-string first?'

Awkwardness overcame Nina as she lay gingerly on

the red bedspread. 'Do you think I could take this gauze off now?'

He looked at his watch and nodded. 'Yes, that'll be a great improvement for the pictures.'

Nina started to pull the white dressing off the tattoo. It hurt.

'Shit, it didn't occur to me it'd be so painful!' she winced. 'It's worse than pulling a plaster off.'

'Do you want me to do it?' asked Andrew. She laughed.

'No way! You can just get a kick out of watching me in pain.'

Slowly she released the gauze and inspected her tattoo. 'Hey, it's a bit red and puffy but it doesn't look bad even now. It's sore, though.'

Andrew surveyed the star shower. 'It'll be great. Let's have a close-up of it.' He zoomed in on the tattoo.

'You know, I felt really jealous of Charles in there, Nina,' he said as he moved the camera up to her face.

'Why? Because he was fingering me?'

'Hardly. I think you know by now that I like to watch you being touched by someone else. No, it was the way he turned you on by talking dirty.'

Nina pouted.

'Hold that expression!' He took several shots of her face.

'I wished I'd been the one to tell you what a nice cunt you've got.'

Again it was like a knee-jerk reaction – or a cunt-jerk reaction, Nina thought, as her vaginal muscles clenched immediately at the word.

'Why didn't I think to tell you how much I wanted to put my cock right up your tight cunt?'

'Yes, why didn't you?' whispered Nina, opening her legs and looking at him. She felt her face relax into an expression of desire, her eyelids lowering and her lips swelling. He moved back and refocused the camera.

'Take your G-string off,' he commanded. She complied slowly, her shaven pubis still feeling strange and exciting.

'Put your fingers up your cunt for me,' he urged. Without prompting Nina started moving lazily in and out. She felt dreamy and weightless, as though she were floating on a sea of decadence. A sea she would be happy to drown in.

'What did you do with the vibrator when you got home on Saturday?'

Nina's tongue flickered lightly over her lips and she remembered for him.

'I pulled it out of the box and turned it on. All these bits and pieces fell out of the box but I wasn't interested in them. I took my skirt and knickers off and went into the bedroom, and worked out how to turn the vibrator full on.'

'Didn't you close the curtains first?'

'Oh yes, I must have done. I lay down on the bed and pushed it in. I was still wet. It felt great; the stiffest cock I've ever had.'

'So you fucked yourself with it?'

'For a bit. Then I pulled it out and tried it on my clitoris. It was like an electric shock. I came straight away.'

'So that was it?'

'Like hell it was. I had to make myself go for a walk on the common on Sunday afternoon, because I thought otherwise I'd just spend the whole day with it.'

'Best present you ever had?'

'I'll say. Are you going to fuck me?'

She was more than ready for him. The combination of Charles's attentions, Andrew's camera and her own fingers was building up remorselessly in her body.

'In a minute. Just take your top off.'

Andrew moved to the vase and took out a handful of the strange red flowers. As Nina pulled her vest over

159

her head he arranged the flowers on her midriff and belly, covering her body between her breasts and her pubic mound and emphasising the creamy flesh of both. She flinched at first as the stems dripped cold water over her warm skin, but once she'd got used to it, she imagined the water trickling over her belly was droplets of come and felt even more horny.

'Great. Just a few shots with the flowers. That'll do.'

He put the camera down and started to unbutton his shirt. Nina watched him, playing with one of the flowers.

'Did you choose these because they've got a little cock on them?' she asked him.

Andrew laughed. 'God, no, I don't choose them. Someone comes and does the flowers.'

'Your daily?'

'No, she just does the housework. It's a florist.'

Nina laughed incredulously.

'You mean you pay one person to do the housework and another to do the flowers? I'm amazed you bother with me. I would have thought it'd be easier to pay someone to come and service your body as well as your flat.'

He approached the bed, undressed. Nina reached out eagerly at his penis, which was as hard as she could have desired, almost as red as the flowers. As she caressed him she looked up and saw the opaqueness of his eyes.

'I do that too,' he said evenly.

She closed her eyes and continued to rub his cock. He moved her hand and lay down on the bed, quickly pulling on a condom.

'Sit on top of me,' he commanded. She didn't need to be told twice. Straddling him, she held the root of his cock and sank thankfully on to its hardness.

'I love whores,' he continued. 'They do what they're told. Although you're getting better at that, Nina.'

160

She moved up and down his shaft. It was delicious. Instead of feeling jealous at the thought of Andrew with other women, she felt turned on. She licked her lips lasciviously as she watched his face as she rose and fell slowly on top of him.

'I love not having to make a woman come if I don't want to,' he continued. 'I like just having a blow job sometimes, without any contact. And I really like having two women at once.'

'So why didn't you walk in on me and Beverley?' she whispered. Losing herself in sensuality, her voice sounded breathy and exciting.

'I told you, I like watching. And that was your thing, you know, making your fantasy come true about having another woman. Next time I'll be there. Anyway, I'd already come with Zandra.'

Nina closed her eyes. 'You wanted to remind me of that.'

His voice was soft and insistent. 'Why not? The thought of her mouth round my dick turns you on, doesn't it? And I bet ever since you found out we were watching you and Bev you've felt horny, haven't you?'

She ignored the question and asked one of her own.

'When you took that photo of Beverley and Ariadne, did you have sex with them?'

She felt her breasts rising as she breathed harder and she started moving imperceptibly faster along the length of his cock. Her eyes were still closed and she felt there was nothing else in the world but her cunt moving up and down on him, fucking him, while she listened.

'They were rehearsing the act, without the actual whipping,' his soft voice said. 'I was watching to tell them what it looked like, playing different music and so on. It was pretty hot. Especially the end, when Ariadne tongued Bev.'

'You watched that.'

161

'Sure. I was as hot as hell, and so was Ariadne. Her mouth was covered in Bev's come. She kissed it all over my face and I decided I wanted some more cunt juice myself, so I put my mouth right in her pussy and brought her off, then Bev got on top of me just like you are now and fucked me. Ariadne stood over her with the whip and told her to go faster or she'd whip her.'

'She was doing this, just like I am?'

'Yeah, but with Ariadne wearing that black mask and black leather standing behind her threatening her. God, that was a real turn-on.'

Nina faltered, making him laugh.

'I'm not making comparisons,' he said patiently. 'I don't want to come right now. But I want you to, and I want to take a picture of you coming.'

He reached and picked up the camera again.

'OK, Nina, you said you liked being choreographed like a porn actress. Now I want you to fuck harder and I want your hand rubbing your clit while I tell you what happened next.'

Her obedient hand moved eagerly to her clit, feeling she could come before he could focus the camera.

'The other hand, so I can see the tattoo.'

He continued with the story when her left hand was rubbing and she was riding him again. 'Ariadne stood behind Bev and gathered her tits in her hands and mashed them hard and told her she was a little slut who couldn't get enough of it.'

Nina moaned as he clicked the shutter just as she rose, guessing the picture would be of his cock just inside her, and her fingers on her clitoris.

'Ariadne forced her to beg me to fill her up with my dick. Then she stood on the bed with her legs apart and her back to me and Bev tongued her while she kept telling her that she was a dirty little slut who was only good for sex. Oh, man, watching Bev's hands round Ariadne's arse while she was still pumping up and down on me, and hearing Ariadne tell Bev that if she didn't make us both come in one minute flat she'd really use that whip on her. Bev was pumping harder and harder and she came. I felt her squeeze me and that was it for me – I couldn't hold it back, especially when I saw Ariadne's arse moving and I knew she'd be coming as well –'

Nina knew that he knew that she too was coming, and as she moaned she heard the shutter click rapidly as he focused on her face, her fingers, her cunt and his cock. The sight of the camera capturing the pulsations of her cunt and the thought of seeing the photographs protracted her orgasm. She heard herself making little mewing noises, and then she heard Andrew moan and he was coming too.

'God, that was intense,' he said, his arm around her as she lay back, still panting.

'Not as intense as your scene with Beverley and Ariadne,' she said.

He laughed. 'Do you think that really happened?'

She sat up and stared at him.

'Did you invent that to excite me more?' she asked.

His eyes looked back at her, unreadable. 'You'll never know, Nina.'

'Shit!' she lay down, exhausted and confused.

'Does it matter?' he asked tenderly, stroking her face. 'It might have done. Or it could happen tomorrow, if you want.'

'You can make anything happen,' she said.

'Sure, that was the premise of our relationship, wasn't it? Me making things happen for you?'

She stretched lazily. 'I feel like the cat who had the cream. And if I wanted more cream, you'd get it for me.'

'Mmm, that reminds me – didn't you want to have a cream tea served on you?'

Nina laughed. 'That was one of my fantasies, true.

Perhaps you'd better get Beverley and Ariadne around for afternoon tea.'

'Never mind tea, it must be time for dinner,' he said, looking over at the clock. 'It's gone nine. I thought I was hungry – how about you?'

'Starving,' she admitted.

'Do you want to go out? Or shall I knock up a gourmet meal out of my modest store cupboard?'

'Difficult one. I don't want to move. But on the other hand, if you're going to start banging pots and pans it'll spoil the mood anyway.'

Andrew raised his eyebrows. 'Do you really see me doing a Rick Stein or a Jamie Oliver? Come into the kitchen and I'll show you what we've got.'

Obviously used to wandering around his flat without clothes, he led the way to the kitchen. Without her pubic hair Nina felt even more naked than usual as she followed him. She took care to stand back from the stainless steel cupboards.

He opened the fridge and started removing items and throwing them on the worktop.

'Smoked salmon. Cold beef. Salad. French dressing. Lemons. Horseradish. Butter.'

The door underneath was the freezer, from which he took half a baguette. 'Bread. Stick it in the microwave, Nina.' He opened another stainless steel door to reveal the oven, then paused and turned to her with the still-frozen loaf.

'Unless you've any better uses for this?'

She laughed. 'Too cold, I think.'

He produced a tray, plates and knives and forks, and two minutes later the feast was arranged. A bottle of wine was opened and glasses taken from yet another stainless steel door and they were back on the bed attacking the salad.

'Better than a takeaway pizza,' said Nina contentedly, breaking off a morsel of the warm bread. 'Do you always keep the fridge ready for an unexpected guest?'

'The housekeeper makes sure there's always stuff in,' he said. 'A lot of the time I don't use it and she takes it home.'

'You're very generous.'

'I'm glad you think so. Does that extend to my treatment of you?'

Spearing a piece of rare beef, Nina looked at him consideringly.

'Well, on one hand, you've given me quite a few new experiences. Not to mention a shave and a tattoo and a few hundred pounds. But on the other, you've withheld a climax for a very long period of time – which is not what I would call generous.'

'Call that another new experience,' he teased.

'Not to mention the fact that you're as generous with your body to others as you are to me,' she added. 'And you've certainly let others make free with my body.'

'Sounds generous to a fault to me.'

Nina looked into his hazel eyes, now warm and relaxed. It was hard to believe that sometimes the light would go out in those eyes and they would look at her as dead as wood.

They finished the meal and Andrew took the tray back to the kitchen. She took the opportunity to examine the photographs in more detail.

Most of the subjects were women in various stages of undress, not many completely naked. She was pleased to see the red bedspread they had just had sex on did not appear in any of the pictures; where the women were on a bed it was certainly not this one.

With a sudden shock she recognised one of the pictures. Almost as she had seen them the previous week, it was the ballet-dancing couple from the strip club.

Just as in their act, the ballerina was wearing nothing

but the ruff of a tutu around her waist. One foot rested on the thigh of the other, exposing her vagina, and the cane of her partner was stretched along the length of her sex.

'When did you take this?' she asked Andrew the moment he came through the door carrying a smaller tray. He looked at the picture.

'Can't remember. Maybe a month ago? Why?'

Nina remembered Max's warning that Andrew was involved in something shady. Possibly owning strip clubs.

'Did you take it at the club?'

'Of course,' said Andrew in puzzlement. 'Where else would I take it?'

'I thought they changed the acts there all the time,' she challenged.

He shrugged. 'There are regular acts. Irina and Sergei aren't on all the time, but they're on a circuit of different clubs. What's the big deal?'

She took a deep breath. 'Andrew, do you own the club?'

He put the tray down. 'What on earth gives you that idea?'

'You seem to know your way around! The rooms upstairs, the two-way mirror – and you said it was a private club! Someone must own it!'

He was looking at her in amazement.

'Sure, someone owns it. Two brothers, actually. One of them came over and talked to us on Friday, if you remember.'

Nina had a vague memory of a white-jacketed man sitting down familiarly with Andrew and Costas, but she had been talking to Beverley at the time.

'Well.' She was at a loss to continue.

'So what makes you think I'm in the strip-club business?'

She took a deep breath and improvised. 'Oh, it was

just when I was telling Max about going to the club, and he said it sounded a bit near the knuckle and I told him it was a private club, and he said maybe you owned it . . .'

Her voice trailed off. It sounded ridiculous, even to herself.

'You told *Max* about the club?'

'Yes, why not? We're quite friendly now.'

Andrew snorted. 'Friendly! He's desperate to get his hands on you, that's obvious to anyone. I'm surprised you're encouraging him. I thought you didn't want your sex life interfering in your work life.'

'I don't! And it doesn't! It's just that sometimes I talk to Max about what I've been doing.'

'From what you told me, until you met me you didn't do anything.'

'Yeah.' Nina hung her head. 'It's just that since I've met you, I've found Max easier to get on with.'

'That's because he's scenting your bloody pheromones.'

'Don't be angry.'

'I'm not angry. I just don't understand how one minute you're moaning at me for making you sexy and that you're fed up that Max is coming on to you, and then you're telling him all about going to the club with me. I suppose you'll show him your tattoo next.'

Nina had to laugh. 'You're kidding. He's just a workmate. Actually, he fancies my friend Angie.'

'Oh yes? Tell me about your friend Angie. Perhaps I'd fancy her.'

She described Angie for Andrew, but in the back of her mind was berating herself for saying she'd mentioned the strip club to Max. It had been stupid, but there was no way she could have told him that her colleague thought he was up to something illegal. Of course it was a ridiculous idea, but all the same she didn't want Andrew thinking ill of Max. She was afraid he could get him in trouble. She remembered what Beverley had said about the power they had . . .

She changed the subject.

'What I don't understand is the ballet dancers – what are they called? Irina and Sergei? – they're obviously proper dancers. Why on earth do they have to do that sort of act? Can't they get jobs as ballet dancers?'

Andrew shrugged. 'They were both trained by a ballet company in Russia, but things are a lot tighter over there now. All the arts were funded by public money, of course, but as I'm sure you know there's not so much to go round now.'

'But surely they could get jobs with ballet companies in England?'

He shook his head. 'Apparently it's not that easy. Still, they're quite happy. They're better off in England anyway than back home.'

'How on earth did they get visas to come here? As much sought after striptease artistes?'

Laughing, he picked up the tray again.

'I expect so. Now, do you want some pudding or not?'

'Mmm – what is it?'

He showed her a bowl full of a yellowish cream. 'Gooseberry fool. It's rich and home-made, and it'll taste delicious off you.' Dipping a spoon into it, he offered her some. It was sweet yet tart, creamy yet light.

'Oh, wow. Can't I eat it off you?'

He frowned. 'Not right now. I'll save you some for later. Now lie down.'

Nina lay perfectly still after Andrew arranged her legs wide apart very much as Charles had placed them for her shave. She closed her eyes obediently and then nothing happened for a couple of minutes. Awaiting the sensation of the creamy confection being smeared on to her breasts or her pussy, she was electrified when she felt the still cold fool on her lips. Small spoonfuls were dropped from one side of her mouth to the other with obvious care, causing her face to tingle. She almost wanted to scratch the sensation but stayed still.

Next she felt the cream dropping in a necklace around her throat and then down between her breasts. Each breast was then carefully circled and each erect nipple was surmounted with a blob of the fool. There was another pause, where she imagined Andrew wondering where to place his pudding next, and then a line was drawn across her waist. Each movement was slow and deliberate and it was driving her crazy. She was straining for each caress of the cream on her body, and imagining where he would decide to put it next.

After her waist he described a line down to her navel, and then there was an even longer pause. She decided he was worried about the tattoo, and eventually he did leave her belly clear of the cream and started to drop it on her pubic mound.

Nina waited breathlessly for it to reach her clitoris, and almost sighed when she felt the firm cream drop softly on to the bud of flesh. Then it followed its obvious path down to her cunt, until finally her whole sex was covered in the mixture. It felt even colder there than it had on her body, as despite her orgasm she was again heated with desire.

Still she waited with eyes closed. The anticipation of Andrew's warm tongue scooping up the cold cream from her body kept her senses straining. But the next sensation was a blinding flash as he took a picture of her outlined with the fool.

At last, when she thought she couldn't wait any longer, his tongue began, first lapping along her lips, then moving from one side of her neck to the other. When he reached her first nipple she moaned involuntarily at the extra attention he gave it, sucking the hard flesh greedily as though to extract every taste of the fool from it.

By the time his questing tongue reached her sex she was straining with desire. In the split second between feeling the warmth of his breath on her pubic mound and the tongue firmly licking the cream she almost felt she could come. And by the time the cream was gone she was trembling from the spasms of the climax which racked her body as the tongue had methodically finished its work.

'Don't you want some?'

Andrew's voice broke into her reverie as she lay shattered on the bed. She hadn't moved, or opened her eyes, for at least two minutes after his tongue had stopped work on her.

She blinked and looked at him. He was kneeling on the bed in front of her and smearing the fool on to his cock.

Once more it was hard and angrily erect. Nina felt jealous just seeing his hand slide up and down as he slathered more of the cream on.

Eagerly she turned over and knelt before him, dropping to her hands and knees to bring her mouth in line with his cream-covered cock. But first she followed his example and made him wait as she teasingly licked the cream from his balls, very gently taking each one in her mouth and sucking it clean. She heard him breathe hard as she licked off the fool that had snaked down from his balls towards his arse, so worked her tongue harder and for longer than necessary to get all the fool.

From his balls she moved slowly up his penis, lapping gently and enjoying the taste and sensation of the cream in her mouth. The almost buttery mixture looked like whipped semen, she thought, as she licked faster, tensing her tongue, towards the top of his distended cock.

Andrew withdrew from her mouth only to slap on more of the mixture. He smiled down at her.

'I'm watching your arse in the mirror,' he said softly. 'Wiggle it for me, Nina. A bit more – yeah, that's nice. Keep on sucking that fool off, though. And keep moving your arse. Oh man – that's it, suck me harder.'

His hands moved out and cupped her breasts. 'Keep jiggling away for me, baby. Oh, that's right, I can see your arse move and I can feel your tits. Keep dancing for me. Open your throat for me. Oh, Nina, that's it, that's it, baby.'

He spurted into her mouth. She still had the taste of the gooseberry fool and so swallowed, the first time she'd taken his semen inside her. As he finished his convulsive movements in her mouth, he withdrew and flopped down on to the bed.

'Your blow jobs are starting to achieve a remarkable standard,' he murmured. 'As Costas would say, it's almost as good as getting head from a man.'

'God, that's a mystery to me,' said Nina, grimacing slightly from the taste of the come.

'Oh yeah? When Beverley was tonguing you, it seemed to me you were appreciating all the little ways she knew how to give you pleasure, woman to woman.'

'OK, quits,' she conceded, smiling. 'My God, that fool's lovely.'

He laughed. 'There's a bit more if you like.'

'I was going to add, "but rich". Maybe a drop more wine?'

Andrew picked their glasses up from the floor and poured a large measure each, draining the bottle.

They drank, Nina nestling against Andrew's chest and feeling that she was home. True, she always felt like she was losing a struggle against his power over her. But she had never had such an incredible evening. Leaning against him she knew that he had completed her life, had found the missing piece of the jigsaw puzzle and put it in place with a confident hand.

'I am so happy, Andrew,' she said simply. 'You've given me more than I could have thought possible.'

He kissed the top of her head. 'Thank you. And thanks for a terrific evening.'

'No, thank you.'

'No, I insist, thank you,' said Andrew gravely. They both laughed.

He looked at his watch. 'Although I'm afraid that when we've finished this, I'm going to call you a cab. I need to do some work before bed. Anyway, I'll be seeing you tomorrow.'

'Will you?' she asked happily, snuggling back against him. 'I thought you said you were going to Rotterdam for a few days.'

'Yes, tomorrow afternoon. First there's this meeting your Max has asked for.'

Nina sprang away from him and looked round. 'Meeting? I don't remember him saying anything about it!'

Andrew shrugged. 'He just wanted to iron out a few queries – didn't he tell you?'

She shook her head slowly. 'I'm sure I'd have remembered. I don't know what he wants me there for, anyway, seeing as I don't know anything about any queries.'

He yawned. 'Oh well, look on the bright side – the trip over to me will give you plenty of time to tell him about tonight!'

She pummelled his chest lightly. 'Yes, I'll show him the tattoo in the taxi.'

On the way home she grinned to herself at the idea of showing Max the tattoo – if he asked nicely enough.

Chapter Eight

'*I* don't really know why you have to take me with you, Max,' Nina said sulkily the next morning. 'As far as I'm concerned this audit's finished. It's your job to pull it together. I'm trying to get to grips with the first stages of the next job.'

'I know, I know.' Max winked at her. 'But I thought in the circumstances we might get a bit more co-operation from your boyfriend if you were there.'

'That's unethical. And I bet you'll get stick from Hal for prolonging this job unnecessarily.'

Hal was the boss, a fast-talking American who expected everything to be done yesterday.

'No, it's OK, he knows what's going on.'

'I hope you don't mean me and Andrew –'

'Jesus, Nina, give me a bit of credit.' He made a face at her. 'Anyway, it's given you a chance to put your new suit on for your boyfriend.'

She had to laugh. It was true, she'd been saving her new outfit for a meeting or a lunch, rather than just wear it for an ordinary day at the office. It was cream linen, a long jacket ending just inches from the hem of the short straight skirt. It had cost a month's money but she had decided it was worth it.

Posing like a fashion model in front of him, she asked for his opinion.

'Great. Nice legs, too.'

'Shut it, Maxie. And let's get a move on if we're going.' She picked up her brown shoulder bag. 'I haven't got any papers with me because I don't really know what we're asking.'

He waved his briefcase at her. 'I hate to say this, but all you have to do is look pretty.'

'Piss off.'

They hailed a taxi outside the office, giving the address of Andrew's firm, not far away on the eastern edge of the City. Nina sat back in the cab. Although she was perturbed about Max's suspicions about the accounts, she knew there was nothing to worry about. He didn't like her boyfriend, which was a shame, but he shouldn't project imaginary improper accounting on to him.

This was the part of the job she normally enjoyed, the investigative nature of the work. The team arriving at a company like a police squad swooping on suspected criminals. She liked the teamwork aspect of auditing, and the fact that the auditors were always treated with deference by the companies they were working on.

She remembered that when she'd first thought about auditing as opposed to being a chartered accountant, someone had told her a story about a certain company who made their auditors wear glasses, whether they needed them or not, to give them an appropriately serious air. That had amused her, and the thought of ensuring you were treated with the proper respect by what were, after all, the customers, had decided her to move in that direction.

Andrew's secretary sat them in a waiting room for a

few minutes before a buzzer sounded and she told them they could go in.

'OK, just cross your legs and pretend you're Sharon Stone and I'll do the rest,' Max whispered.

Nina glared at him but didn't have the chance to say anything as Andrew opened the door and smiled at them.

'Hello! Come in. Nice to see you again, Max.' He shook his hand and as he shut the door on the secretary he turned to Nina and kissed her briefly on the cheek.

'Hope you've recovered from last night.' He turned to Max. 'I understand you know all about our relationship so there's no point in pretending otherwise.'

Max smiled blandly. 'It's none of my business, Mr Marnington. Now, if we can just recheck a few invoices and documents with you, I'm sure you'll be able to clear up our little problems. Your accountant seemed a bit vague as to some of these bills.'

Nina let her mind drift away from the business in hand. She had not even seen the problem documents so contented herself with watching Andrew and Max, heads bent over the paperwork her colleague had pulled from his briefcase.

Andrew was looking as handsome as ever. His face was set in a patient smile which emphasised the delicious lines that ran from the corners of his eyes down to his finely chiselled mouth. On the other hand Max was talking earnestly, unsmiling, seriously looking at Andrew as he showed him various pieces of paper. Andrew was tanned, compared with Max's pale face. And Andrew's lean face, dominated by his broken nose, had an aristocratic air, compared to the other's slight roundness and snub nose. All in all, she decided, Andrew looked like a man, while Max, despite his twenty-nine or was it thirty years, still looked like a boy.

'You found no problem with the cargo documents, did you, Nina?'

Max's voice broke in on her reverie. She crossed her legs and looked up, then almost laughed out loud as she remembered his Sharon Stone comment.

'No, none. Although I know you said you found documents in the other files that I should have had – but the samples I checked were all in order.'

'I think you'll find our accounting team will be able to clarify this, Max. Let's see if Jim's at his desk.'

Andrew made a quick phone call, then nodded to Max. 'Yes, he can see you. You know where to go, of course. Now, Nina, can I get you a coffee while Max clears up his problems?'

'Please,' said Nina, as Max picked up his briefcase and left the room.

But Andrew made no move towards getting her a drink. As the door closed behind Max, he stood up and walked over to her, lifting her to her feet.

'You look fantastic. That's a terrific suit!'

He kissed her lips longingly.

'How's the tattoo?'

'Not bad, actually. It hardly hurts at all.'

'Let me see.' He started to lift the linen skirt.

'Andrew, Max'll be back any minute.'

'No he won't. He'll be at least ten minutes with Jim, probably longer. Come on, let's have a look.'

Nina felt last night's fire rekindling in her as Andrew lifted her skirt higher.

'Oh, man,' he breathed. 'That is beautiful.'

'The tattoo, or the shave job?' she enquired.

He laughed. 'Both. And those little lacy knickers. They're like the ones you wore when you were my whore.'

'God. Andrew, what if someone hears?'

'They can't. Hey, you hold the skirt up and let me have a proper look.'

Uneasily Nina took the hem of her skirt from his hands and stood holding it at waist height, trying not to crease the linen but fearing it was a lost cause. Andrew took a few paces back and stood watching. She couldn't help feeling excited as he drank in the sight of her exposing herself like a tableau in a Victorian sex parlour.

'Stand with your back against the desk,' he said huskily.

'Look, my skirt's getting creased –'

'Just stand where I tell you,' he said sharply. Nina obeyed, fearing that if Max were to walk through the door she would be right in his line of vision, her skirt hiked up around her waist, scarred by the fresh tattoo and with an obviously shaven pubis barely covered by a tiny scrap of lace.

That thought turned her on even more.

With two strides Andrew came towards her. She was expecting a kiss and made to drop her skirt, but before she could he lifted it higher.

'I'm going to fuck you, Nina. I need to be right inside you.'

She breathed hard. 'No way, Andrew.' But as she said the words his fingers were working their way inside the lace and massaging her naked pudenda.

'I need you, Nina,' he said insistently. 'I won't see you for three days after today. I need to remember what your cunt feels like.'

With his right hand he was undoing his zip and she felt his already hard cock nudging against her as he pulled a condom from his pocket and ripped it open with his teeth.

'Max will come in.'

'I told you, he'll be at least ten minutes. You want it too.' His fingers were inside her. She was starting to feel horny but she knew her brain hadn't had enough time to translate her arousal into a wet and ready pussy.

'I really do not want it, Andrew.'

'You do,' he insisted. 'And the longer you pretend

you don't, the more chance there is of Max walking in on us. Just get your backside on the edge of the desk.'

Nina started to panic. 'Andrew, I so do not want Max to see this.'

'So move your arse!'

Almost numbly Nina did what he said, lifting her skirt at the back and sitting, bare apart from the lacy string bisecting the cheeks of her bottom, on the polished wood of his near-empty desk. She felt helpless to refuse him, knowing that as usual he would get his own way, and knowing he was right when he said that delay would just increase the chances of being caught.

She knew too that the excitement she was feeling was due to that fear, and not due to Andrew. And despite the fact that she would have hated Max to see her being used like this, a part of her shivered with excitement at the thought of Max being turned on by seeing her having sex. Turned on while knowing he couldn't have her himself. Wanting her more than ever . . .

'Lay back on your elbows – oh, man, that's right.'

Above her Andrew watched her, his eyes narrowed as, moving the lace briefs aside, he pushed inside her. Although her vagina was starting to feel excitement she wasn't as wet as she would have liked to have been. For a brief second she was reminded of the men she'd had before Andrew, who had pushed inside her before she was ready.

But she couldn't help feeling turned on by leaning back on the desk. Andrew lifted her thighs and wrapped her legs around his waist, but while she was excited by the position and the fear of discovery, she wasn't concentrating on him. Instead she was imagining Max begging her to let him have his turn afterwards, promising to do anything for her if she'd just let him have her once, eagerly pleasing her with his tongue, his fingers, his lips.

She felt almost guilty at thinking of Max while

Andrew was inside her, but he deserved it. After last night he couldn't be exactly desperate for it. It wasn't her body that turned him on, she guessed, but was the possibility of being caught.

Andrew came and withdrew, efficiently removing the condom and re-zipping.

'God, that's better. How about you?'

Nina stood and smoothed her skirt down. It was, of course, creased.

'Yeah, no-contact sex. I remember how much you said you liked it.'

He laughed. 'Exciting, isn't it? Don't tell me it didn't turn you on.'

'I wasn't very keen on the idea.'

'But you got wetter, didn't you? I was there, after all. You can't deny it.'

That's because I was thinking about Max, she didn't say. Instead she gave him an enigmatic smile.

'Don't worry that I didn't come. I'm going out with Angie later and we're hoping for a really hot night.'

'Oh shit, I'm sorry you didn't come.' Andrew looked remorseful. 'I thought you'd get really horny at the prospect of being caught.'

'Not to mention the prospect of pointing out to Max that I'm your sexual property.' She indicated the creased skirt.

He looked dismayed. 'That wasn't on the agenda. I wonder if Janice will notice?'

Nina felt the explosion coming and let rip. 'Christ Almighty, you're worried that your secretary will notice that I've had my skirt up round my ears, when it'll be bloody obvious to Max that you've took the chance to get rid of him and fuck me on the desk! Don't you ever think of anyone but yourself?'

'Come on, Nina, you know that's not true. Yeah, I suppose I was thinking of myself, of how much I wanted to fuck you, but I didn't know you weren't

179

going to enjoy it. I didn't just take the chance to get rid of Max, as you put it. He was the one who wanted to come over here. This meeting wasn't for my benefit. I didn't engineer it just so I could have you on my desk.'

'Oh no? All these new experiences you're so kindly providing for me, let's not pretend that they don't usually involve me dancing to your bloody tune.'

'Hey, calm down. It's a pretty good tune, isn't it?'

'Yeah, fucking Beethoven. How about getting that coffee you mentioned five minutes ago? In Max's hearing, what's more.'

He picked up the phone and ordered coffee from his secretary.

'Anyway, you've got your vibrator now,' he added when he'd put the phone down. 'You can just feel horny all afternoon and then go home and sort yourself out.'

Nina laughed bitterly. 'Thanks a bunch. No, I think I'll just wait and see what Angie and I can pull.'

Andrew was looking at her, amused. 'Why not? You can tell me all about it when I get back. If you still feel like seeing me, that is.'

She wrinkled her nose at him. 'Depends what you've got planned. How about I tie you up to your bedposts and whip you before making you my slave for the night?'

'No thanks. I'm sure I can come up with something better than that.'

The door opened and Nina crossed her legs and pulled her jacket down in an attempt to hide her wrinkled skirt. It was the secretary with the coffee.

'OK, we've got our coffee, so Max won't suspect a thing,' he said, smiling sarcastically as she sipped her drink. 'He'll probably think we've just been exchanging sweet nothings.' He leaned back in his chair and looked at her appraisingly. 'I'll be back on Monday. While I'm away I'll think of something special for our reunion. I'll come over to your place about eight.'

Again the door opened and Max walked back in.

'All right, Max? Has Jim answered your queries?'

'Sorted,' said Max, looking anything but. 'It seems there was a bit of a problem with the filing system.'

Andrew nodded sympathetically. 'Sorry about that. You know what happens – holidays, temps, everything goes missing until somebody notices there's something wrong, just as you did. Thanks a lot for pointing it out.'

'It's my job,' said Max briefly. 'OK, Nina, ready to get back?'

Andrew rose. 'Well, how about coming for lunch, if you've nothing planned?'

'Sorry, no can do,' said Max, avoiding Nina's eye. 'I've got to finish my report on your accounts, and Nina's already been complaining about being taken away from the next job to come here.'

'Oh, what a shame. Nina, I apologise if I've distracted you from more important tasks,' said Andrew smoothly, his eyes laughing as he looked at her. She stood up, blushing fiercely, half because of Andrew's look and half because she saw Max's eyes travel down to her creased skirt.

'If you need any more information, don't hesitate to give me a call next week,' Andrew told Max. 'I'm away until Monday lunchtime, but after that, anything I can do –'

'Going anywhere nice?' asked Max.

'Rotterdam. New ship just finishing her maiden voyage from Korea.'

'Congratulations,' said Max. 'Bit of a boring place from what I can remember. Now Amsterdam, that's a completely different city.'

'Oh yes, I'm very fond of Amsterdam,' said Andrew. 'But Rotterdam's not so bad. I've got a couple of friends there, and we'll probably go out to a harbourside fish restaurant in Scheveningen they usually take me to.'

'OK, have a good time.' Max shook hands with Andrew and left, followed by Nina.

Max said nothing until they were in the taxi on the way back to the office. Then in a neutral voice he said, 'That skirt was a mistake, Nina. You've only been sitting down for about twenty minutes and it's well creased. Actually, it looks like you've been wearing it as a belt instead. I'd take it back if I were you.'

'Shut it, Max.'

'Just trying to help.'

'So you got your queries resolved?'

He sighed and rubbed his hands over his eyes.

'Oh yes, no loose ends. That is, all the queries the accounts department had no idea about last week, suddenly they knew exactly what was wrong. This invoice was in the wrong file, that one was made out incorrectly and they'd got the right one from the shipper, the other document was dated wrongly and related to stuff from the previous year – everything was accounted for.'

Nina smiled triumphantly. 'I told you he wasn't dodgy.'

'So you say.' He shook his head. 'It's all too pat. The accountant's shit scared. He's been given a real bollocking for not sorting it when I first asked, I'd put money on it.'

'For God's sake, Max. Why on earth do you think there's something funny going on?'

His constant suspicions were starting to get on her nerves. Although Andrew wasn't in her good books at the moment, as far as business was concerned she couldn't see any reason for Max's witch hunt.

Max sighed again. 'Everything odd is to do with Limanos Hellas. There's money coming in that doesn't make sense. I'm convinced they're laundering money, but why? And what's the connection between them?'

Nina gave him a withering look. 'Laundering money

– bullshit. You don't know anything, Max. I know how they're connected. Andrew and Costas Limanos are like family. Costas looked after Andrew and his father's business after his parents were killed.'

He stared at her, shaking his head. 'Well well. So Mr Sleaze is part of some Greek *Cosa Nostra*.'

'Oh, please. Every time I tell you something you turn it round. And do not ever again call Andrew Mr Sleaze!'

Max grimaced and held his hands up in mock surrender.

'OK, sorry, I promise. Don't be cross. Please don't. But one more thing – I promise, I'll let it go after this. I don't remember coming across any reference to this new ship he's gone to Rotterdam to see. He had a new ship delivered last year, the *Lady A*. Do you remember seeing any contracts, invoices, anything to do with another one?'

Nina sighed with growing impatience. 'No. But maybe it wasn't even started last year, Max. We're working a year behind the times. Just do not tell me you think he's lying about going to Rotterdam, or about why he's going.'

He shrugged. 'No, doesn't make sense. You're right, it must have been started after the accounting period we're looking at. Unless he bought it half built or something.'

'Look, you're just being paranoid. Whatever it is there's a reasonable explanation. And this laundering money idea is just ridiculous.'

He really is a pain in the arse, she decided, as she turned to look out the window. She heard Max sigh and he laid a hand on her arm.

'Don't be angry with me. Let's go and have lunch before we get back.'

'We haven't got time, as you just told Andrew,' she reminded him.

'Yes, well, I wanted to have you all to myself,' he replied cheekily.

Nina laughed, and remembered her fantasy about Max walking in on her and Andrew. Their quickie had left her unsatisfied, but there was no way she was going to get her own back on Andrew by having sex with Max. They had a good working relationship now, with an edge of sexual tension which made them a good team. There was no point spoiling their friendship for a quick revenge fuck.

Although the thought of actually having sex with someone else, someone not set up by Andrew, was tempting. The only time that had happened in the last couple of weeks was when she and Angie had dressed up and her friend had tried to seduce her.

Why was it that the two people she fancied most apart from Andrew were her best friend and her closest colleague?

She reminded herself that despite the session in the office, she really still was happy with Andrew.

'There's no way I'm coming out to lunch,' she said to Max. 'As you said to Andrew, you've got to get his report finished. Why don't you go over to Veggie World and get us a healthy organic sandwich? I'll get some coffee, and we can sit in the office and pretend it's the wine bar.'

'Cheers,' he said ruefully. 'You can have a healthy organic sandwich if you want. I'll get it for you on my way back from the pub. I need to sit down and have a cigarette.'

He cast a baleful eye at the THANK YOU FOR NOT SMOKING sign in the cab.

'Are all taxis non-smoking now? I certainly never get in one that isn't.'

Nina laughed. 'I'm surprised you get in many taxis at all. I'd have thought most of them would refuse to go to the wilds of Hackney.'

'Very funny. Anyway, seeing as I spend most of my nights out in Hackney, I don't need to worry too much about it.'

'So you're not interested in clubbing with me and Angie tonight then?'

Max sat bolt upright. 'Are you kidding? Are you asking me?'

'No way!' she teased. 'Just thinking that you probably wouldn't be up for it anyway, if it took you off your own patch.'

The cab pulled up outside their office. As Max paid the driver, he turned eagerly to Nina.

'Look, brilliant idea. Why don't you and Angie come over to Hackney tonight? I don't think there's much in the way of clubbing on, but there are some really cool pubs.'

Nina raised her eyebrows. 'I thought I was the one doing the asking.'

'Yes, but you're not saying the right things,' he riposted. 'Wouldn't it be nice to have your best friend and your best workmate hitting it off together? That means you'd be able to include me in your social life without me trying to pull you all the time.'

She burst out laughing. 'You're a real case, Max. I'll think about it.'

'Well, I'll be in the Tavern on the Park in Edinburgh Road at about half-nine. I won't say any more than that. If you turn up, great, if you don't, I'll be with some mates anyway.'

He walked a few paces up the road and turned back and winked at her.

'You can't resist me, Nina, you know you can't,' he said. 'I'm just going for a beer and a sandwich. I'll bring you some rabbit food back.'

Nina couldn't help smiling to herself as she got the lift up to the fourth floor. In some ways she couldn't resist him. His humour, his little-boy-lost look, his cockiness – they all contrasted with Andrew's polished manner and worldliness. Not necessarily favourably, but refreshingly.

Perhaps it would be fun. And Angie was certainly hoping to pull tonight. She'd put it to her, anyway.

'Hackney! You're joking, aren't you?' said Angie.

Nina had taken the chance to phone her before Max got back from the pub.

'Yeah, yeah, I know. But Max seems to have a crush on you. I thought you might be interested.'

'Oh, does he?' Angie's voice had decidedly perked up. 'He's quite a cutie, isn't he?'

'Not bad, if you like that sort of thing,' said Nina non-committally. 'No, I'm not being fair. He's sweet. And funny. Though he can't stand Andrew.'

'You're joking! Why?'

'Oh, I'm not going into all that now. So what do you think?'

'Don't mind. Just as long as we have a good night I don't care where it is. Look, I'll come over to you about eight and we'll take it from there.'

Nina finished the call and sat contemplating the computer modem. She called up the Clyde, Surrey and Co. accounts but she wasn't thinking about it at all.

Her thoughts were veering all over the place. Standing holding her skirt up for Andrew to inspect her. That had been exciting. Being penetrated when she was still unwilling. That had not. Fantasising about Max begging for his turn with her. That had been exciting. Max still suspicious about Andrew's accounts. That was annoying.

If they went to meet Max it would be the first time she had socialised with anyone from the office, apart the two occasions recently she'd had a drink with him after work. The last thing she wanted was to mix work and pleasure.

It's only a drink, she told herself. If only she could banish the image of Max pleading with her to let him satisfy her, she would admit to herself there was no harm in it.

There was also no doubt that she didn't want to spoil anything with Andrew. From the way he'd reacted when she'd lied to him and told him she'd told Max about the strip club, she knew he wouldn't be impressed by the thought of her going out with him, even if it was completely innocent.

He won't find out, she told herself. She wouldn't have to lie to him. Of course he'd want to know if she and Angie did make out that night. Once she told him that she hadn't, he would lose interest in her evening.

She couldn't decide if her attraction to Max was because she felt that she could dominate him if she wanted to. It was such a contrast to her relationship with Andrew, where she was helpless to do anything but his will. Andrew bathed her in a warm bath of decadence but Max awoke a triumphant power in her that she liked. A lot.

Turning back to the screen, she tried to concentrate, only to be interrupted when Max came in with roasted aubergine and hummus on ciabatta for her. She ate quickly, her eyes still on her work. The next project was unfortunately not going to be very inspiring, but at least it deserved her undivided attention. She was due at the hairdressers at half-past five, so there were only four hours of work to go. However interesting her sex life, she should be able to give her next client that much of her time.

'You look fantastic!'

Nina pirouetted in front of her friend. 'You're right,' she conceded. 'He did it even better than I expected.'

Instead of a smooth bob, her hair had been layered all over and the strands teased outwards to halo her head. Although it was almost as long at the back as it had been before, the layering meant that it had a rounded look rather than the bell-shaped effect of the bob, which had always rather irritated her. Her fringe too had been feathered and looked softer and sexier than the heavy helmet she'd been wearing for years.

'Have you got highlights in it?' asked Angie.

'No. It looks like it, though, because of the way the light catches the sticky-out bits.'

Nina had gone in to her hairdresser with a rough idea of something 'a bit wild' but still suitable for work, and he'd succeeded brilliantly.

'The only thing I want to know, Heinz, is why you didn't suggest something like this before,' she had said as she studied the results after the mousse and blow-dry.

The hairdresser had frowned.

'To be totally honest with you, Nina, your hair always suited you as it was. You seemed to be the perfect neat bob person,' he answered in his stilted Germanic English. 'But something's happened to you, is it not so? You are now more of a wild teased person. Why is that?'

She had giggled. 'It's a long story, Heinz. Perhaps I'll tell you next time.'

Angie laughed as Nina related the story to her as she poured them a drink.

'Well, wild teased person, have you decided what we're doing tonight? It sounds as though we ought to stay in and watch reruns of *Whose Line Is It Anyway*?'

'Ha ha. Well, you look as though you've dressed for clubbing rather than boozing in Hackney.'

Black hipster pedal pushers and a black bandeau top left Angie's midriff and stomach bare. Her tan had deepened slightly since Nina had seen it so close up the previous week, but was still golden and sexy rather than a tacky bronze. A tight-fitting crochet cardigan in deep crimson covered her arms and shoulders, and her lipstick matched the lacy top.

'I'm dressed for pulling,' said Angie with a wide, lazy smile. 'And so are you, by the look of it. Though it sounds as if this man of yours is keeping you occupied in that department.'

Nina had dressed all in white, contrasting with Angie's black and red. Inspired by the chiffon-clad Carmen lookalike in the strip club, she was wearing a calf-length finely pleated chiffon skirt which was not, however, transparent. Its double fabric prevented it from being see-through. On top she wore a knitted silk vest, low enough to show her cleavage, which came tightly down over the chiffon at hip level. The ballerina effect was finished by a pair of white pumps.

'What do you think?' she asked anxiously. 'I bought this to go out with Andrew last week. I thought I was going to get my first chance at eating à la Marco Pierre White but instead he suggested I have a tattoo done. I didn't really want to walk into a Soho tattoo parlour dressed like a reject from the corps de ballet.'

Angie was laughing. 'I don't see why not. I'm sure all sorts of people have tattoos done. Why didn't you tell me straight away? Let's have a look at it!'

Nina felt hesitant about showing Angie her hairless sex, but could think of no reason not to show her the tattoo. She compromised by pulling her skirt down slightly and her top up, and exposing the whole of the meteor shower without revealing that she had been shaved.

'Wow! That's fantastic! Do you remember when we thought about having our shoulders done?'

'Yes, and we decided it was too common. But I saw this on somebody and I thought I'd really like it.' She looked down herself at the crescent-shaped star shower on her belly. As predicted, there were hardly any scabs and the puffiness had gone already. 'And as the bloke

189

in the tattoo place said, it'll make me think before I stuff myself or I'll end up with the Milky Way instead of a few stars.'

'Do you know, I think I might get one done myself – especially now you can recommend a good place to go,' said Angie. 'Hard to know what to have done, though.'

'Yeah, it took me ages looking through boring designs. Why don't you have your belly button pierced instead? Or how about a labial ring?'

'Nightmare! There is absolutely no way I want anything sharp going anywhere near my private bits, I can tell you!' exclaimed Angie, horrified. 'You haven't got one as well, have you?'

'No way,' said Nina. 'He didn't even suggest it, though I must admit I wouldn't have been surprised.'

'Don't you feel as though that tattoo's like – well, it's like he's branded you?' asked Angie curiously.

'Yes,' said Nina blandly. 'But that's because I know it was his idea, and so do you. It won't occur to anyone else; they'll just think, Wow, what a sexy tattoo. So it's not important.'

Angie nodded. 'Mmm, that's cool. Anyway, tell me about your night of lust at his flat.'

'Penthouse, if you don't mind . . .'

They finished off the bottle of Chardonnay while Nina told Angie about the photographs and the gooseberry fool – 'very Women's Institute,' remarked Angie tartly. She had to return as well to the episode with Beverley, which Angie insisted on hearing in full and graphic detail.

'Christ, Neen, I'm feeling horny already,' she said, wriggling provocatively in her black pants. 'So are you going to take me to Hackney to shag your Max? Or are we going to hit town and take our chances there?'

'Only one way to decide.' Nina took a pound coin

from her purse and flicked it in the air. 'Heads Hackney, tails town.' She uncovered the coin. 'Heads. Might be your lucky night. Or should I say Max's?'

Angie winked. 'Well, if you say he's meeting his mates there, you might get lucky as well, unless you're being faithful to lover boy.'

'We never said we'd be exclusive,' said Nina, deadpan. They both laughed.

'I've never actually been to Hackney. Don't suppose a taxi'd want to go there from here.'

'That's just what I said to Max,' Nina snorted. 'No, we'll get the tube to Old Street and a bus from there.'

'It'll be just like going to work for you,' laughed Angie. 'Come on, then, let's hit the East End.'

On the way to the station they passed 'Be Happy' and his pal, but they had nothing to say to the girls, too busy with their sherry bottle. Nina had been apprehensive when she saw them and still felt too embarrassed to tell Angie about the lewd comment of the previous week. She laughed inwardly at the thought that she could now have replied that she did not have a hairy mary any more.

Instead she filled Angie in on Max's dislike of Andrew and his suspicions about his business. As an accountant herself, Angie dismissed the idea of Anmar Shipping's accountant being anything less than completely straight.

'Oh and the other thing about Max,' she remembered to tell Angie as they got off the 55 bus and walked towards Edinburgh Road, 'is that he's got this fantasy that we're bisexuals. He said he could manage us both at once.'

Angie giggled. 'I hope you told him that we don't like labels.'

Nina snorted with laughter. 'Actually, isn't Hackney a bit of a gay enclave? Better watch out or Max won't stand a chance. We might get off with a couple of women.'

'I wouldn't mind one bit, especially after hearing your story about Beverley,' said Angie. 'Would you do it again?'

Nina considered. 'If it was someone like Beverley I would. I just really fancied her because she was so beautiful and so friendly. But I wouldn't have another woman just for the sake of it.'

'Yeah, that's how I feel,' said Angie. 'Still, I wouldn't mind teasing Max a bit. Best way to get a man going is to let him think he's in with a chance of a bit of lesbian action.'

She linked arms with Nina as they turned a corner to see a park laid out before them.

'I don't know why Hackney gets such a bad press. It looks quite a lot like Clapham to me,' she observed.

'Yes, or Regent's Park – only joking!' added Nina.

Angie laughed. 'Perhaps Max'll take us back to his penthouse after the pub and it'll be a mirror image of Andrew's.'

'Bet he won't have a housekeeper to make him goose-berry fool, though.'

They heard the pub as soon as they saw it. People had spilled outside and laughter and conversation hung in the air. It was a young-looking crowd, and Angie noted with glee in her voice that men easily outnumbered women.

'Don't think we need your Max,' she said to Nina. 'At least we've got a few alternatives here. This is going to be a good night, Nina.'

Max lit up and scanned the room.

'What's up, Max? You expecting anyone?'

'Not really, George. I just felt lucky tonight. Like, the next love of my life's going to walk through that door any minute.'

George laughed. 'Seeing as the loves of your life only last a couple of weeks, I don't suppose it'd matter too much if you missed one.'

'Yeah, you're right. Anyway, I thought Jed and Al might be in tonight.'

'They'll probably be in the Ark by now. Fancy moving on?'

'In a minute, mate. One more here?'

'OK.' George shrugged. 'Another lemonade, if you like.'

Max turned towards the bar to order a bottle of Becks and a lemonade. It was after ten o'clock and he was pissed off. Although he'd told himself not to expect Nina and Angie, he couldn't put it out of his mind that they were going to turn up. But he couldn't hang around all night in the Tavern. After all, they weren't going to come all the way from Clapham for an hour's drinking.

It was probably just as well for him not to see Nina anyway. He knew there was something seriously wrong with Mr Sleaze. He'd had another check through the files and there was definitely nothing about the new ship there. A call to Lloyd's List turned up no trace of a new building in Korea just making its maiden voyage to Rotterdam, still less any connected to Anmar Shipping.

So why was lover boy going to Rotterdam – if indeed he was going there, or anywhere?

George's excited voice interrupted his moody reverie.

'Max, getting those drinks was a bloody good move. I think I've just seen the next love of *my* life. If I can get to her before every other dirty sod in here.'

Max turned round with the drinks in his hand, which was just as well because he would have embarrassed himself by punching the air. George was looking transfixed at Nina and Angie, who were making their way to the bar arm in arm.

'Which one, George?' he asked, trying to keep the laughter from his voice.

'The one in white, mate,' said George, making in the girls' direction. 'I'm moving in quick.'

'No point,' said Max, catching Nina's eye and waving. 'They're coming over here.'

'You lying bastard, you set this up!' said George gleefully. 'I love you, mate.'

Max laughed. 'I didn't set anything up for you, I can tell you.'

He made the introductions as the girls reached them.

'I expect you've heard me mention Nina,' he added to George.

As he turned back to the bar to order Red Bull and vodka for the girls, George put his hand under Nina's elbow.

'I don't know why but although Max goes on about you all the time I didn't think you'd be so bloody lovely,' he said.

Nina smiled. 'Why, what's his taste in women usually like?'

'Rubbish,' said George, laughing.

Max handed over the drinks. 'You should have seen her a few hours ago, George. Executive hairstyle and linen suit. She's had a fairy godmother make her over.'

He decided not to use the word 'crumpled' to describe the linen suit. Smiling hugely at Nina, he touched her hair. 'This is great! Though I don't think you look much like an auditor any more.'

She laughed. 'No, I think I'll have to see about getting a pair of glasses. Anyway, I don't suppose you'd have guessed that Angie's an accountant.'

'Not if I didn't know already. I wouldn't mind auditing your accounts, Angie.'

George grimaced. 'Oh God, he's off. Pass the sick bag.'

Max felt his arm hovering somewhere above Angie's

shoulders and he tried to tone down his wide smile, but knew he'd have to give it up as a bad job. She was laughing at him and there was something throaty in her laugh that spoke sex to him. This is a magic night, he decided, as he joined in with her laughter while watching George and Nina get acquainted.

'What do you do, George?' she asked.

He looked faintly embarrassed. 'Well, I'm in the police.'

'Don't sound so apologetic,' she laughed. 'Don't tell me, you're on duty and that's why you're drinking lemonade.'

He nodded. 'Sort of. I'm not on yet, but I will be later, up in Soho after the pubs close.'

'What, trying to find drunk and disorderlies?'

'No, thank God. I left the uniform behind a long time ago. Actually, this is my uniform.' He indicated his T-shirt and combats. 'I'm checking out a few clubs and so on.'

'As it happens, Nina, George was doing a bit of digging into your mate Costas,' interrupted Max. He couldn't help taking a slightly malicious pleasure in seeing her start. 'You helped him out, actually. He didn't know that he was your boyfriend's godfather.'

Nina glowered at him. 'I didn't think I was helping in a police investigation when I told you that little snippet, Max.'

'Hang on,' said George, obviously confused. 'I don't think you've given me the full story, Max. Does that mean you're going out with Andrew Marnington, Nina?'

'Oh sorry, George, I thought he'd given you the complete lowdown on my life and loves. Didn't he get that far?'

Max shrugged. 'Wasn't relevant.'

He suddenly remembered George's face when he first laid eyes on Nina and could have kicked himself for pointing out that Nina had a boyfriend, especially when it was Mr Sleaze.

'Anyway, he's not here tonight,' he said lamely. And of course George was going off to work in a couple of hours.

Tonight wasn't going to be the night for George and Nina, but once she had got rid of Mr S, they could all start again.

Nina shook her head and turned back towards George. She liked him straight away although he wasn't the usual Latin type she went for. He had a pronounced but soft Scottish accent and his brown hair had an auburn glint which presumably had something to do with his Celtic heritage. But his dark brown eyes had a sincere, trusting look to them, and his face was lit up with a flashing smile. He was tall as well, which was nice, seeing as Andrew wasn't much taller than she was.

'Max has got this thing about Andrew,' she told him. 'He just doesn't like him.'

'Probably jealous because he's going out with you,' said George.

'No, I don't think so. So why are you investigating Costas?'

George took a swig of his lemonade. 'Difficult to say, really – have you met him?'

'Yes, a couple of times. He seems OK, for the oldest man in the world, that is.'

'He's that all right. Where did you meet him?'

She thought quickly. 'Well, the first time I was having a drink with Andrew in some hotel in Belgravia. The second time it was a club in Soho.'

'And have you met Madame Saphianos?'

'His niece? Ariadne? Just briefly. She's a very imposing woman.'

'That's her, all right. She's got a finger in a lot of pies.'

196

Little does he know that I've had my finger in one of her pies, thought Nina flippantly, thinking of Beverley.

'Like what, exactly?'

'Oh, a model agency, a couple of clubs, PR – you name it.'

'While Costas and Andrew are just into shipping, right?'

'Yes, though Costas seems to be tied up with his niece in a few things.'

'But all legal, right? So what's the problem?'

George shook his head and smiled his wide smile. 'Maybe something, maybe nothing. But you know we have to pursue all lines of enquiry, even if it looks like we're on a hiding to nothing.'

'This must be where Max has got it from. He's been a pain in the arse over Andrew's accounts, and at the end of the day there wasn't anything out of order at all.'

He shrugged. 'That's the way it goes, Nina. Look, do you want another one here, or shall we move on? We normally go off to the Ark next. It's a brilliant place, music, late licence, few more mates –' He broke off and looked seriously at her. '– Though come to think of it, I don't really feel like being in a crowd.'

She couldn't help reacting to his frank gaze. He was letting her know in no uncertain terms that he was interested. And she knew she was melting under the look in those deep brown eyes. His Scottish accent gave his voice a gravelly, caressing timbre which she felt she could listen to for hours. She imagined him talking dirty to her in that voice, that accent.

And maybe she'd watched too much TV, but the mere fact of his being a policeman was decidedly exciting.

Hell, she was telling him all this by the look in her eyes, she knew. But she was quite happy for him to read it there.

Anyway, he had to go to work. No danger there.

Chapter Nine

*I*t really was one of those magic evenings. The chemistry between the four of them made the conversation sparkle. Nina thought she'd never seen Angie laugh so much. Maybe it was the influence of alcohol but it seemed that the repartee between herself and Max scaled witty heights it had never reached before, and George proved to be as amusing as he was attractive, with a dry sense of humour that she put down to him coming from north of the border.

The Ark was an oddball, laidback place. Its backstreet location meant it was less crowded than the parkside Tavern, and the clientele was a bit older and more mellow. They draped themselves on overstuffed settees and drank beer from the pub's own microbrewery. A pianist was playing jagged, funky jazz when they went in and after a while he was joined by a guitarist and a black woman who sang a mix of old Tamla tunes and jazz standards in an impossibly deep voice. It was almost too cool, thought Nina.

'I mean, Hackney! I thought the height of sophistication here was the Hackney Empire and the greyhound stadium.'

Max grinned at her. 'Just because you're stuck in a time warp in post-Sloane Clapham, doesn't mean the rest of the city hasn't moved on,' he said. 'Mind you, when one of my mates moved to Hackney a few years ago I thought he was mental – till I came out for a drink with him. Bet you'll be moving in before long.'

'No way! This is great, but you've got that horrible rundown main road just round the corner. There is no way that compares with Lavender Hill and its delis and restaurants.'

'Shops and restaurants aren't much good to Max,' said George. 'Greasy spoon caffs and pubs are the places he spends his time in, eh, Maxie?'

'Yeah, mostly,' Max admitted. 'But we have got a deli down the road, and as it happens I do use it from time to time. And we've got Marks and Spencer, so what more could anyone need?'

'And you have to admit, Nina, that you're not exactly a gourmet cook,' said Angie treacherously.

'Bitch,' laughed Nina. 'OK, Ange, you move to Hackney and I'll think about joining you.'

'Not another Clapham girl?' asked George.

'Almost – more Balham borders,' said Angie. 'What I'd miss is the tube. Waiting for buses is all right in this weather, but in winter, nightmare!'

George looked at his watch. 'Talking of transport, I'd better get going,' he said.

'Oh yeah, George has got his transport problems sorted,' said Max. 'Work shifts, be a cop and have a new Alfa.'

'Very impressive,' said Nina. 'I like cars. You'll have to give me a ride sometime.'

George stood close to her and fixed her with his deep brown eyes. 'I will. And that's a promise.' He gave her and then Angie a peck on the cheek. 'Enjoy the rest of the night. See you later.'

Nina felt a mixture of annoyance and relief that he

had had to go. Of course she wasn't interested, she told herself, because of Andrew. And it was a bit unnerving that he was investigating Costas. But she had definitely felt vibes coming from him, and they were nice ones.

The three of them still managed to have a good time without him and they were surprised when last orders were called at ten to midnight.

'Sod it! I really don't want this night to end,' said Max, as Angie went to the bar to get the last round in. 'Having fun, Nina?'

'Oh, you noticed? I suppose you're trying to get me off with George because you don't approve of Andrew?'

Max looked at her innocently. 'Are you kidding? I thought me, you and Angie were a threesome. George just happened to be in The Tavern.'

'Amazing coincidence, since he's investigating Costas.'

'Oh well. Don't tell me you don't like him.'

'Probably not as obviously as you like Angie.'

He laughed as she came back with the drinks. 'Yeah, but don't tell her, I don't want her to think I'm a pushover.'

'Who's a pushover?' Angie enquired, shaking her hair back from her face. 'We don't like that sort of talk, do we, Neen?'

She put her arm round Nina and looked at Max archly. He groaned.

'Are you ganging up on me?'

'I think we might be, what do you think?' Angie asked Nina conspiratorially. They both laughed.

'Look, I'm an innocent. I can't cope with women. Walk all over me, do what you want!'

'Sounds interesting,' said Angie. 'How about it, Nina? Fancy walking all over him? Or are you only up for being walked all over yourself?'

Nina looked daggers at Angie.

'Sorry,' she apologised. Nina hoped Max hadn't caught the allusion, or put two and two together from the state of her skirt that day.

'As I was saying,' Max said, 'I don't want tonight to end. How about coming back to mine for a nightcap?'

For the second time that week Nina was impressed by a man's flat. While it was nothing like as opulent as Andrew's penthouse, Max's place was stylish in a different way. It was on the top two floors of a four-storey Victorian house which had its back to the canal. The first floor was an open-plan sitting room and kitchen, and Max opened the door at the back of the room to reveal a small balcony overlooking the water, which lapped seductively in the light breeze. A hammock was slung across the balcony, which was decorated with two tall aluminium containers planted with stiff-leaved purple grass plants.

Max turned on two black contemporary-style standard lamps which lit up the room's deep yellow walls. There was a black marble fireplace with three settees ranged round it and a Quad hi-fi with a massive selection of CDs towering next to it.

He went into the surprisingly clean and tidy kitchen alcove to get drinks and Nina followed him.

'Beer? Vodka? Wine?' He opened the fridge to reveal a stash of Becks beer, two bottles of white wine, three cartons of orange juice and one of milk. The freezer compartment on top held a bottle half full of Absolut and a few ready meals.

'I'm stunned, Max. I assume this wasn't laid on for our benefit? So you must always live like this.'

He laughed easily. 'Yeah, a fridge full of beer. Is that a cliché or what?'

'I suppose you have a daily to keep this clean and tidy?' asked Nina drily, thinking of Andrew's army of decorators, designers, florists and housekeepers.

'Yeah, you could do that on our salary? I'd rather spend it on booze and get the duster out from time to time.' He grinned. 'So what's it to be?'

Nina and Angie both decided they could manage another vodka and he poured the ice-cold liquid for them and uncapped a beer for himself. The girls sat on one of the settees while Max pored over his music collection. As the voice of Sharleen Spiteri filled the room, he sat down opposite them.

'Your neighbours must be pretty accommodating,' said Nina, as the music increased in volume. He beamed.

'That's the beauty of this place. The flat downstairs is upside-down, if you see what I mean. We're above their living room. And even better, the couple who live there go off to their country cottage every weekend, so I can make as much noise as I like. This house is an end terrace so there's no one on that side, and on the other the staircase is in between my rooms and theirs. You can't hear a thing.'

He reached into a drawer and pulled out a tobacco tin. 'How about a smoke?'

'That's something I haven't done for ages,' said Nina dubiously, remembering feeling distinctly paranoid the last time she'd smoked dope several years ago.

Angie laughed. 'Didn't you tell me that the last time you did something you hadn't done for years it turned out to be an amazing experience?' she said wickedly.

Nina made a face at her. 'So it was!' she exclaimed in a falsely bright voice. 'Go on, Max. I'll try a quick drag and see if it's better than I remember.'

Sipping her vodka, she watched Max's dark blond head bent over as he rolled the joint intently. He brought the same concentration to it that he brought to his work, a diligence that belied his casual charm. She was struck by exactly how fond she had become of him lately.

After the joint had gone round a couple of times she was feeling no pain. Max was running his finger down his CDs, saying he was looking for something more mellow. Suddenly the sound of REM playing 'Everybody Hurts' filled the room.

'Oh, wow, this was one of our favourites at college,' said Angie, putting her arm round Nina's shoulders. 'Do you remember we were all singing it around finals time?'

'Don't I just,' giggled Nina. 'Amazing, though – I was just thinking I was feeling no pain and then he puts on "Everybody Hurts".'

They swayed and sang together while Max took another drag of the joint and passed it over to Angie.

'Getting a bit hot,' he advised.

'You, or the joint?' asked Angie.

Max sat down on the settee next to her.

'Dope always gets me going,' he said. 'Added to the sight of you two sitting there with your arms round each other, I don't know how I can control myself.'

Nina felt the same way. The joint had certainly taken effect on her and she knew that if she had been with anyone but her best friend and best workmate she would now be surrendering to the desire to lock tongues, move her hands all over them and rub her sex against them and beg them to fuck her. But she wasn't playing that game with Max and Angie.

She was playing a totally different game. And the thought of that excited her even more.

'You don't have to control yourself, Max,' she said silkily, 'because I'm in charge here. You just be a good boy and do what I tell you.'

Angie turned towards her, raising her eyebrows and smiling, her tongue between her teeth.

'How about me?' she purred. 'Do I get a say in this?'

Nina winked and smiled at her. 'Yeah, I reckon – as

long as you say the right things. How about a bit of a replay of last week?'

Angie's smile widened. 'Oh yeah, that's OK by me. I think it'll be OK by Max as well.'

Nina nodded. 'Probably. Let's just hope he behaves himself, or we'll just have to go back to Clapham and carry on at my place.'

Max sat on the settee as though he had been turned to stone. There was obviously no way he was going to spoil whatever was coming next.

The girls both knew exactly what to do next. Their mouths met gratefully, the memory of the previous week's kisses adding greater depth to this one. Under the spell of the marijuana, their tongues probed even more insistently and abandonedly than before. Nina felt she was losing herself in the kiss and quickly took control. She shifted Angie round slightly so that she could push her down, her head on Max's lap, as their lips worked against each other's. Nina herself felt the heat from Max's crotch as she leaned over Angie. Slowly she disentangled her tongue from her friend's and licked lightly around Angie's lips. Max was breathing hard.

'OK, Maxie?'

He nodded. 'Oh yeah. Definitely,' he breathed, still not daring to move.

Nina laughed. 'Good boy. I think he's got a hard-on, Angie. Can you just check?'

Angie smiled teasingly and rubbed her head gently up towards the obvious bulge in Max's trousers.

'Wow, no problem there, Neen. Are we going to let him use it?'

Still leaning over her friend, Nina looked consideringly at him. Not daring to speak, he implored her with his eyes.

'I'm thinking about it. But only if he's a good boy. I

think you're going to be a good boy, aren't you, Maxie? Are you going to do everything I tell you?'

'Sure thing, Nina.'

She sat up then stood, looking down at both of them. 'I think Angie's dying for a bit more attention, Max. What do you think, Ange? How about having your tits squeezed?'

'Yeah, great,' whispered Angie. 'Hang on a minute.' She reached both hands behind slowly and, lifting her neck, unclasped the back of her top, throwing it on the floor. Her tanned breasts were revealed, framed by the crimson cardigan.

'Nice, eh, Max? What are you waiting for?'

He didn't need to be told twice. Looking down at his cropped blond head bent over Angie as he rubbed her breasts, all in compliance with her bidding, sent a shockwave of excitement through Nina. Her friend's nipples had stiffened under his first touch, and knowing that they were both excited turned her on even more.

'You can talk, you two,' she ordered. 'How's he doing, Angie? How does she feel, Max?'

'She's bloody gorgeous,' said Max obediently.

Angie wriggled under his hands. 'Lovely hands, Max. He's got a nice firm touch, Nina. Aren't you going to try it?'

Nina laughed. 'Maybe. How would that be, Max? Can you manage both of us?'

He blew his cheeks out hard. 'Oh yes, Nina, whatever you want. You just say the word.'

'Good boy. Take your T-shirt off. It's not fair that Angie's the only one exposing herself.'

While Max lifted his T-shirt over his head, Nina put her fingers lightly on Angie's nipples. As he drew it down over his arms she heard him breathe in sharply as he saw her. She laughed.

'Actually, Max, you might as well unzip and get your cock out while I'm taking over here,' she teased.

'Oh God,' he groaned. 'I'm in heaven.'

'Not yet. Still, I reckon you could be in with a good chance of getting there. As you can see, Angie doesn't care who's touching her up, as long as someone is. She came out looking for a shag tonight, and I expect you'll do.' She surveyed him. 'Nice body! Great cock!'

Although Max didn't have a six-pack stomach, his arms were well enough muscled and his chest lightly tanned with a fair sprinkling of straight hairs, slightly darker than his head. And his cock was very nice. Not incredibly long but really quite thick, Nina was surprised to see – much thicker than Andrew's. It was a nice smooth honey colour, too, crowned with deep brownish red. A clear drop of pre-come squeezed out of the eye.

'Have a look, Angie! And you could just lick that little dribble off if you like.'

Angie turned her head slowly.

'Mmm, nice one, Max,' she said appreciatively. 'I tell you what, even if madam here doesn't let us fuck tonight, we can always get together on our own another time.'

Max closed his eyes as her tongue snaked slowly up his cock from as near the base as she could get with his jeans in the way, and lapped round the glans and swallowed the clear liquid.

'He tastes nice, Nina,' Angie informed her, snuggling round to face Max's penis. 'Want a go?'

'I think I'd like you both with less clothes,' observed Nina. 'Get up and get your trousers off, Ange. And you –' she pointed at Max '– can strip right off.'

How sweet it was that they both immediately obeyed her. She soon had Max lying full length on the settee while Angie stood next to her wearing only a pair of black lace knickers and the cardigan on her arms and shoulders.

'Surely you're going to take something off,' said Angie, her arm sneaking around Nina's waist. 'I bet Max would like to see your tattoo.'

Nina sighed with mock irritation.

'I might not have wanted him to know I had one,' she said sharply. 'Honestly Angie, I think maybe you'd better do what you're told as well as Max.'

'Sorry,' said her friend meekly.

Nonetheless Nina peeled her silk vest off, revealing her breasts spilling out over a half-cup white satin bra. She registered Angie uttering a small 'Oh!' because she knew that the other half of the outfit was the crotchless briefs. But while Angie thought she knew what was coming, she wasn't expecting her shaved sex, Nina remembered with satisfaction. She turned to her friend and put a finger on her lips.

'Quiet, Angie,' she said, and then again her mouth closed over her friend's. She imagined what Max was feeling, watching the two girls kiss, one dressed in nothing but a pair of black briefs and cardigan and the other in a cleavage-revealing bra and skirt.

She fondled Angie's breasts and let her friend touch hers, her fingers snaking inside the cups to touch her erect nipples. Then her hands moved to Angie's bottom and she pulled her closer. She told herself it was for Max's benefit as their sexes ground tantalisingly together.

'Are you getting wet?' she murmured to Angie. 'Go and show Max if you are.'

Angie giggled and obediently went to stand next to Max's head. She hooked her thumbs into her knickers and slowly wriggled them down and stepped out of them.

'Oh boy,' breathed Max, as his hand reached towards her black fleece almost falteringly, as if expecting Nina to tell him to stop. She watched him and shivered with desire as at her command his fingers probed Angie's wet sex.

'So tell me, is she wet or what?' she asked impatiently. Max closed his eyes and continued to push inside Angie.

'She's well fucking wet,' he answered. 'She is absolutely soaked.'

Nina unzipped her skirt and stepped out of it as it fell around her feet. She moved over to stand next to Angie.

'What about me? Am I as wet as her?'

Max opened his eyes and Nina watched him triumphantly as he closed them again involuntarily as he gasped at the sight of her. Angie looked down, thinking she knew what she was going to see, and she too gave an appreciative gasp.

'Wow, Nina. Why didn't I think of that? God, that's brilliant.'

'Max!' said Nina threateningly. He seemed to have forgotten what she'd asked him. With a beatific smile, his fingers moved from Angie's vagina to stroke along Nina's sex.

'Yes, Nina, you're just as wet,' he said. 'I have gone to heaven, haven't I? Anyway, I'm seeing stars.'

Nina laughed. 'Nice one, Max. Haven't you got two hands? Can't you touch us both at the same time?'

'Oh my God. Can't I sit up, though?'

'No, I want you on your back. I tell you what, get on the floor.'

Max rolled eagerly off the settee and on to the floor. Nina knelt on one side of him and motioned to Angie to do the same on the other side. They smiled at each other and spread their legs.

'Go on, Maxie. Make us come.'

* * *

Slowly, he moved each index finger from each seriously wet vagina and stroked firmly up to each swollen clitoris. Then down again. Then he fretted each clitoris with each thumb. He moved his head to the left. Angie's thighs were tanned and just a little plump. Her fleece was straight and dark and silky, and her juice on his fingers was slightly creamy. He moved his head to the right. He still couldn't believe what he was seeing. Nina was still wearing her white satin knickers, but they were split to reveal a silky shaven pubic mound. Her cleft was revealed from clitoris down to arsehole. He had never seen anything like it. And just above the knickers she had a tattoo of a shower of stars pointing right down to it.

He pushed two fingers inside each of them. Nina made a small noise of appreciation.

'Doing good, Max. Are you having fun?' She didn't wait for an answer. 'Keep concentrating.' He saw her arms move out and moving his head back to the centre saw her caressing Angie's breasts. Then he saw the two girls' mouths move towards each other. He dipped further and faster inside them, his thumbs working their swollen buds, Angie's almost hidden in the dark hair while Nina's stood proud. He was so hot that he thought that maybe for the first time since teenage wet dreams he was going to come without even a touch on his dick. The only caress he'd had had been Angie's tongue lapping at him for about five seconds, but he felt as though he'd been brought almost to the point of orgasm by imagined touches and sucks.

This is probably the best moment of my life, he thought as he stroked and kneaded both girls, desperately wanting to bring them off, not to fail in carrying out Nina's orders.

He felt, more by intuition than by touch, a shudder run through Angie's body. He knew she was nearly there. He didn't know about Nina, but knew for some reason that he should move both hands together. Plunging once more inside each hot, slithery, delicious cunt, he stepped up the pressure and speed of thumb pads on clitorises, and was, thank God, rewarded with a cry from Angie as her sex pushed towards him, and her muscles clutched around his fingers. His hands had been working in unison for so long that he had to close his eyes and concentrate hard so as to keep the pressure up on Nina while allowing Angie to dictate the moves she wanted from him as she stayed his thumb while gripping his fingers. It wasn't long before his concentration paid off and Nina too was bucking against his hand. Angie had slid to the floor away from him and he was able to give Nina his full attention, watching his wet hand working at her and watching her bare mons slamming against his thumb as she came.

'Mmm, Max, pretty good, pretty good,' she crooned breathlessly, still rubbing lightly against him. 'OK for you too, Ange?'

'Too right,' murmured Angie contentedly, snuggling up with her head on Max's chest, her eyes closed. 'I could just go to sleep now.'

Max started to feel a bit worried. His prick was massive and he knew he couldn't go without coming for much longer. If the girls turned over and went to sleep, what was he going to do? It seemed a bit pointless having to wank himself off with two babes naked either side of him.

But Nina was tutting and reached over and smacked Angie lightly on the bottom. 'Don't be so bloody selfish,' she told her. 'What about poor Max?'

Angie opened her eyes again. 'Oh, sorry, Max. Just a minute, though, eh? It's only because you did such a good job that I feel so shagged.'

Nina laughed. 'Yeah, when they called you a right wanker in work I didn't believe them –'

'Hey! Who did?'

210

'I'm winding you up, idiot.' She turned and punched him on the arm. 'I didn't mean to let you do that, but it just seemed fair that I should get the same as Angie.'

He smiled at her. 'And am I going to get the same in return?'

'Might manage to do better than that. Let me think about it – while you get something to drink. I'm dead thirsty.'

Max padded into the kitchen, pleased to feel the cool vinyl floor underfoot, although he didn't want to cool down too much. He still didn't believe what was happening. It was definitely the best night of his life.

He poured a carton of orange juice into a jug and put it on a tray with three glasses. On second thoughts he decided to go for another beer. And on third thoughts he got the vodka bottle out of the freezer and put that on the tray as well.

You're a perfect host, Max, he told himself as he picked up the loaded tray and headed back to the sitting room. Let's just hope you get your just rewards. Something tells me you will.

'I feel guilty now,' Nina said as soon as Max left the room. 'I don't think I'll tell Andrew about this.'

'Couldn't resist it – or him?' teased Angie.

'Not him. He's a mate, that's all. I just really wanted to come. At least –' She leant back against the settee '– I couldn't resist ordering him to make us come. Then I was fantasising that I didn't come and had to punish him.'

Angie whistled. 'Punish how?'

'Well, tie him up, tease him for hours, make him beg for it, go off to the bedroom and go to sleep and leave him here waiting for it, that sort of thing.'

They laughed together.

'You know, Nina, I think there's definitely a latent dominatrix hidden in you somewhere,' said her friend.

211

'Not exactly a dominatrix – I think I just like a little power,' mused Nina. 'I wouldn't really want to whip anyone but I do like the thought of being the one calling the shots.'

'Sounds like you're modelling yourself on Andrew,' said Angie sarcastically.

'That's the trouble. I don't know if I'm wanting to get my own back on him through Max, or whether I do really want to be the one in control – in which case, how on earth am I going to carry on as I am with Andrew?'

Angie shrugged. 'You're still hot for Andrew so why not carry on and have someone else on the side you can push around?' She looked mischievously at Nina. 'What about someone like George? You were wetting your knickers for him.'

'Cheek! I was not!'

'Oh no? I saw the way you were looking at him. Don't blame you, though. Sexy voice.'

'Who, me?' Max walked in with a tray loaded with glasses, jugs and bottles held just above his still hard cock, like a male version of a Playboy bunny.

'No, your mate George. I was telling Nina they could be made for each other.'

'Piss off, Ange.' Nina helped herself to a glass full of orange juice and drank deeply. 'That's better. I would like to remind you both that being brought off by Max just now notwithstanding, I have a very good relationship going already. This night's a one-off.'

'Shame,' said Max, grinning. 'Hope that means you're going to make it one to remember.'

'Thought I already had,' said Nina with raised eyebrows. 'I suppose you're thinking of your own selfish orgasm.'

Max picked up a beer and took a long draught. 'Up to you,' he said simply. 'It's still fucking unreal, lying around naked in my sitting room with you two, having just brought both of you off. If you just got dressed and walked out the door I could hardly complain.'

'Oh, what a sweetie,' said Angie. 'There's no way we'd do that. Well, I wouldn't. I don't think Nina's planning to either, though she might make you beg her not to.'

'I'm not too proud to beg,' said Max. Nina started to feel the sense of power course through her again. It was the strongest turn-on she'd experienced in the last few shattering weeks.

'That won't be necessary,' she said crisply. 'Anyway, Max, I think your cock's doing its own begging.'

Both girls surveyed Max's hard-on.

'I think I liked you best on your back.' said Nina, pushing him down. 'Close your eyes.'

He didn't need telling twice.

She picked up the freezing cold vodka bottle. Angie screwed up her eyes in sympathy for Max, lying there unwitting and eager, as Nina laid the bottle square on to his penis.

'Jesus!'

'Shut it, Max,' ordered Nina. 'I don't want a sound out of you until I say so.'

His cock had subsided slightly under the assault of the ice-cold bottle. Nina slid the glass up and down on it, revelling in the way he screwed up his eyes and clenched the muscles of his cheeks to stop himself from making a sound. Before he could get used to it, she pushed it down further over his balls and snuck it in between his thighs, rotating it against his perineum. His Adam's apple moved as he swallowed frantically to stop himself from shouting.

'I think he likes it, Ange. How about it? Do you fancy some more vodka?'

'Depends,' teased Angie, who had obviously picked up what was going through Nina's mind. 'I've left my glass over there somewhere.'

'Never mind,' said Nina, unscrewing the top. 'Have some from this.'

Slowly she trickled the liquid over Max's cock, which still had not completely recovered its full solidity. It bucked slightly as the cold vodka hit it, and Nina guessed the shock wasn't as great as the freezing bottle had been.

Angie leaned over and lapped her tongue up Max's cock, licking off the vodka.

'Enough, Angie?'

'No, more, please.'

This time Nina poured more of the drink out of the bottle and Max almost gasped, then remembered in time he wasn't supposed to. From the head of his prick right down to the balls, a double measure at least. Shame it was dripping on to the carpet.

'Vodka doesn't stain, Max, so don't worry,' she told him as she motioned Angie to carry on licking. Her friend started this time at the balls, gently sucking the booze off them, and then made her way up to the crest of his rim. Once again he was completely, gloriously hard. Nina almost wished she could impale herself on that thick chunk of dick but knew she would enjoy watching Angie do it almost as much. When she told her to, that is.

'I think it's dribbled right down to his arse, Ange. Not that I want to make you lick his arsehole –'

'Not much,' laughed Angie. 'I've gone nearly all the way there. He seems to like it.'

'Wonder if he's ever had a cock up his arse?'

Max made to speak but as quick as lightning Angie put her hand over his mouth.

'Good girl! I bet he hasn't. You think he might like it, though?'

Angie's index finger moved around Max's hole. 'Wriggling a bit. Could be pleasure, could be fear.'

Nina reached behind her and picked her bag up off the settee.

'Turn over, Max. I want you on all fours. And as a reward for doing what I say, you can open your eyes and look at Angie.'

She thought for a second or two that Max was going to refuse, and the game would be over. Sickeningly, she realised that if he did, there was nothing she could do. This was her first chance at this game and she was loving it. If he stopped it now she knew she would never have the nerve to try it again.

But Max obediently turned over on to his hands and knees. Now he was in the position she had been in so many times with Andrew, and she was behind him. With the power.

Angie entered fully into the spirit of the game and lay back tantalisingly, her knees wide apart, fondling her breasts and smiling teasingly at Max. He groaned and Nina slapped him lightly on the buttocks.

'You are still in silent mode. I'll tell you when you can speak.'

She saw Angie's eyes widen as she pulled her new vibrator from her bag. Carefully she fitted on the attachment she had so far had no use for: a long, thin finger of rubber, about five inches long and slightly less than finger thickness. A tube of KY Jelly was the next item out of the bag.

She squeezed the jelly on to her forefinger and smeared it liberally on Max's arsehole, which was already wet from the vodka. He seemed to be holding his breath. More lubricant on the rubber finger and then she turned it on.

He started and grunted as he heard the vibrator buzz into action. Gently Nina pressed it against his slippery hole. Without much effort she pushed it in a little way.

'You've got about an inch inside you, Maxie. If you

215

hate it you can speak now. If you like it just keep on watching Angie.'

Silence. Angie moved her hands down and parted her black fleece to show her own wet opening. She sucked one of her fingers provocatively and pushed it inside. Nina watched while she slowly moved the vibrator back and forth, gradually pushing further inside.

'Two inches, Max. Does he like it, Ange? Is he still hard?'

'Rock hard,' said Angie, her finger still moving inside her. 'Hard and thick and pointing straight at me. Can I have it, Neen?'

'I'm thinking about it,' said Nina, pushing in further. 'Three inches. Max, if you just get down on to your elbows, I think you might be able to give Angie a bit of attention with your mouth.'

He moved so quickly she guessed he was only too happy to oblige. Angie brought her sex up to meet his mouth and sighed blissfully as he started tonguing her.

Nina pushed the vibrator all the way in and out again, and again and again. She turned up the speed so that it jolted against his arse as it went up to the hilt. He didn't object; from the up and down movements of his cropped blond head he was more interested in doing a good job on Angie.

She fucked him harder with the vibrator, wishing for a cruel second that she could pull the attachment off and thrust the whole lot inside him. But she didn't want to spoil the game. At the moment she was in command, and that wasn't going to change. If she pushed too hard he might stop playing, and she didn't want to risk that.

Nina realised that apart from the sense of power she was enjoying the calculation of how far she could go, when she would have to stop. She hadn't expected this aspect of taking charge. How many times had Andrew done this? Played her to the limit and known when to relent, when to stop pushing, when she was going over the edge?

Instead, she pulled right out. Removing the finger attachment, she adjusted the vibrator to full speed and stroked it up and down Max's perineum, feeling the shudder run through his body. She moved it over his balls and ran it up and down his cock, then swivelled round so that she was kneeling next to Max's head and Angie's cunt. Lightly, she ran the buzzing vibrator across Angie's pubic mound.

'Jesus, Neen, I'll come if you do that again,' said Angie throatily. 'I'm nearly there now.'

'So stop it, Max,' said Nina, tapping him on the shoulder with the vibrator. 'Get your mouth out of there.'

Max raised his head, moustached with juices. Nina tutted and quickly darted her tongue around his mouth. Taken by surprise, Max stayed stock still at first and then responded by crushing his tongue into her mouth. Nice, thought Nina. But no thanks.

'I didn't say you could kiss me. I was drying your mouth off, that's all,' she said sternly.

'Sorry,' said Max, looking quite unrepentant.

'Who said you could speak?'

He closed his mouth.

'The music's stopped. Go and put on something sexy, turn it down a bit and come back here.'

While he was sorting through his CDs Nina went out to the balcony and tried the hammock for comfort. Not bad. The balcony was dark and looking into the illuminated sitting room was like watching a film. Just what she wanted.

The sound of M People came over the speakers.

'Down a bit more, Max, and say something – I want to hear you speak.'

'How's that?'

'Can't hear. What did you say?'

She had heard him, but she wanted to be sure to hear clearly. He moved the volume and adjusted the bass and then looked at her.

'That's got to be right.'

'Yeah. OK, kids. I want a show. A real sex show. Fuck the arse off each other, and take your time. I want to see a real live porno film, and I don't mean a silent film, either. What do you think?'

'You're fucking weird, Nina,' said Max, but he was beaming. 'What do you think, Angie?'

'About bloody time,' said Angie. 'You've got a lovely mouth and useful hands, Max, but what I really want is that great fat cock inside me.'

'That's good, keep talking,' ordered Nina, settling herself on her hammock. 'Just don't forget you're doing this for me as well as for you. I want to come as well as you two. Just imagine you're really in a skinflick.'

Max knelt in front of Angie. 'Ready, co-star?'

'You better believe it,' said Angie, opening her legs.

'So beam me up, Scotty,' said Max.

Nina set the vibrator purring and as Max slid his cock inside Angie's wet opening, she settled back in the hammock, opened her legs and started on the first sweet climax.

If she'd been casting a porn movie she couldn't have chosen a better team. The contrast of Angie's long black hair and tanned body with Max's clean blond looks and sturdy frame made a perfect picture. Max's excitement had been building up for so long that he came fairly quickly after pumping strongly into Angie, who came vociferously before him. She was doing a great job at a running commentary for Nina, and it must have been partly due to that, as well as her caressing hands, that Max was ready for action again so quickly.

Nina herself had come almost the minute she turned

on the vibrator. Her performance with Max had made her more than ready for it. But she was ready for more when her own live porno movie started up again.

This time they were indefatigable. Angie was on top for a while, then Max had her from behind, then he turned her over and lifted her thighs high over his shoulders while he ground away, and lifted her on to his cock and walked round the room with her bouncing up and down on top of him. They sucked as well as fucked, fingered and tongued, and Nina watched and fucked herself with the vibrator until she'd had enough. She understood why Andrew was hooked on voyeurism.

Max had just come for the second time and she walked over to them.

'Great show. Think I've had enough now.'

'Me too,' yawned Angie. 'How big's your bed, Max?'

'Or are you sleeping on the settee?' added Nina.

He laughed. 'King size, of course. So was that all right for you, Nina?'

'Yeah. You're a superstud. I'll start spreading the rumours on Monday.'

'Don't mind if you do.'

Nina stood over him and put her foot on his stomach.

'I certainly won't. And neither will you. If you ever, ever mention anything about any of this at work, you will be very, very sorry.'

He raised his hands in submission.

'Hey, I was joking! Of course I won't say anything.'

He sat up and kissed the foot that was resting on his body.

'I swear, Nina. If there might be the remotest chance of this happening again, there is absolutely no way I would spoil that possibility.'

She laughed shortly. 'I said this was a one off, Max. Don't try to blackmail me. You will not say anything about this even if I tell you right now that there is no chance this will happen again.'

'I didn't mean that. Anyway, me and Angie might get together again, even if you don't want to be involved.'

Nina nodded. 'OK. Now bed for me.'

'And me!' Angie put her arms round Nina. 'Wish you'd joined in a bit more. Can't we get Andrew to play too?'

The thought of Max and Andrew in a foursome made Nina laugh. 'Which of you two would hate it more?' she asked Max.

He shook his head. 'No chance, Angie. Sorry, but no.'

Max led the way to the bedroom. Nina was the only one who had any clothes on and despite everything that had happened she felt a bit shy about taking off her low-cut bra and crotchless knickers, despite the fact that she was hardly revealing anything more by stripping off. Just before she went to sleep, she realised that they had added to her authority by setting her apart from the others. The teacher rather than the pupils, the choreographer rather than the dancers. Or the film director rather than the actors.

As opposed to her relationship with Andrew, where she was the pupil, the actor, the puppet. Tonight had proved it was possible to have the best of both worlds, though she didn't think that would prove to be an ongoing option. Perhaps Andrew would let her play the puppet master sometimes.

If not, so what? She was happy with him as things were.

She was too tired to think about it any more. Snuggling down next to Angie, she gave in to sleep.

Chapter Ten

*T*he last thing Nina had expected when they were en route to Hackney the night before was that all three of them would wake up at some incredibly late hour in Max's bed.

For one awful moment she thought he was after a replay of last night but he wasn't stupid. He showered quickly and told them he wasn't into making breakfast and they'd better get dressed to get down to the café.

'I don't really feel as though I've got the right clothes on for breakfast,' said Nina after her shower, looking in dismay at her chiffon skirt. 'Max, got a pair of jeans I could borrow?' she shouted from the bedroom.

'And I need a T-shirt,' said Angie as he came back into the room.

'Great,' said Max, pulling a pair of faded jeans and a neatly folded T-shirt from the wardrobe. 'How do I know you two didn't just set this up so you could steal the clothes from my back?'

'It's not that – I just want to go to work on Monday and tell them I finally managed to get into your jeans at the weekend,' said Nina, deadpan.

'Shame you haven't got a bra I could borrow as well,' said Angie. 'Still, I'll just swing.'

Nina pulled on the jeans. 'Not a bad fit – bit loose, but they'll do. Though I expect he's a bit disappointed, Ange. After all, if we went to his local caff wearing last night's gear, all his mates would know that he'd pulled us last night.'

Max winked. 'Yeah, so now you're wearing my clothes they'll be really fooled,' he said solemnly. 'I'll tell them you came all the way from Clapham this morning half dressed in men's clothing to have a late breakfast with me.'

'OK, smart arse, right as usual,' said Nina. 'Does anyone else have a hangover, or is it just me?'

'I bet I feel worse than you. After all, you didn't have that treble vodka you poured all over Max's cock for me,' grumbled Angie. 'I suppose Mr Becks is feeling fine?'

Max grinned. 'Beer's definitely better for you than spirits.'

'Actually, it wasn't the vodka. I never get a hangover from vodka. It was that bottle of wine we drank before we came out,' claimed Nina. 'Either that or the grass.'

'Certainly wasn't lack of sleep,' said Max, looking at his watch. 'If we're not careful it'll be lunch instead of breakfast.'

'No, I want a greasy fry-up,' said Angie. 'With fried bread. And mugs of tea.'

'Scrambled eggs with bacon and lots of coffee,' said Nina. 'Nothing like a hangover to give you an appetite.'

'Just watch out for the Milky Way,' threatened Angie, laughing.

'What's that?' asked Max.

On the way to the café they explained to him about the tattoo turning into the Milky Way if Nina ate too much. Calling in at a newsagent, they bought reams of Saturday papers, but the noise in the crowded café was several decibels too high for reading and they contented themselves with chat.

It amazed Nina that despite the events of the previous night they were just as at ease with each other as if nothing sexual had happened. It was like being out for a drink with Max after work, with Angie along too. Maybe they were all being splendidly adult about it, she thought. Certainly she wasn't embarrassed about it, and she didn't think the others were either.

In fact, as she ate her scrambled eggs, she felt pretty good about it. She thought maybe she'd mimicked Andrew a bit, but it was her first time. The next time she'd probably be a bit more inventive.

What next time?

'Jesus, mate, you look rough!'

As if by magic, Nina was thinking about the next time and George had just walked into the café.

Max was right, he did look rough. He had dark circles under his eyes and it looked as though he'd been using a garden rake for a comb.

'Twelve hours straight and no sleep for thirty-six hours – what do you expect?' retorted George. But though he was talking to Max, his eyes were on Nina. 'Hi.'

'Yeah, but trawling round the fleshpots of Soho isn't really work, is it?'

George smiled briefly at Max. 'No comment. So what have you been doing since I left you?'

Max gave him a blissed-out smile. 'Just chilling, mate.'

George ordered himself a mug of black coffee and a doughnut. 'Great. I'm not going to be much company. I've just spent the night with two tarts. One's black and blue. And someone's been seriously wounded for putting me in touch with her. So, breakfast and bed.' He swallowed his coffee.

There was a silence.

'Well, you've managed to bring a note of urban reality into our little fantasy world,' said Nina with a brittle laugh. 'I think it's time we got back to Clapham.'

'Don't go on account of me,' said George through a mouthful of doughnut. 'I mean it, I'm off to bed.' He smiled at Nina. 'You're welcome to join me, though.'

She was actually blushing. How could she still do this? It was so embarrassing.

'After a night surrounded by sleaze and violence, the thought of a clean bed with a wholesome, beautiful woman is almost too much.' He was still looking at her.

Nina winced. Andrew enjoyed associating with whores. And now the only other man she could possibly be interested in was forced to.

She wondered if George would still think she was wholesome if he knew more about her – even about last night. Would Max tell him? Men were supposed to be worse than women when it came to boasting about their exploits to their mates.

'I wouldn't have associated Soho with that sort of thing,' Angie was saying. 'I mean, we all think of prostitutes on street corners in the provinces – or even in Balham, come to that – with pimps controlling them, but I thought Soho was full of independent French girls with poodles and their own flats.'

George laughed bitterly. 'You're way out of date, Angie. Most of the prostitution in London now is controlled by pimps, the ones who get the girls from Eastern Europe. Ever since the Iron Curtain collapsed there's been a boom market in bringing in girls from all the former Communist countries. Of course, the Balkans are the latest great source of women, especially from Kosovo and Albania.

'Some of them know what they're coming to and are just happy to get out of a refugee camp, but most of them are told they have to pay off the cost of smuggling them here by working as prostitutes. As far as I can see, that takes for ever. Basically, they're slaves.'

Angie shook her head, horrified.

'God, just think, Nina, it's there but for fortune. I mean, there are women just like us out there who just happen to have been born in Kosovo.'

Nina had taken in what George was saying but she was having trouble fitting it into her world view. Her head couldn't get round the effort of reconciling the fact of Andrew visiting prostitutes with the cowed sex slaves George had just described. She had acted as a whore for Andrew; what a farce that apparently was compared to the real world.

'So why do they bring all these girls to London?' Max asked. 'Are Londoners the best customers for prostitutes? Seems like it's reinforcing the Victorian stereotype of the repressed Englishman.'

George shook his head. 'It's not just London, mate, it's all over Europe. Germany, Holland, especially. They're nearer, of course, and overland. It's a bit harder to smuggle them into England with false papers, or no papers at all.'

He stood up. 'Sorry, I've got to crash. Nina, are you sure you won't come back with me?'

'Really, no. Sorry.'

'No worries. Hope I'll see you soon. Max, Ark later?'

'Yeah, mate. Have a good kip.'

'Well, that was a bit of a downer,' said Max after he'd gone. 'Almost spoiled my breakfast. How about you two?'

Nina stirred. 'I think I'll be getting back home.'

'Shame to break up the party. How about a livener first? You can't leave Hackney without one in the Bluebird.'

Angie laughed. 'Maybe we ought to, Neen, then we can say we've done Hackney and we won't have to come back.'

'Hey! That's definitely not on! There are loads of places you have to come back to. Especially mine.'

'Only joking.' Angie sparkled at Max. 'What do you think, Nina, one for the road?'

'No way. I'm not into lunchtime drinking, but you carry on. You might as well stay and keep Max company, Ange.'

'Yes, stay,' urged Max, his face serious now, his hand on Angie's arm. 'We can just have a couple and then walk over the park, read the papers – how about it?'

'Yeah, you two lovebirds get acquainted.' Nina stood. 'I'll have my skirt first, though, then I'm going home to sleep off this hangover.'

She dismissed the thought that she could have done that lying next to George. With no plans for the rest of the weekend, she was probably being stupid going home. It would be fun, hanging out in the park, then meeting George in the pub later.

But right now she needed to get her head together. Sleep, then a swim. A night in front of the telly, and she'd go to her mum and dad's for Sunday lunch. Then it would be Monday, and Andrew would be back.

She wondered what he was doing in Rotterdam right now. Looking round his precious ship, no doubt.

Lots of prostitutes in Rotterdam, by the sound of it. He wouldn't have any trouble mixing business with pleasure. Still, she'd done pretty well on her own account.

On the bus she tried to weigh up the pleasures of last night compared to those of one of her encounters with Andrew.

There was no doubt she had her submissive side. While she had been horrified by the thought of sexual contact with Costas, obeying him and Andrew had turned her on too. And while she had been humiliated at being an unwitting performer with Beverley, part of her had revelled in the shame of it.

But she had enjoyed the power of ordering Max and Angie around more than she could have imagined. The only thing that had spoilt it was the fact that they were the two people in the world she was determined not to fuck. They were too close, and she was no way prepared to risk losing a good friend and the loyalty of a colleague like Max.

So say she was in the dominant position with somebody else? If Andrew would just once in a while let her call the shots, it would be fantastic.

Perhaps she would be able to persuade him on Monday. If not ... Andrew had been the one to say they weren't exclusive. If not, maybe she could see George from time to time. It was obvious just from two short meetings that he didn't have Andrew's controlling streak, and he must have seen enough exploitation of women to make him a pussycat in bed.

Too many maybes, she told herself as she got off the bus at Old Street Station. And this was too close to the office to be on a Saturday afternoon. She disappeared as quickly as she could into the subway and a peaceful weekend.

Luxuriating in home life proved too tempting. Although Nina had only intended spending Sunday afternoon at her parents' house, she had been easily persuaded to stay until Monday morning.

She didn't get home very often, despite the fact that Hemel Hempstead was only a short train journey from London, so every time she appreciated her mum's insistence that she sit back and relax and not worry about the washing up. This visit was especially nice because of the good weather, and Nina spent most of the afternoon in the garden.

Her flat was terrific, and there was no way she would want to have to come home from work and tend to a garden of her own, but lazing on the lawn in a sun lounger with the Sunday papers while her dad watered and weeded was the perfect antidote to Andrew, Max and George's prostitutes.

On the way to London on the train on Monday morning, she wondered idly if there would be any awkwardness between Max and herself about Friday night. She thought not. However, she didn't find out. Max wasn't there.

At first she thought he'd probably slept in – still with Angie, maybe. Then time went on and she got a bit concerned. She tried phoning but got no answer.

Hal came by halfway through the morning to discuss how long the next audit was going to take, the one she'd been doing preliminary work on.

'Is Max coming in on this one with me?' she asked guardedly.

'Sure. He'll be back in tomorrow.'

'So where is he? I was worried about him.'

'He called in this morning and said he had some things to check out. He may be in later, if not tomorrow morning.'

'Someone could have told me,' said Nina indignantly. 'I didn't know whether he'd taken a day off or fallen under a bus.'

'Yeah. Look, no shitting me, Nina, are you having a thing with Max?'

'*A thing?* What, you mean an affair?' She chose the word carefully.

'Yeah, that's more or less what I mean. A couple of the guys reckon you two are too close for comfort, if you know what I mean.'

Nina didn't know if she was more furious with herself for almost giving way to Max or more furious for not going all the way.

Either way, she was fucking furious.

'Sure I know what you mean. But what you should know, Hal, is that I would think it unprofessional to have an affair with Max. And another thing you should know is that a couple of the guys were not long ago putting round rumours that I was frigid or a dyke just because I wasn't screwing anyone in the office. I wouldn't be surprised if those were the same couple of saddos. And I have to say I resent you not standing up for me straight away.'

'Whoa!' Hal was taken aback. 'Shit, Nina, I had to ask you. I know you're professional, though God knows I wouldn't blame Max for trying. But once someone's put that sort of idea forward, I have to ask, you must appreciate that.'

'Yes, so now you know, just tell those sad tossers to get off my back. Sorry,' she added.

Hal laid a hand on her shoulder. 'Hey, calm down. You and Max make a great team. I just didn't want anything interfering with that.'

Yes, a wonderful team, she thought crossly. So wonderful he hasn't even told me what he's doing today.

He probably hadn't told her because he was following some wild goose chase to do with Andrew's accounts. Maybe he was even at the Anmar Shipping office.

Well he could shove it, as far as she was concerned. She didn't want to know. She had the next audit to concentrate on and tonight to plan.

Black leather, she thought, contemplating the spreadsheet on the screen. It was tempting to break the journey home and visit the sex shop in Soho to get some handcuffs, but that might be over the top.

Silk scarves would do. She would tie him up and tease him. Could she force him to beg? Although she'd fantasised about Max begging her, she hadn't made him – but then it would have been easy. It certainly wouldn't with Andrew, but the thought really got her going. She was just going to have to try harder, that was all.

Abstractedly, she moved the cursor over the computer screen, imagining herself wearing the black leather, a whip in her hand. Black gloves. High heels. Andrew spreadeagled on the table, tied with thin silk scarves. Still wearing his grey shorts, which he begged her to take off, but she wouldn't. The bulge of his erection straining angrily at the cotton of the shorts.

The coolness of her black leather gloves massaging oil into his heated skin. Except the skin of his cock. Everywhere else, the whole of his body tingling with the sensation of her touch, except his cock. She made him beg to let him satisfy her and she finally gave in and stripped off her shorts and lowered herself on to his face. She instructed him to tongue her nice and slow so that it lasted. It took ages to come and she knew then he thought she was going to reward him, release his cock from its prison and let him fuck her.

The hell she was. Now she was satisfied, he could wait even longer. She got herself a beer from the fridge and drank some from the bottle. He was thirsty too, so she trickled some over his mouth, though not enough to satisfy even a tiny thirst. She didn't want him satisfied, not in any way.

She wondered aloud whether the bottle was too big to fit up his arse. Maybe too dangerous, she decided. Perhaps the vibrator would be best. He was swearing at her. She hit him, not hard, but with authority, and he stopped.

When he was nice and quiet she pulled his shorts down to his knees. His prick sprang out angrily and she decided she wouldn't mind some of it after all. In an impersonal way. She straddled him backwards and grabbed the root of his dick and fucked herself with it as though it were a vibrator, her finger rubbing hard at her clit because she didn't want him to come before her and lose the erection.

She came just moments before him and he was still

pumping into the condom and crying, 'Oh God!' when she got off. So, it would have been good if he hadn't come, but she supposed he deserved it. As long as he thanked her nicely, she might just let him do it again later.

She had barely got home and laid out on the table the silk scarves she'd bought from the Sock Shop en route when the entryphone buzzed.

Hard to believe Andrew would be so early. She picked up with a sharp 'yes?'

'Max. Can I come up?'

'What the hell are you doing here?'

'Let me in, for Christ's sake, and I'll tell you.'

She pressed the buzzer and shook her head. Surely, after her indignant denial to Hal, Max wasn't going to make a real play for her. What had gone wrong with Angie? And why couldn't he phone? He'd never been to her place before; she didn't even know he had the address.

As she unlocked the flat door he appeared at the top of the stairs, dressed as though he'd just come from work. Except she knew he hadn't.

'What the hell are you playing at? You don't go in to work, you don't let me know though you tell Hal, now you turn up here when I've got things to do. And I've had a grilling from Hal, who wanted to know if we were screwing.'

'What did you say? Only with a vibrator up the arse?'

She burst out laughing. 'Actually, it was a bit difficult. He asked if we were having a *thing*, and I said diplomatically and frightfully Britishly, "Hal, surely you don't mean are we having an affair?" Which of course I could deny.'

'What on earth does he know?'

231

'A couple of the guys have apparently put him on to it.'

Max blew out through closed lips. 'Yes and I think we both know who. I'm going to get those bastards.'

'I think Hal might beat you to it. What made me so mad was I didn't fuck you because I didn't want to spoil our working relationship but if the whole office thinks we're an item I might just as well have jumped in between you and Angie.'

He laughed. 'Never too late!'

'Yeah, yeah. Nice time on Sunday afternoon, by the way? Did Angie get home at all?'

'I had to kick her out in the end, I was too exhausted. No, seriously, we just had a drink and a walk round the park, smooched a bit, boy-girl stuff, then she went home.'

'For now.'

'Mmm. Thanks a lot for coming over on Friday. Not to mention coming across, sort of.'

'Cheers. Anyway that digression hasn't got you off the hook. What are you doing here?'

'Any chance of a drink first? And a seat?'

'It'll have to be a quick one. Andrew's coming round at eight.'

Max looked uncomfortable. 'Yeah, well, I had to come here to tell you this. No way could I do it anywhere public.'

Nina got a beer out of the fridge for Max. She made to close the door but decided to join him and got another out. It made her remember her earlier fantasy.

'What do you think about a beer bottle up the arse, Max?'

'Not a lot,' he said, nodding his thanks as he took a draught of the beer. He sat in one of the dining chairs and absently fingered one of the silk scarves. 'Nice. New image?'

'No, substitute handcuffs. What do you think?'

He looked up, surprised, then laughed. 'I'll ask George. Reckon he'd go for it. Talking of whom ... that's partly why I'm here.'

She sat in the chair opposite. 'Why, what's the matter?'

He sighed. 'This case he's on. Well, I suppose you've guessed he's vice squad. This prostitution racket ... fuck it, Nina, there's no easy way to tell you this. Your boyfriend's involved in bringing these women in from Eastern Europe. Seriously involved. And not just to London, but all over. Like Rotterdam.'

She felt as if she'd turned to stone. 'That's ridiculous. You are not honestly sitting there telling me Andrew's a pimp?' For the second time that day anger started to rise in her.

'No, I'm not. It's not as easy as that. He doesn't actively pimp the prostitutes once they're here, he gets them here from contacts in Albania, Serbia, Kosovo, you name it. Sorts out the wheat from the chaff, if you know what I mean. Organises false visas, transportation.

'He's not on his own in this – his fucking godfather is in on it, and I bet you anything he's in charge of the whole bloody shebang. Oh, and Madame Saphianos. I think you know her – she's involved as well, though I think she's a bit more hands-on this end. She's not known as a Madame for nothing.'

Nina's anger was red hot and rising.

'You fucking shitbag! You're making this up. You've had it in for Andrew from the moment we first walked through his office door. I bet you've put George on to him with no evidence whatsoever and he's just swallowed this bloody fantasy.'

She was too angry to stay seated any longer and paced up and down the room.

'You've no evidence, have you? It's all a big stupid conspiracy theory. God, I hate that shit! You find one invoice out of place and all of a sudden it's money laundering, so you go running to your cop friend.'

Max shook his head. 'You could just listen to me, Nina. George was on to Costas and Andrew before we even knew we were going to audit Anmar Shipping. I just happened to mention we were moving into Onassis land when we started the job and he was right there on my case, wanting to know which company. When I told him he just told me to be very careful. Very careful indeed.'

'Oh, for Christ's sake, what on earth are you talking about?'

'We're talking about pimps getting stabbed and girls being beaten up. Girls whose only crime is to go to a local crim for false papers to come to England. You know they're not much different to you, Nina, they just by an accident of birth happen to be completely bloody destitute, maybe living in a refugee camp.

'They think they're getting away from a shit life and then end up shut in a room having sex with an endless procession of punters. And they don't see any of the money. They're told it's paying off their debts.

'And we're talking about police informers being killed. Get real, Nina. We're talking serious crime here.'

Nina was shaken with sobs. 'I can't believe Andrew is involved in anything like that. It can't be true.'

Max stood up and put his arm round her.

'I wish it wasn't. But George has spoken to girls who've identified him as the middle man. One of them is the one who was beaten up the other night.'

'Don't tell me Andrew did that!' screamed Nina. 'Don't tell me he's beating up women!'

'Sshh, no,' he said tenderly, taking hold of her wrists. 'No, he's not actively involved in violence. But he is involved with people who are. Calm down,' he said soothingly, as Nina gave way to tearing sobs. She felt his arms wrap round her and he rocked her gently. 'Sshh, Nina. I'm sorry. I'm really sorry.'

'Don't lie,' she forced out through her tears. 'You're not sorry. You were determined to prove he was bent. I bet you're made up you've found something wrong with him. If it's true,' she added, sniffing.

He stroked her hair. 'George says it's true. I wish to God it wasn't. Whatever I think of him, I hate to see you upset like this.'

'Upset!' Nina burst into a fresh storm of sobs. Upset was a feeble word to describe how despairing and empty she felt.

For the first time in her life, she'd felt as though she'd met someone she could fall in love with. Now Max was telling her he was a complete sleazebag. Her entire world was shattered.

'It's getting more competitive, apparently,' Max continued. 'The Albanians are trying to take over the whole vice racket. It could get dangerous.'

'Now what are you trying to say? You want me to feel sorry for him?'

He snorted. 'You must be joking. I'm just telling you that things are getting out of hand. God knows what'll happen if the different vice rings start fighting each other. It's not going to be a friendly dividing up of territory. George thinks it'll be a fight to the death.'

Nina snivelled quietly. Her head was throbbing.

She was still shaking her head in denial of Andrew's involvement in the prostitution racket, but somewhere inside her mind she was registering that it was true.

The vice squad believed it was true. Could she really stick her head in the sand and refuse to believe it?

'So what do you want me to do?' she asked dully.

Max looked at her pityingly. 'It's up to you. If you want to carry on seeing him, there's nothing I can do about it. I'll still be your friend.'

'I didn't mean that. Do you want me to help you get him put away? What should I do?'

He shook his head. 'They can't pin anything on him. George got a positive ID from those women but not in a statement. Nobody's talking now. George's contact is in hospital after having a knife stuck in his ribs. He's probably not supposed to be alive, and God knows if he will be for much longer. They've got a couple of pimps for living off immoral earnings. There's nothing to stick to Andrew.'

'But that's ridiculous! Either he's guilty of it or he isn't, and if he is, he should be punished for it.'

'In a black and white world, he would be,' said Max gently. 'It doesn't work like that any more, Nina. They're trying to get co-operation with the Albanian police but it's impossible to clamp down on.

'Apparently, sex trafficking generates about five billion pounds a year. Not much compared to the drugs trade, but still pretty big business. That's why it's run by organised syndicates.'

'Like Andrew and Costas.'

'Yeah, and all the others. Globalisation's got a lot to answer for. It's too easy to smuggle anything across borders these days – drugs or women.'

'What about the audit? Won't that raise some questions?'

Max shrugged. 'That's what I've been doing today, going over my report with the vice squad and the fraud squad. But there's no conclusive evidence there, particularly after the accountant conveniently tied up all those loose ends. It sure as hell is shady, but nothing that'd stand up in court.'

'So they'll carry on?'

He finished his beer. 'They'll probably lie low for a bit after they find out about these pimps getting busted and the stabbing. But they'll be back on the job after a while. They're not operating much on home ground, so it's almost impossible to get them.'

Nina nodded, tired. She looked at her watch: ten to seven.

'I think you should go now, Max.'

She could hardly bear the look he gave her. Pity, tenderness, concern.

'Are you sure you want me to go? I'm worried about you confronting him.'

'You said he's not into violence.'

'No. If you're sure . . . see you tomorrow.'

He leaned over and kissed her gently on the cheek. Suddenly feeling frighteningly lonely, she put her arms round him and clung to him. He hugged her back.

'Go on, Max.'

She had to get ready. She had to scrub the tears from her face and sort her head out in an hour. Before then she had to decide how she was going to play it.

Chapter Eleven

A long hot bath was what Nina most wanted. She needed to lie in a cloud of scented bubbles with a drink and run a housekeeping check over her mind.

But it was too hot and too late. Instead she stood under the shower set to lukewarm and after soaping herself and washing her hair, let the water run over her while she tallied up a few facts in her mind.

Innocent-seeming facts, such as Andrew liking prostitutes. Knowing the strip club with the mysterious upstairs rooms. His familiarity with Charles the barber's special shaving jobs.

Sharing her with Costas, who turned out to be his 'godfather'. Watching her and Beverley with Ariadne, another member of his surrogate family.

The Russian ex-ballet dancers now working – willingly? who could say? – as strippers. A woman called Katya.

All those things merely proved that his taste in sex was dark and decadent, quasi-incestuous. It had thrilled her.

But when those facts were set against what she had just learned they led to another picture of her lover. A slave trader up to his balls in filth, corruption, exploitation and sleaze.

She shivered under the cool water and got out of the shower.

Mr Sleaze. Very good, Max. His instincts had been a lot better than hers.

Then there were other facts to bear in mind.

She'd discovered great sex. They had fun, too. He was gorgeous. And rich.

But where did the money come from? Obviously not just shipping. How much of his penthouse was paid for from his legitimate earnings, and how much from trafficking in prostitutes?

She could close her eyes to it and ask no questions, like other criminals' women presumably did.

If he was robbing banks or dealing in drugs, it might be possible. But he was dealing in women; human beings. Could she really live with that knowledge and stay with him?

One thing she was going to do was stick to her original plan for the evening, at least up to a point. It might be the last fuck, so it had better be a good one.

And if it was going to be the last one, this had to be the one she would control.

Nina dried her hair, holding her head upside-down to give the layers volume. Suddenly tears came to her eyes again. After her outburst with Max she had felt brisk and matter of fact about the situation, but it was a flimsy veneer. She allowed the tears to well up and fall, then wiped her face. They could be confronted later.

She did the whole body lotion and perfume bit, then put on the black leather halter and shorts. It was the first time she'd worn them since trying them on, and she immediately felt better when she saw herself in the mirror. Her body had tanned slightly since she bought the outfit and her exposed flesh looked good.

She made up with dark grey eye shadow and lined her lower lids with kohl, adding lots of mascara and red lipstick. Every addition made her feel more confident and powerful. She contemplated putting on black stockings but rejected them as whore's clothes. Instead she found her black winter boots in the back of the wardrobe. Unfortunately they weren't stilettos, but had a small kitten heel that was still quite sexy. She found her black gloves, made of fine stretchy leather, and pulled them down as far as she could over her wrists.

Time for a glass of Dutch courage before Andrew arrived. Shame there was no vodka – she felt the need of the strength of 70 per cent proof hitting her bloodstream. She made do with a large glass of fourteen per cent Rioja drunk very quickly, which helped, followed by a sip from another glass. Andrew could assume that was her first drink of the evening. The beer bottles were thrown in the bin.

She put the silk scarves out of sight on a chair drawn up to the table and added a bottle of massage oil labelled as 'Relaxing'. The buzzer went.

'Oh, man. What a welcome!' He surveyed her leather outfit then drew her into his arms and kissed her. 'Missed you.'

'Me too. Good trip?'

'OK. It was nice to be by the sea; cooler than London.'

'How was the new ship?'

'Fine, fine. You've changed your hair – it's terrific. But are you really going out in that outfit?'

Nina laughed, watching him closely. His eyes were affectionate, his smiling face folded into its familiar lines. Dressed in a cream linen collarless shirt and khaki pants, he looked like a successful businessman out to play rather than a sleazy sex trafficker.

'Looking back on the places I've been to with you recently, I thought it was most appropriate,' she replied. 'But if you're planning to go somewhere respectable, I can change.'

He grinned wryly. 'Actually, I've booked a table at the Mirabelle for nine.'

Just the place she'd kill to get to. Why now? she thought furiously.

'Wow! But first you have to have your welcome home present.'

He raised his eyebrows. 'That reminds me –' He picked up the black leather bag he'd put on the floor when he came in. 'A little perfume and some Dutch ginever for you.'

'Thanks.' She took the bag from him.

'Oh, and the bag. It's Prada.'

'Thanks again.'

'I like the gloves. Very sexy.'

She ran the fingers of her left hand across his sculpted lips and down his chin and throat to his neck. 'Feel nice?'

'Mmm.'

'So why not take this lot off and feel them all over?'

A half-smile on his face, Andrew unbuttoned his shirt and took it off and laid it over the back of a chair. Nina watched him, hands on hips, as he unzipped his trousers and took them off, together with his shoes and socks. He was wearing snug white Calvins and she could see his penis was just stirring to attention inside them.

She moved towards him and ran her gloved hands over his chest. The supple leather moved easily over his lean, muscular body.

'Do you remember the last time we fucked?' she asked him in a low, slightly breathless voice.

'Are you kidding? It was terrific. But not for you.'

'That's OK. I just think that I'd like to have you sit on the table, like I did on your desk.' She patted the end of the table.

He smiled easily and moved backwards against the table, rested his buttocks on it and leaned back on his elbows.

'That suit you?'

'You'd better take your pants off, I think,' she said consideringly. 'Or maybe I will.'

She unpeeled the white trunks from his body and his erection sprang out at her eagerly. Leaving the trunks at mid-thigh level, she took his long slender cock in one gloved hand and toyed with it.

'Lie back on the table,' she suggested, still in the low, breathy voice. 'Move your arse up a bit – that's it. I thought you might like a bit of a massage to relax you after the stresses of travel,' she continued, picking up the bottle of oil. 'Just close your eyes and relax. Pretend you're in a massage parlour.' She picked up a cushion and placed it under his head, turning it to the side.

Andrew stretched and yawned. 'That's not a bad idea. I did get a massage in Amsterdam, actually. It wasn't that great, though.'

Nina poured oil into one gloved palm.

'Thought you were in Rotterdam?'

'Yes, but we went over to Amsterdam for the day.'

She massaged the oil in slow circles on his chest. 'I don't suppose this massage had anything to do with visiting a prostitute as well, did it?'

His lips curved into a smile. 'Do you want me to tell you?'

'Actually, no.' She picked up one of the scarves and ran it lightly across his chest. 'I thought we'd agreed that when you came back I'd tell you about my weekend.'

His smile became broader. Nina passed the end of the scarf around the table leg and brought both ends up and crossed them lightly on his forearm, then picked up another scarf and started running that over him.

242

'Did you pull, then? Why do you think I want to know?'

She duplicated the move with the other scarf. 'I think you'll be interested. After all, there were three of us.'

Andrew chuckled and Nina deftly knotted first one scarf, then the other, securing him to the table. He gave no indication that he'd noticed.

'So what happened?'

She resumed her massaging action on his thighs, eliciting little sighs of anticipation from him. At the same time she picked up a third scarf and as she circled slowly down his legs, she slipped it round his ankles.

'Well, first of all me and Angie started fooling around, then I got her to undress, then Max wanked us both off at the same time, then I got them to perform for me.'

'*Max!*' He tried to sit up but the scarves held him on the table. At the same time she swiftly tied the third scarf round his ankles.

'What the fuck are you doing? Let me go. And what in Christ's name were you doing with Max?'

'Just playing with him a bit,' she said smoothly, running her leather-clad hand around his balls. 'Lie down, Andrew. If you keep moving around like that your balls could get crushed.'

'Don't threaten me. And get these bloody ties off me, it's ridiculous!'

'Oh, I don't know,' said Nina, laughing softly. 'I think it's quite nice. Surely you don't mind being on the receiving end for once.'

He glared at her. 'So what the hell were you doing with Max?'

'I fucked him up the arse. Hey, do you fancy that?'

'Like hell!' he spat out.

'Well, you were planning to do it to me,' she said reasonably. 'Look, you can't mind this too much, your cock's getting even bigger.'

243

It was true, too. It looked as though it was ready to burst out of its skin. Nina poured a little more oil on to the palm of her gloves and ran her hands up it caressingly. He shuddered.

'It's turning you on whether you like it or not,' she observed, moving her hands up and down in slow motion. 'Angie said it was a shame you weren't there, because I didn't want to go all the way with either of them.'

Andrew made a strangled noise in his throat. 'I thought you said he wanked you.'

'Yes, I was a bit annoyed at myself about that little weakness. It was pretty good, though, especially as I was kissing Angie at the time.'

She felt his groin muscles shudder under her hand and immediately moved her hand from his cock.

'God, I thought you were going to come there. It's not time for that.'

'Why the hell not?' he demanded.

'Because I want a bit of attention!' she said scoldingly. 'You can be selfish, Andrew.'

Unzipping her shorts, she wriggled them off and advanced towards his head, pleased to see his eyelids lower involuntarily as he set eyes on her shaved crotch embellished with the tattoo above it.

'Bet you'd forgotten how nice it looks,' she said huskily. 'I think seeing you tied to that table has got me a bit excited.'

He watched dumbly, upside-down, as she put one foot up on the chair behind him and slowly pushed a finger into her cunt.

'Mmm, nice,' she said, pushing it back and forth a couple of times, then inspecting it. 'Juicy.' She sucked on it.

'I tell you what, I'll untie you if you're good,' she continued, carefully moving her foot along the chair and lifting her other foot up so she was standing on it.

'I'll let you lick me till I come, and if you're as good as Max, I'll untie you and you can fuck me.'

'You fucking bitch!' he roared, straining up but unable to release himself. 'How fucking dare you, you stupid cunt!'

Her hand shot out and she slapped him as hard as she could, one, two, across the face. 'Don't you ever, ever call me that again,' she said furiously. 'Or any woman, for that matter.'

'Don't be so bloody stupid,' he howled. 'That fucking hurt.'

'Good,' she said, as calmly as she could, although her heart was racing, not only with anger but with fear at her temerity in cracking him so hard. 'It was meant to. Now I want your face making love to my cunt.'

'Oh, so it's all right for you to say it. Anyway I thought you loved hearing it,' he said sulkily.

'I love hearing you talk about it. It's not the same as being called one. Do not, repeat not, do it again.'

She carefully knelt down, her shins resting on his forearms, positioning her pussy right over his mouth.

'Now, do I have your co-operation here? Are we understanding each other?'

'Only too well. If I perform as well as your little boy at the office, I'll get a pat on the head too.'

Nina laughed and lowered herself on to his mouth. 'At least you'll get to fuck me, which is more than he did.'

His tongue flickered over her clitoris. 'Oh, yes, I think you're getting to be almost as good as a woman at this,' she said sarcastically. 'Anyway, I thought you'd quite like the idea of me screwing Max's arse with your vibrator.'

She felt his tongue stop moving, as though he were clenching his jaw in anger. Amused, she carried on.

'Not the whole thing, just the thin little finger bit. He quite liked it. I think maybe I wouldn't mind that little bit up mine, though I don't know if I would fancy a whole cock. Especially Max's, because it's really thick.'

A choking noise came from Andrew's throat, but he didn't stop plunging his tongue tip inside her and then lapping down to her arse and back. She was having a great time.

'Anyway, what I really wanted to tell you about it is that I know why you like watching so much now. I sat on a hammock on the balcony in the dark with my vibrator, and they performed for me inside the room. It was better than a porn film. Well, I think it was. We haven't got round to watching one of those yet, have we?'

His tongue was sending a tingling electric current from her clitoris into her cunt. It wasn't going to be long.

'I think maybe you could get me some videos, Andrew. I mean, like now, while you're working away down there, it'd be great for me to have something to look at. I bet you of all people can get hold of porn.'

She tensed her muscles and moved against his tongue. The thought of watching porn was sending her over the edge. Despite his bondage, Andrew responded to her movement, hardening the point of his tongue and licking as hard and rasping as a cat, and the release flooded through her like a tidal wave.

With the climax came, for only the second time in her life, post-coital tears. She sat motionless while the muscles of her sex wrung the last drop of pleasure from her orgasm, tears coursing down her face, feeling completely bereft. As her contractions trailed off, she wiped away the tears and slowly lifted herself off his face.

'Nice one, Andrew. At least as good as Max.'

'Thanks a lot. Does that mean I can get untied now? My arms are killing me.'

She raised each leg in turn and clattered her heels on to the chair behind her, then stepped on to the floor.

'That's better. I have to say, Andrew, there's one way in which you weren't as good as Max.'

He was looking ugly.

'The thing is, you're not enjoying it, are you? You hate being tied up. You hate me being in charge.'

'You're not kidding. Did you tie up your office boy, then?'

'No. I didn't have to. He was quite happy to do what I told him.'

'Yeah, well, that's the difference between a man and a boy.'

'There's a bit of a problem, though,' she said. 'You see, I really liked being the one giving the orders for once. But if you don't – where does that leave us?'

Andrew sighed. 'Untie me and we can discuss it.'

She laughed shortly. 'You were going to make all my fantasies come true, but you haven't exactly helped with the one about tying a man up and making him do my bidding.'

'I'm here, aren't I?'

'Yes, but if you'd realised what I was doing you wouldn't be. What about the fantasy where I make you beg for it?'

He snorted. 'I'll do without, thanks.'

'Exactly. It has to be your way, doesn't it?'

'There's not much point in me pretending otherwise.'

'No. We just keep coming down to the fact that you only do what you want to do.'

'Very succinct,' he said sharply. 'Now can you just untie me?'

'No! For once, no, you're not getting just what you want!'

She paced up and down in front of him. He lay back wearily.

'Nina, you're just making yourself look ridiculous.'

'Well, you've made me look ridiculous often enough! I think it's better if I do it to myself.'

He shrugged. 'Whatever. Don't pretend you haven't loved every minute of what we've done together.'

'Yes, including just now. Which you didn't.'

'The problem is, Andrew,' she went on, 'since I've found out about your nasty little business affairs, some of the things we've done together, as you put it, have taken on a different dimension. Not a very nice one, either.'

His eyes went as dead as driftwood. 'What nasty affairs?'

'Your – what would you call it? – import business?'

'What are you talking about?'

'*"What are you talking about?"*' she mimicked. 'Don't be coy, Andrew. I know all about it. Your whores. Or should I say sex slaves?'

'Oh, for God's sake. Now we're into melodrama.'

'What the fucking hell do you expect?' she shouted, losing the control she'd tried so hard to hang on to. 'What do you think a girl's supposed to do when she finds out her lover makes money out of selling girls into prostitution against their will? You fucking shit, you make me sick.

'That must have been a real laugh, making me be your whore at the hotel. You've got your pick of them, haven't you? The ones you force into prostitution. Do you get first shag with all of them?

'And taking me to the strip club. How many of them work for you as well? And those photos in your bedroom. I bet most of those are your bloody harem.'

'Nina, calm down. It's really not like that.'

'Oh, no, of course not. It's all honest, legal and above board, is it?'

He shook his head impatiently. 'Of course not. But I swear I have absolutely nothing to do with the women after arranging for them to get here.'

'You mean you sell them to pimps.'

'No, I don't sell anybody. Really. It's just a business arrangement.'

Nina pulled out a chair and slumped down. She suddenly felt tired to the bone. Her eyes swept dispassionately over his face, the face she'd got so fond of. Funny that Max had always seen him as Mr Sleaze; ironically, he had turned out to be just that, but she still couldn't get it. He still looked like the man she thought she might have loved.

'You said you'd untie me and let me fuck you,' he reminded her.

'Yes. I sort of meant that to happen before I told you I knew about your alternative career.' She felt lost. 'I don't know what to do now.'

'Untie me, then.'

Why not? she thought. She picked at the knot she'd tied in one of the scarves. Andrew's straining had pulled it impossibly tight.

'I can't do it,' she said.

'You're going to have to do it,' he said darkly.

She laughed derisively. 'Go easy on the threats. I meant I'll have to cut it.'

The kitchen scissors made a quick job of it. Three quick snips and Andrew was sitting up on the table, rubbing his wrists.

'God, you've cut right into me.'

'I didn't, it's only because you kept trying to get away.'

'And my face stings like hell.'

She examined him closely. 'I might have bruised you.'

He put his hand out to touch her face as she looked at him. 'Shit, I deserved that. I was really out of order.'

'Yes.'

'Sorry.'

He was stroking her face, and she nuzzled into his hand.

'I've got a horrible feeling you're going to dump me.'

'Ten out of ten.'

'Look, don't act on the spur of the moment. Think about it. You could get used to it. Really, Nina, you can get used to anything.

He swung his legs over the table and stood up, pulling her towards him and kissing her closed lips and cheeks gently.

'I really want to be inside you,' he breathed. 'Let me fuck you, baby.'

'No!' She pushed him away, glaring at him indignantly. 'You must be out of your mind. How can you expect me to screw you now I now you're involved in this sort of thing?'

He smiled cynically. 'Probably because you were happy to let me eat you. I'm a bit confused as to the difference.'

'Oh please. You know exactly what the difference is. No way did you enjoy that.'

'Right, so that was a punishment?' He raised his eyebrows. 'You've found out that I'm involved in – in this business, so you decided you'd teach me a lesson for being such a naughty boy.'

He was recovering his equilibrium, Nina noted with distaste. Moving towards her again, he put his arms around her waist and rubbed his hard cock against her.

'See how much I want you.' He reached up and pulled at the zip of her leather top. 'God, you're sexy.'

'I said no.'

Ignoring her, he moved his hand down and pushed his fingers inside her still-wet slit.

'I'm not one of your tarts,' she said coldly. 'No means no. Don't think you're going to play out a rape fantasy.'

He pulled away from her, anger on his face. 'Jesus, Nina. Whatever you might think you know about me, you can't suddenly cast me as a complete monster.'

Nina shook her head disbelievingly. Was he really outraged, or putting it on?

'You have got to be taking the piss. Do you honestly think I can just carry on with you as though nothing's happened? I mean, God knows what else you might be into. Like, extortion or violence.'

'You're the one doing the hitting. And for someone who's pretending to be afraid of me, you've just taken a few chances, haven't you? Tying me up, ordering me about, slapping me –'

'OK,' she interrupted. 'But get real, Andrew. I've known about your extra-curricular business activities for approximately two hours. I've gone through the crying and screaming bit and calmed down, but I don't think it's really sunk in. So don't expect me to act as though nothing's happened.

She sat down abruptly and took her boots off, then pulled on the leather shorts.

'Why don't you get dressed and out of here?'

He closed his eyes and shook his head. 'Please, don't say that. Think about it, Nina. You could get used to it. I mean, you wouldn't have to know anything about it.'

'God, you must think I'm a complete bloody idiot.'

She picked up her glass of wine and drained it. 'That's better. I need another one of those.'

'I suppose there's no point me asking for one?'

Shrugging, she went into the kitchen and came back with the open bottle and another glass. She filled her own glass and put the bottle and fresh glass on the table.

'Help yourself. And don't forget to cancel your dinner reservation.'

He sighed. 'Oh, come on, I know you want to go to the Mirabelle. Come with me, please.' He poured some wine and drank. 'I think we ought to talk about this a bit, Nina. Don't just kick me out and end it.'

'Yeah, you're right. We ought to talk. Maybe you could convince me that it's not such a big deal after all.'

He winced at the sarcasm in her voice.

'You work on that while I get changed. I don't feel right somehow wearing a whore's outfit.'

Closing the bedroom door behind her, she stripped off her leather gear and put on jeans and a T-shirt. The bed invited her in for a long sleep, making her realise how exhausted she felt. It was tempting to tell Andrew to get out now and crawl into bed, hoping she would sleep until morning.

Still, she wanted some sort of explanation from him, however lame. And she wanted to get totally and completely wrecked.

'They can't prove anything.' They had finished the wine and moved on to the next bottle.

'Yes, I know.'

'OK, so you know everything. How on earth did you find out?'

Nina explained with some economy about Max's vice squad friend.

'Anyway, he thinks you need to be careful. The Albanians want you out. They want to be the London vice kingpins.'

Andrew watched her, an amused expression on his face. 'Thanks for your concern.'

'Don't be sarcastic. I don't really give a shit.'

He took her hand. 'Sorry. I really do appreciate it. You know, you could get used to it, Nina. Think about it. It's not like I get really involved.'

She sighed. 'Let's get this quite clear. What you do is just bring these women over and sell them to the pimps?'

He looked uncomfortable. 'More or less.'

'Which do you mean? More or less?'

'OK, we sort of – sort of lease them, rather than sell them.'

'Oh, just like cars,' she said angrily. 'Sorry, Andrew, I don't think I could really get used to it. It's a bit like little pimps having bigger pimps on their back, isn't it?'

He was silent.

'I had you figured for a nice, decent person. I think that's basically what you are. You make enough money from the shipping business. God knows I've audited your accounts, it looks profitable enough to me. Just tell me why on earth you're involved in this –' she flapped her hand contemptuously '– this racket?'

'Drop it, Nina,' he said quietly.

'Are you kidding? Don't you think I deserve an explanation?'

He grabbed her wrist. 'I said drop it,' he repeated, with menace in his voice.

She glared at him and tried to move her arm away, but his grip tightened. It hurt.

'Give it up, Andrew, and I might stay with you. And let go of my wrist. Only a few minutes ago you were pointing out you haven't turned into a thug and now you're hurting me.'

He released her.

'I can't give it up.'

'Why not?'

He was avoiding her eyes.

'Why not?'

'Look, you know everything. You know this is to do with Costas. It's not up to me.'

'So tell Costas you want out.'

'Jesus, everything's so easy as far as you're concerned, isn't it? I think I told you once, I owe Costas. Big time.'

She shook her head disbelieving.

'You're telling me that just because he looked after

you when you were a kid, you have to follow him into a life of crime? That's ridiculous.'

'It isn't ridiculous to me. He didn't just look after me, Nina, he looked after the business till I was older, then he taught me everything he knew about shipping.'

'Yes, that was nice of him. But look, say your father had lived and you'd taken over the business from him, you wouldn't have felt obliged to go into the vice game if he'd had an urge to go in that direction, would you? I can't believe anyone's kid would feel they'd have to do that.'

Andrew moved restlessly in his chair. 'Sure, if he was my father. But what he did for me makes him more than that.'

'Yeah, I said before. Your fucking godfather in a fucking Greek Mafia.'

He smiled wryly. 'Put like that, yes. I suppose that's it in a nutshell.'

'Jesus.'

They drank in silence.

'You know, I remember after I had the tattoo done, I said I might as well have had "No Free Will" tattooed on my forehead.'

'Yes?' he said warily.

'That's you, not me, isn't it?'

She smiled at him across the table. At last the wine had relaxed her, or maybe the tension had left her because she understood now.

Why he had to dominate her. Why he couldn't let her take control.

Because his life wasn't his own – except in relationships with women. It was only in the bedroom that he could get rid of the frustratons he had at being Costas's puppet.

'OK,' he said wearily. 'Yes you're right. I'm sorry. I'm sorry, but there's nothing I can do. Except,' he was watching her carefully, 'except when Costas dies. You said yourself he's the oldest man in the world. He can't live for ever.'

'So you're proposing I hang around and put up with the fact that my boyfriend's a pimp and a slave trader, because when his godfather dies he's going to give it all up and go back to running an honest shipping company?'

'Well? Think about it.'

'And what if you get knifed by the Albanian gang in the meantime?'

'Unlikely. There might have to be some arrangement between us, we realise that. But there's enough business to share.'

Nina sniffed. 'That's a relief,' she said contemptuously. 'But it's not just Costas, is it? What would Ariadne think if you wanted to get out?'

'Ariadne would be absolutely delighted, and I can tell you, she's more than capable of running the whole show herself.'

'I can't believe that. Surely she needs a bit of muscle behind her.'

He snorted dismissively. 'Muscle is the easiest thing in the world to buy. She's got what it really takes, brains and loyal workers.'

He put his hand on hers.

'I swear to you, I'll get out. As soon as Costas goes, I'm out. Ariadne can have it.'

'That's sick, Andrew. Just waiting around for him to die.'

'Yeah, maybe. But think about it.'

'No way.'

She drained her glass. A headache was starting slowly just above her eyes.

'Every time you went off on a business trip I'd wonder if you were really going to Albania or somewhere to arrange another cargo. Every time we had sex

255

I'd think about some girl having her tenth punter that day.'

She felt a shudder go through him.

'Even if you gave up tomorrow, you can't cancel out the past. I couldn't live with the knowledge of what you've done. I don't see how any woman could.'

'OK, it's hard to accept. God knows when I first found out about the business from Costas I felt the same way. But I got used to it, and so could you.'

Nina shook her head. 'No. If you were dealing in guns or diamonds or maybe even drugs I might think I could get used to it, though quite honestly I doubt it. But we're talking about human beings here.'

She stood up. 'I don't think there's anything else to say, do you?'

'Oh, Nina. If you ever change your mind . . . I know I won't meet anyone else like you.'

She laughed softly. 'I bet you do. But you will tell her, won't you? Before it gets too serious? About your business affairs?'

'Yeah, if you like.'

'Yeah. Look, I feel awful. Please go.'

'Just like that?'

'Just like that.'

She saw him to the door. 'Goodbye, Andrew.' She kissed a finger and touched his beautiful lips with it. 'Be careful.'

'Can I call you some time?'

'Yes. But not for a while, OK?'

She opened the door and stood holding it. He kissed her cheek tenderly and started walking slowly downstairs.

If he looked back, she didn't see it. She closed the door behind him and let the tears fall again.

Chapter Twelve

*H*er head was playing host to a sumo wrestling match and her mouth tasted like a Chinese restaurant's dustbin. Big mistake, she thought, squinting at the alarm. Seven thirty. Time to get up and go to work. On automatic she rolled out of bed and into the bathroom. Her hair was sticky with sweat. No doubt the drink had contributed to that as well as the heat.

The needles of water falling from the shower hurt her face. If only she hadn't had that vodka.

After Andrew left she had cried, curled up on the floor behind the door. Then with the clarity of logic of someone who had already drunk more than enough she knew that what she needed was a drink. A proper one, not just wine. She needed to drink to forget.

So she'd splashed her face with cold water and gone down to the off-licence for half a bottle of vodka and four cans of Red Bull. The cheerful Irishman had been behind the counter and she'd joked with him as usual. She had impressed herself by her ability to talk to him as though nothing had happened.

So much for drinking to forget. She remembered perfectly finishing off the vodka, amazed that it had gone so soon and wishing she'd bought a whole bottle.

How stupid, she told herself. Only the other day she'd decided that it was the mixtre of vodka and wine that had given her a hangover. She should have stuck to wine. Now she felt sick.

Of course she hadn't eaten, but she had cried a lot, and played all the weepy songs she could find.

She swallowed two Paracetamol. She had to get to work. Life goes on.

Thank God for work. She'd have hated to be stuck in the flat with her own thoughts. And thank God for Max, who would understand and be nice to her. Maybe they would go to the pub at lunchtime. She thought a hair of the dog might help.

Her eyes were puffy but gel helped and she put dark glasses on before she went out. She felt a bit unsteady walking past the common but her nausea vanished in the fresh morning air.

A woman was begging in the subway as she got off the tube. She was dressed all in black, a baby in her arms, mutely holding out her hand. Nina emptied her purse into the woman's outstretched palm.

'Thank you,' she whispered in heavily accented English, looking at Nina with surprise.

Nina shook her head. 'It's the least I can do.'

'You OK?'

Max was obviously surprised to see her at her screen when he got in ten mintues early, probably for the first time ever. She was touched, presuming it was because he was concerned about her. But she'd arrived even earlier.

'Sort of. But hungover.'

He smiled. 'Not surprising. You sure you're OK?'

'Yes, I said so.'

He shrugged and switched on. 'New job going all right?'

'Yep.'

'Still hot.'

'Yep. Think there's a storm coming, though.'

'Me too.'

They sat in silence. Max clicked his mouse more times than could possibly be productive.

'I've finished with him.'

'Oh, great. I mean sorry.'

'So can you do some work now?'

He grinned at her. 'And you're really OK?'

'Christ, Max, how many times?'

'All right.'

No more than twenty seconds went by before he jumped up. 'How about a coffee?'

'Black, lots of sugar.'

'OK.'

When he'd left the room she shook her head. What did he have to be so restless about?

He came back with the coffee. 'We should go out at lunchtime and celebrate,' he suggested.

'Not yet,' she said sipping the sweet liquid. 'God this is disgusting.'

'Too much sugar? Shall I chuck it away and start again?' He was hovering by her desk.

'No. Max, why are you so restless?'

He smiled. 'Well, I'm sort of, like, excited. I phoned Angie last night.'

Nina laughed. 'And?'

'Well, first of all, she's really worried about you.'

'But as you know, I'm fine. So what else?'

'We're going out tomorrow night.'

'Great!' She patted his arm. 'Really, I'm pleased.'

'Yes, isn't it great!' He sat down and looked over at her. 'You didn't mind me telling her about Mr – Andrew, did you?'

'No. Saves me from doing it.'

'Good.'

He moved his eyes back to the screen and tapped away at the keyboard for a minute.

'Why don't you come too?'

She sighed. 'Is that what all this is about? You're trying to set up another famous threesome?'

'No!'

'I told you that was a one-off. I'd rather you didn't even talk about it in this room. And I really think you better get up to date on Clyde, Surrey or this job's going to take forever. We should be going out on site now.'

'Yes, I know all that. But it's just that we're going to see Iron Heel at the Artshare, and there's a spare ticket.'

Nina looked at him in bemusement. 'I sometimes think we don't talk the same language, Max. No, I know we don't. Is there any reason why I should have the faintest idea what you're talking about?'

'God, you've led a sheltered life, Nina. They're a band, sort of crossover hiphop jazz kind of thing, really cool. All women in leather, fantastic.'

She stopped the smile that was playing at the corner of her mouth. 'And why do you think I'd be interested in that?'

'Because they look just like the sort of women who'd like to shaft a bloke up the arse,' he said, laughing. 'And there's a spare ticket.'

'Take George,' she said non-committally.

'George is already going,' he said patiently. 'He's got a thing about women in black leather. I mean we've got four tickets.'

'I suppose this Artshare is in Hackney?'

'Need you ask?'

'Why did you get a spare ticket?'

He smiled smugly. 'Because I got two tickets hoping that Angie would come. In the meantime George got two tickets for me and him. It's not a set up.'

Nina raised her eyebrows. 'Did I say I'd mind if it was?'

So how about it?'

'I'll think about it.'

She carried on scrolling down the screen, though George's face was floating between her eyes and the figures she was supposedly studying. She saw his warm brown eyes and heard his deep, Scottish voice. He like women in black leather. She clicked back to reality. There was work to do.

But Max interrupted again.

'So?'

'So what? Are you going to let me get any work done today?'

'Sure, after you say you'll come tomorrow.'

Nina walked over to Max and swivelled his chair round to face her, putting her hands on his shoulders.

'Of course you've told him all about Friday night.'

'Yes.'

She was taken aback by his honesty.

'Oh.'

He shrugged exaggeratedly. 'I knew you'd think I had even if I hadn't, so I thought I might as well. He hated me for a bit, but he's sort of got over it. As long as you come over tomorow.'

'And it's all back to your place afterwards, I suppose?'

Max shook his head. 'It doesn't have to be, if you don't want. It's up to you.'

'I'm in charge?'

'Definitely.'

She hardened her voice. 'In every respect?'

He nodded earnestly. 'Absolutely. George knows that too.'

'Do I have your word on that, Max?' She leaned closer to him.

'Oh, yeah,' he breathed. 'Nina, I'm getting a hard on. Please, just say you'll come tomorrow, and we'll do some work.'

Satisfied, she backed off.

'Yeah, I'll come tomorrow.'

She certainly would.

Visit the Black Lace website at
www.blacklace-books.co.uk

FIND OUT THE LATEST INFORMATION AND TAKE ADVANTAGE OF OUR FANTASTIC FREE BOOK OFFER! ALSO VISIT THE SITE FOR . . .

- All Black Lace titles currently available and how to order online
- Great new offers
- Writers' guidelines
- Author interviews
- An erotica newsletter
- Features
- Cool links

BLACK LACE – THE LEADING IMPRINT OF WOMEN'S SEXY FICTION

TAKING YOUR EROTIC READING PLEASURE TO NEW HORIZONS

BLACK LACE

Black Lace Booklist

Information is correct at time of printing. To avoid disappointment check availability before ordering. Go to www.blacklace-books.co.uk. All books are priced £6.99 unless another price is given.

BLACK LACE BOOKS WITH A CONTEMPORARY SETTING

☐ SHAMELESS Stella Black	ISBN 0 352 33485 1	£5.99
☐ INTENSE BLUE Lyn Wood	ISBN 0 352 33496 7	£5.99
☐ A SPORTING CHANCE Susie Raymond	ISBN 0 352 33501 7	£5.99
☐ TAKING LIBERTIES Susie Raymond	ISBN 0 352 33357 X	£5.99
☐ ON THE EDGE Laura Hamilton	ISBN 0 352 33534 3	£5.99
☐ LURED BY LUST Tania Picarda	ISBN 0 352 33533 5	£5.99
☐ THE NINETY DAYS OF GENEVIEVE	ISBN 0 352 33070 8	£5.99
Lucinda Carrington		
☐ DREAMING SPIRES Juliet Hastings	ISBN 0 352 33584 X	
☐ THE TRANSFORMATION Natasha Rostova	ISBN 0 352 33311 1	
☐ SIN.NET Helena Ravenscroft	ISBN 0 352 33598 X	
☐ TWO WEEKS IN TANGIER Annabel Lee	ISBN 0 352 33599 8	
☐ PLAYING HARD Tina Troy	ISBN 0 352 33617 X	
☐ SYMPHONY X Jasmine Stone	ISBN 0 352 33629 3	
☐ SUMMER FEVER Anna Ricci	ISBN 0 352 33625 0	
☐ CONTINUUM Portia Da Costa	ISBN 0 352 33120 8	
☐ FULL STEAM AHEAD Tabitha Flyte	ISBN 0 352 33637 4	
☐ A SECRET PLACE Ella Broussard	ISBN 0 352 33307 3	
☐ GAME FOR ANYTHING Lyn Wood	ISBN 0 352 33639 0	
☐ CHEAP TRICK Astrid Fox	ISBN 0 352 33640 4	
☐ THE GIFT OF SHAME Sara Hope-Walker	ISBN 0 352 32935 1	
☐ COMING UP ROSES Crystalle Valentino	ISBN 0 352 33658 7	
☐ GOING TOO FAR Laura Hamilton	ISBN 0 352 33657 9	
☐ THE STALLION Georgina Brown	ISBN 0 352 33005 8	
☐ DOWN UNDER Juliet Hastings	ISBN 0 352 33663 3	
☐ ODALISQUE Fleur Reynolds	ISBN 0 352 32887 8	
☐ SWEET THING Alison Tyler	ISBN 0 352 33682 X	
☐ TIGER LILY Kimberly Dean	ISBN 0 352 33685 4	

☐ RISKY BUSINESS Lisette Allen	ISBN 0 352 33280 8	£7.99
☐ OFFICE PERKS Monica Belle	ISBN 0 352 33939 X	£7.99
☐ CAMPAIGN HEAT Gabrielle Marcola	ISBN 0 352 33941 1	£7.99
☐ MS BEHAVIOUR Mini Lee	ISBN 0 352 33962 4	£7.99

BLACK LACE BOOKS WITH AN HISTORICAL SETTING

☐ PRIMAL SKIN Leona Benkt Rhys	ISBN 0 352 33500 9	£5.99
☐ DARKER THAN LOVE Kristina Lloyd	ISBN 0 352 33279 4	
☐ THE CAPTIVATION Natasha Rostova	ISBN 0 352 33234 4	
☐ MINX Megan Blythe	ISBN 0 352 33638 2	
☐ DIVINE TORMENT Janine Ashbless	ISBN 0 352 33719 2	
☐ SATAN'S ANGEL Melissa MacNeal	ISBN 0 352 33726 5	
☐ THE INTIMATE EYE Georgia Angelis	ISBN 0 352 33004 X	
☐ SILKEN CHAINS Jodi Nicol	ISBN 0 352 33143 7	
☐ THE LION LOVER Mercedes Kelly	ISBN 0 352 33162 3	
☐ THE AMULET Lisette Allen	ISBN 0 352 33019 8	
☐ WHITE ROSE ENSNARED Juliet Hastings	ISBN 0 352 33052 X	
☐ UNHALLOWED RITES Martine Marquand	ISBN 0 352 33222 0	
☐ LA BASQUAISE Angel Strand	ISBN 0 352 32988 2	
☐ THE HAND OF AMUN Juliet Hastings	ISBN 0 352 33144 5	
☐ THE SENSES BEJEWELLED Cleo Cordell	ISBN 0 352 32904 1	
☐ UNDRESSING THE DEVIL Angel Strand	ISBN 0 352 33938 1	
☐ THE BARBARIAN GEISHA Charlotte Royal	ISBN 0 352 33267 0	£7.99
☐ FRENCH MANNERS Olivia Christie	ISBN 0 352 33214 X	£7.99

BLACK LACE ANTHOLOGIES

☐ WICKED WORDS Various	ISBN 0 352 33363 4
☐ MORE WICKED WORDS Various	ISBN 0 352 33487 8
☐ WICKED WORDS 3 Various	ISBN 0 352 33522 X
☐ WICKED WORDS 4 Various	ISBN 0 352 33603 X
☐ WICKED WORDS 5 Various	ISBN 0 352 33642 0
☐ WICKED WORDS 6 Various	ISBN 0 352 33690 0
☐ WICKED WORDS 7 Various	ISBN 0 352 33743 5
☐ WICKED WORDS 8 Various	ISBN 0 352 33787 7
☐ WICKED WORDS 9 Various	ISBN 0 352 33860 1

To find out the latest information about Black Lace titles, check out the website: www.blacklace-books.co.uk or send for a booklist with complete synopses by writing to:

> Black Lace Booklist, Virgin Books Ltd
> Thames Wharf Studios
> Rainville Road
> London W6 9HA

Please include an SAE of decent size. Please note only British stamps are valid.

Our privacy policy
We will not disclose information you supply us to any other parties. We will not disclose any information which identifies you personally to any person without your express consent.

From time to time we may send out information about Black Lace books and special offers. Please tick here if you do <u>not</u> wish to receive Black Lace information.   ☐

Please send me the books I have ticked above.

Name ....

Address ....

....

....

....

Post Code ....

Send to: Virgin Books Cash Sales, Thames Wharf Studios, Rainville Road, London W6 9HA.

US customers: for prices and details of how to order books for delivery by mail, call 1-800-343-4499.

Please enclose a cheque or postal order, made payable to Virgin Books Ltd, to the value of the books you have ordered plus postage and packing costs as follows:

UK and BFPO – £1.00 for the first book, 50p for each subsequent book.

Overseas (including Republic of Ireland) – £2.00 for the first book, £1.00 for each subsequent book.

If you would prefer to pay by VISA, ACCESS/MASTERCARD, DINERS CLUB, AMEX or SWITCH, please write your card number and expiry date here:

....

Signature ....

Please allow up to 28 days for delivery.